CW00517756

RULES BETWEEN
ROOMMATES

Thanks to my mum, who wouldn't stop asking me to finish this. Your enthusiasm gave me the boost I needed.

Thanks to Dan for lending his personality to these pages. It's my favourite.

Thanks to my brother, Jay, for sharing his drunken antics with me. They made their way into this story. Ste, Steph - I'll be using you next.

Finally, thanks to Lauv, whose song I Like Me Better got me through many slumps.

CHAPTER ONE

C all me a time-waster because that's what I am. My best friend, Holly, would also agree with you. She currently sat on the bed to my right, and, from her huffs, I knew she was trying and failing to be patient.

Me? I was trying and failing to ignore her.

"Would you just open it?" she demanded, finally voicing her frustration.

I wanted to. I really, really wanted to. So much so that I couldn't.

I'd waited for this email all summer. Every day, I'd switch on the computer, open up my emails, and feel disappointed to see no new ones. Not today. The surprise at seeing the email sitting there is why I called up Holly.

I regretted that now.

"Open it!" she said again, this time with a shake of my arm.

I read over the subject of the email once more.

Important: Application for Graduate Position.

My stomach whirled with nerves.

"I can't do it," I groaned, covering my eyes like the coward

I was.

"What has gotten into you?" she wondered aloud.

I was wondering the same thing.

Was it nerves? Or more than that? Deep down, I knew I'd be devastated if I didn't get this job, so part of me was afraid.

At the beginning of the year, I graduated with first-class honours in Games Development. The first-class part came as a surprise to everyone, although Holly at least had the courtesy to act as if she'd expected it. I put it down to my love for gaming. I'd loved it for as long as I could remember, so going into games development was always an obvious and easy choice for me.

And the obvious and easy choice of career was with Bluebird Gaming, the largest games developer in Europe. The headquarters was in London. Perfect. Except not perfect–because they were almost impossible to get into. I was surprised I even made it through the applications, let alone the interview stage.

And now I couldn't even open the email.

It was true that this was my dream job, and if I got rejected, I probably wouldn't be able to handle it. But that wasn't the only reason I was afraid–I also *needed* this job. I needed the money. I needed to move out.

I lived with Holly. As my best friend, she was the first to offer me a place to stay when I moved out of university halls. I didn't have anywhere else to go, and, unlike the other lucky students in my year, I didn't have a job lined up. That was months ago, and I was well aware I'd overstayed my welcome.

Holly wasn't the problem–I was rarely made to feel

unwelcome by *her*–it was Nick, Holly's long-term, uptight boyfriend, who I had issues with. While he didn't say anything to my face–and I'm sure I had Holly to thank for that–his eyes said it for him. *You're not welcome here; when are you leaving; get your hands off my milk.*

He definitely hated me.

I was more than happy to leave. For one thing–I didn't like him either. He always looked miserable. Would it kill him to crack a smile? And for another, I hated being the third wheel. Pizza night was no longer fun when two out of the three obviously needed some privacy.

My problem: I couldn't afford to rent a place on my own. This job solved that problem.

"*Aargh.* If you won't, then I will."

I peeked through my fingers as Holly grabbed the mousse. Seeing that I was about to protest, she pushed my chair out of the way. Her mouth stretched into a triumphant smile. "See, nothing to worry about."

"What do you mean?"

"You got the job, Dani!"

"I–what?"

"Look!" she pulled my chair back and pointed at the screen. The word *congratulations* caught my eye.

Oh my goodness, she was right.

I did the first thing I could think of–I jumped to my feet and screamed. Holly, the great friend that she is, joined in with me. I was so happy I felt like I could celebrate all night. I would have celebrated all night if not for Nick and his complaints. We heard his grumbling from down the hall.

"Crap," Holly pulled me to a stop, eyes darting to the door.

"He has work tomorrow."

I glanced at the time and felt a sudden wave of guilt. "So do you."

She waved her hand like that fact didn't matter. "It's fine. I can be tired. We need to celebrate your success! Just quietly," she added, glancing back at the door.

"We can celebrate tomorrow," I told her. She opened her mouth to argue, so I faked a yawn. "I'm tired anyway. Honestly, you should go. Before Nick falls back asleep, and you wake him again."

She chewed her bottom lip. "Tomorrow," she promised before disappearing into the hall.

I closed the door behind her and took in the silence. It didn't match my current elated mood. I wanted to scream for joy and pop open a bottle of champagne. With effort, I climbed into bed instead. Nick hated me enough already–no need to poke the dragon.

I wished I was even a little tired, but my thoughts whirled back and forth as I stared at the ceiling. While I was excited and afraid to start working, the excitement outweighed my fear. Because the dream to start my career at Bluebird was about to become my reality.

I must've drifted eventually because the sun shone through the cracks in the curtains when I opened my eyes again. I glanced out of habit at the clock on my bedside table and almost fell out of bed in surprise. I hadn't been awake this early since... ever? Had I entered some alternate reality where I, Dani Scott, was now an *early bird*? I tested my brain. It felt wide awake–none of the usual grogginess. Well, there was no point in wasting this rare feat. I jumped out of bed, grinning at how alert I felt.

Holly and Nick hadn't left for work yet. That's how early it was. I heard them bustling around in the kitchen below.

The smell of cinnamon wafted up the stairs as I crept onto the landing.

As I made my way down, I realised they were having a heated discussion. I turned away, not wanting to get involved, but something Nick said caught my attention.

"She is never going to leave, Holly!"

He was talking about me. I edged closer to the door.

"I told you she has a job now," Holly whispered. "She always said she would move out when this happened."

"But you've been too nice to her. She isn't going to leave unless you tell her to. Why won't you tell her to move out?" He let out a long, despairing groan. Always the dramatic. "You want her gone as much as I do."

This was news to me. Holly wanted me gone?

"But it's so awkward," she complained. "What am I supposed to do–tell my best friend that she isn't welcome? You know I can't do that."

"Well, you don't need to say it like that. Just ask her when she's leaving and go from there. Or you can just tell her to do one," he added, as though he preferred that option. I shot daggers in his direction. "I don't think I can deal with this for much longer, Hol. You know she drives me crazy. I need our privacy back."

Holly's sigh hurt me, but not as much as her next words. "She drives me crazy, too."

That was as much as I could handle. Turning quietly, I crept back up the stairs, shutting the bedroom door behind me.

I needed a moment to think.

I climbed back into bed and stared at the wall opposite, my mind spinning.

What could I do now? What *should* I do now?

I couldn't stay here. That much I did know. Nick wanting me gone was no news to me–it was almost a daily occurrence that he made this clear–but Holly was a different story. I'd had no idea she felt that way. How humiliating that they *both* felt that way.

I wondered for the first time what my best friend actually thought about me. Why did she let me stay here if I drove her crazy? Was it out of pity?

I pressed a pillow to my face and screamed.

Okay.

It was okay.

If they wanted me gone–I would leave. I'm sure I could find a place to live somewhere. The *where* part was just something I needed to figure out.

Scrambling out of bed, I loaded up the computer.

Keeping my new job in mind, I searched for flats to rent in London. There had to be hundreds of places up for rent in the city, and I could afford one now that I had a job.

By the time Holly and Nick were due home, I had over ten viewings booked in.

I hoped Holly would arrive home first so I could tell her the news privately. But, when I entered the kitchen, it was Nick with his face in the fridge.

He noticed me enter and frowned, eyes darting to the empty seat he'd forgotten to occupy. I quickly sat on it before he could throw his bag down, as was his custom when it was just the two of us in the house.

"Hey, Nick. Good day at work?"

He turned his attention back to the fridge. "I see you've used my milk again."

You didn't seem to care when you used mine. "Do you know when Holly's back?"

"No idea."

Knowing this was as far as our conversation would go, I settled in, silently watching as he made himself a sandwich. I could tell my presence irked him. It was the only reason I stayed.

He was just cutting his bread in half when the front door opened.

"In the kitchen!" he called out, simultaneous to my,

"Welcome home!"

Holly entered the kitchen warily. It didn't surprise me, considering Nick and I usually avoided being in the same room together.

"What's going on here?" she asked.

"I just came in to make a sandwich," Nick answered. His eyes flashed to me as if to say *I don't know what her problem is.*

I grinned back at him. "I actually have some news for you both."

Holly put her bag on the table and sat. "News?"

This was the hard part. Saying it out loud made it real.

"I'm moving out."

They exchanged a glance. I tried to ignore the joy flashing across their faces.

"Moving out?" Holly repeated.

"Yep. I'll be out of your hair in a couple of weeks." My only hope was that I'd given myself enough time.

"That's amazing!" Holly quickly checked her enthusiasm. "I mean, only if that's what you want?"

Nick, ever the charmer, swiftly nudged her chair. "Good for you, Dani," he smiled. It was the first genuine smile I'd ever seen him give me, and I couldn't help but feel offended. "And congrats on the job."

"Thanks, Nick." *I won't miss you, either.* I turned to face Holly, whose pained expression caught me off guard. She flew towards me, enclosing me in a hug. "What's this for?" I asked, bewildered.

"I'm going to miss you," she whispered. Despite what I'd overheard in the morning, I could tell she meant it. I gave her a squeeze.

"I'll miss you too. And thanks for everything."

Over the next few days, I noticed Nick watching me with more interest than he'd previously shown. It was like he was a spectator at a magician's show, waiting for the moment I disappeared. I tried to ignore him. Most of the time, it was easy. But that's because I was out of the house and searching frantically for a place to move into.

The flats I viewed weren't just questionable–they were downright hideous. I quickly realised that I wouldn't be living in anything comfortable with my price range. If there weren't stains on the carpet–there were stains on the walls; if the plumbing didn't have issues–the electrics did. I couldn't bring myself to put an offer in on any of them. But my time was running out, and Nick continued to watch.

Luck seemed to strike at the end of the first week. Perhaps it was because I'd seen so many terrible ones before it, but I could visualise myself living in this one-bed flat. It wasn't perfect by a long shot–but there wasn't anything glaringly wrong with it. I took that as a deal maker.

"I'll take it," I told the agent.

And then it was the day of the move.

Packing came easy for me. I packed light, so to speak. The entire contents of my wardrobe fit easily into two bags. A third I filled with a collection of games and books I liked, and I was finished. Holly was not impressed. Somehow, my lack of belongings offended her.

"This cannot be it," she accused, eyeing my three bags with a frown.

"This is it, and I'm surprised you're surprised." I hoisted them onto my shoulder and switched off the light. The upper floor was now empty of all things me.

Holly followed me downstairs and to the front door. I could hear Nick in the front room, watching football. For one second, I expected him to come out and say goodbye. He didn't.

"Do you have to leave?" Holly complained.

"Don't let Nick hear you say that."

"You know he loves you, really."

I couldn't help but laugh. "Definitely don't let him hear you say *that*."

Holly smiled. "I'll make sure I come and visit you soon. Oh, and let me know how your first day at work goes!"

"I will. Thanks for everything." I gave her a parting hug and left, casting a quick eye over the front window in case

Nick decided to wave. He didn't.

Thankfully, the estate agency wasn't too far away. I headed there to pick up the keys and felt my phone buzz in my pocket.

"Hello?" I answered, wondering why the agent needed to speak to me before our meeting.

A female voice echoed through the phone. "Hi, Miss Scott. Is now a good time?"

"Now is a perfect time," I told her. "I'm on my way to you."

"Oh, I was hoping you wouldn't say that."

Something cold trickled through me at her tone. I stopped walking. "What's wrong?"

"Well, I have some bad news about the flat. The landlord is no longer willing to give it up."

A pause.

"Is that allowed?" I demanded.

"He's given the flat to his sister. Says she's desperate. He won't give up the keys."

"Can't you make him?" I choked. "I mean, I signed an agreement. I already sent the deposit!"

"He's sent the deposit back to us. It will be with you in a few days. Miss Scott, I'm very sorry, but he isn't someone whose hand we can force. We manage a number of his properties, you see-"

"But I have nowhere to live now," I interrupted, feeling frantic. I couldn't turn back to Holly's. I wouldn't.

"We have several listings that are available to move into soon. Should I send them to you?"

"Please."

She put the phone down. I sat on the curb and waited for

the email to come through, my legs shaking. Wrapping my arms around them, I willed myself to relax, jumping to my feet when the email finally pinged.

Horrible.

Horrible.

Horrible.

I continued scrolling and then stopped when one caught my eye. A two-bed house, one hundred times better than any of the others I'd seen. A thousand times. It even had a little garden out front. And it was close to the city centre, where my new office was.

It was perfect.

I rang the agent back.

"That two-bed house," I said as soon as she answered. I needed to confirm one thing first. "Is it really only that much a month?" It looked like it should have been double, even triple the price. I waited for her to confirm my doubts.

"The house? Oh, yes. Sorry, I didn't realise I sent that to you. It's just come in. The price should be correct, let me see..."–I heard her rustling through some papers–"yes, it's correct."

"Can I see it?"

An obvious pause. "I didn't think this was something that would interest you."

What kind of an answer was that? "Of course it is. The house is beautiful."

"I'm not sure if I should... I mean, I'm not sure if you're..." she trailed off.

"Not sure if I'm what?" I pressed.

"The landlord is usually out of the house at the weekend,"

she said suddenly. "And he's fully booked next week. I could try to get you in the week after..." she trailed off again.

I knew what she was doing. She was delaying me. We both knew the house would be gone if I waited over a week. The only thing I didn't know was why she didn't want me to have it.

"So the landlord is living there?" I asked.

"Well, yes. You have read–"

"And he needs someone urgently?"

"Yes. You do realise–"

I put the phone down.

CHAPTER TWO

This was probably stupid. It certainly wasn't rational. But what did I have to lose?

That's what I asked myself as I raced to the station. I couldn't allow myself time to stop. If I stopped, I'd think; and if I thought, I'd probably convince myself that this was a bad idea. I needed to keep moving.

I reached the station and headed straight to the Underground, where I jumped on the first train to Kings Cross. According to Google, the house was a thirty-minute walk from here.

I knew my decision to view the house without the agent was risky. That's why I reasoned it out. First: there was no chance she was willing to show me this place herself, so going alone was my only option.

Second: if I did wait, as she said, someone would definitely get the house before me.

And third: the listing said it was available immediately, and I needed somewhere immediately.

My mission had a setback. If the agent had been honest when she said the landlord went out on weekends, he most likely wasn't home. But something in my gut told me not to believe her, and I was willing to cling to any hope.

What I would say when I got there was another question. I hadn't thought that far ahead.

Using the listing as a reference to find the house, I walked down the street, searching for a blue door. Neat houses flanked me on either side, with perfectly pruned gardens and flashy cars. Not the kind of neighbourhood I grew up in. Where were the screaming children? The trash on the floor?

I found the blue door at the end of the street. The house was tucked into a corner, half-hidden by bushes. I paused with my hand over the latch on the gate, my nerves picking up.

What were the chances I'd be a good fit for this place? Why would this person choose *me*? I looked down at my baggy sweats, and the doubt grew. I shook it off. Either I got the house, or I didn't. I had nothing to lose. And the clothes were irrelevant.

Twisting the handle, I raced down the little stone pathway before I could chicken out, stopping to knock on the door. I turned to the doorbell when no answer came. It pinged, reverberating throughout the walls inside.

"What the hell," I heard someone grumble from within. A curtain pulled back an inch at the front window. I looked in, but it closed swiftly. The sound of footsteps moved through the house.

The door swung open.

I hadn't given much thought to who the landlord might be. If I had, I might've imagined an old man in a turtle neck, with a kind face and wrinkles beneath the eyes. This person was the opposite. Young (early to mid-twenties), smooth-skinned (not a damn blemish in sight), and... shirtless.

As quick as thunder, I diverted my eyes from his bare chest and down to the floor. The only item of clothing he wore was a pair of loose-fitted grey joggers.

"Do you want something?" he demanded.

I looked back at his face. It seemed the safest place, even with his angry eyes. There were faint circles beneath them, and his golden-brown hair was scruffy and dishevelled.

"Did I wake you?" I asked. Not a great first impression.

"No. Do you want something?"

I buckled at his harsh tone. His eyes didn't seem unfriendly as they bore into mine, but they didn't seem friendly either. I reminded myself of why I was here and not to feel intimidated.

I looked down at his feet again–his exposed toes helped with the intimidation–and then smiled up at him. "I wouldn't be here if I didn't."

He blinked. "Well, are you selling something?" his eyes moved down to my bags and back up to my face before moving slowly over my hair and clothes. He raised a brow. "Or are you here to ask for money?"

Now that was uncalled for. "Why would you think that?" I demanded, no longer smiling.

He shrugged. "You look a bit rough, that's all. No offence," he added quickly, as though that helped.

It was with extreme effort that I didn't throw a 'no offence' comment back at him. But I wanted this house, and he seemed to be the person with the power to give it to me. "Well, I wasn't expecting to be doing this today, and I have just been on the Underground, so I'll allow that."

"What does that have to do with me?"

Again with the rude tone.

"I saw your advertisement online." *Don't lose your temper now, Dani.* "You're urgently looking for a tenant, right?" His eyes narrowed in confusion, making me panic that this wasn't the right place. But, before I could worry too much, understanding seemed to clear them. I took it as encouragement. "Well, I'm also looking for a place to live, and it's pretty urgent. Doesn't it make sense to save each other the effort of looking for a tenant and landlord when both landlord and tenant are here now?" I commemorated myself on the brilliance of the question.

But he seemed to be unwilling to speak. Instead, he continued his silence, staring at me with unreadable eyes. "I promise I'll make an excellent tenant," I said, too desperate to my own ears. "I'm extremely clean; I can fix a broken shower, de-clog a toilet... although I'm not saying I'll clog it in the first place! You'll always get your payments on time, and, what's more, I'm ready to move in now." I smiled my best smile. He stared at it for a long second before his eyes moved to my bags on the ground.

Only then did I realise what an idiot I must look to him. Knocking on a stranger's door, bags ready to move in. The audacity of it almost had me laughing. And to top things off, I'd made myself look desperate. The advertisement might've said *immediately*, but had I needed to take that so literally? After all, didn't he need to move out before I could move in?

"I don't need to move in straight away," I said quickly,

hoping to reverse any damage caused. "Whenever you're ready for me."

His lips finally curled into a smile. My heart leapt, but his following words made it shatter into pieces.

"Yeah, that's not gonna happen."

The door started closing in my face.

Without thinking, I quickly slammed my foot in the way, jamming it open. He glared at my obstructing shoe in anger and shock. I didn't care–I wasn't feeling nice anymore.

"Why isn't it going to happen?" I demanded.

"You've got it wrong," he said shortly, tugging on the door. I didn't budge.

"This is 54 Mill Avenue, isn't it?"

"So?"

"I have the right place, see?" I shoved my phone under his nose and pointed at the advertisement. "54 Mill Avenue, looking for a tenant..."

"Let me see that." He plucked my phone from my hand before I could stop him. "Yeah, you're reading it wrong." Clearly triumphant, he shoved it back to me.

"What, no, I'm not!"

He pointed. "Joint-tenant. It says I'm looking for a joint-tenant, i.e. roommate."

"Oh." I looked down and saw that he was right. My cheeks burned. "Well, why didn't you put that in the title? Then I would never have made this mistake or wasted my time coming here."

"Don't blame me," he defended. "I never wrote that. I left it with the agent to deal with. Speaking of an agent," he frowned, as though just realising something. "Shouldn't you have gone through one before coming here? Isn't that how this works?"

I cleared my throat. "Yeah, sorry about that. I've not had the best of luck, so I thought I'd come straight to you." Bad idea, I now knew.

He eyed me for a long second before his eyes flashed to my bags again. "You must be desperate. I'm sorry that I can't help." His apology sounded sincere. It made my heart sink.

"Yeah. Thanks anyway." I moved my foot from the door, but then something hit me. "Wait!"

"What now?" he groaned.

What now was that it didn't matter to me if I had a roommate or not. In fact, it was better. It meant bills were halved. And there was no way I could afford a place like this living on my own. Being a joint tenant was actually perfect.

"Can't I be your roommate?"

He looked at me like I'd gone mad. "You? You be my roommate?" I didn't like the way he said *you* as though there was something wrong with me.

"Is there a problem with that?"

"You're just not what I'm looking for."

"Why the hell not?" I was too offended to keep my voice calm. He raised his brow like that was the reason.

"Well, for starters, you're a girl."

Now I raised my brow. "What's wrong with me being a girl? Are you being sexist–should I report you?"

"Hey, there is nothing wrong with a guy wanting a guy for a roommate. And how can you report me when you didn't even go through my agent?"

That stumped me. "But I can do everything a guy can," I

complained. It was probably true. "Do you game?" I asked, hoping to find common ground. His eyes did seem to light up. "I love gaming. We could play co-op if you wanted." I pressed my hands together and pouted. "Please let me be your roommate." For a second, he looked like he could be swayed; it was only for a second, and then he shook his head.

"See that," he pointed at my lips with a frown. "A guy wouldn't do that. No. Having a girl for a roommate would just get too complicated. I'm sorry. Now can you please move your foot out of the way? I'm getting cold."

"You shouldn't answer the door half-naked, then," I sighed.

He closed the door without another word. As if that wasn't enough, I heard the *clink* as he locked it. That was fair. I'd do the same if I was him. What crazy person jabs their foot in a stranger's door and begs them to let her live with him?

But I tried, and that's what mattered.

That's what I told myself as I turned away from the door, trying not to feel too disheartened by my failure.

Maybe I should come back and try again later. I wasn't one for giving up, but the mental image of his face, upon opening the door to me once more, quickly convinced me not to. He'd probably call for aid.

"Excuse me, but who the hell are you?"

Spinning, I found a girl standing by the gate. She was tall, auburn-haired, gorgeous.

Girlfriend, perhaps?

"Just someone minding my business," I said, bending to

hoist up my bags.

"In Will's garden." I heard her retort. Her arms were folded when I turned back to her. I didn't like that.

"Can't I mind my business here?"

She laughed once. "If this is why he's been ignoring me, I will kill him."

She marched down the path and banged on the door, ignoring me as I stood in front of it. Too astonished to move out the way, I stayed put. Her long, slim arms reached around me to bang again.

The door swung open, revealing Will and his angry face.

"Didn't I tell you to l-" he started and then stopped. His eyes moved slowly from me to the newcomer. They widened in horror.

"Hi, Will." Her tone was pleasant, but I felt a sudden wave of fear for him.

"What are you doing here?" he choked.

"I came to see you."

"I told you that I'm busy."

"I can see that." Her eyes flashed menacingly to me. I shrank back, increasing the space between us while simultaneously closing it between the door... and him.

"This isn't what it looks like," he said quickly, casting a panicked glance down at me and frowning at our nearness. We were almost touching.

"Oh, I think this is exactly what it looks like," she replied.

I wasn't sure, but she looked ready to explode. I eyed her up, just in case, assessing her as an opponent if it came to that. The difference would be that she looked ready for a fight. I wanted to sit down if anything.

And this was his problem, not mine.

Suddenly, I wanted to swap places with him. I wanted to be the one on the inside. It was safe there. He could slam the door and shut us both out if he wanted. I thought of the possibility of pulling him out and barricading myself inside instead. Sure, it was illegal, but it seemed the better option.

As though he could read my mind, he grabbed my shoulders and moved me in front of him. I looked up, affronted, and then realised what he was doing: he was using me as a human shield. If the girl decided to pounce, it would be me who she clawed.

"*Hey!*" I hissed at him.

"Rather you than me," he whispered before saying aloud, "What's it to you who she is? In fact, why did you even come here?"

"Are you sleeping with this girl?" she demanded, ignoring his questions.

That was enough for me. I struggled against his grip. He held me tighter when he realised what I was doing, so I settled for glaring at her instead.

"*Excuse* me. I am not some booty call who sleeps around. I'm-"

"Are you sleeping with her?" she repeated, cutting me off as though I weren't here. My dislike for her increased tenfold. "Because if you are, you will never see me again."

"I don't even know who sh-" Will cut off as though an idea had just hit him. He smiled down at me. "I mean, yes. Yes, I am. She's my girlfriend." He squeezed my shoulders and winked. I wondered if he was actually insane. Opening my mouth to say as much, he quickly whispered, "Go along, and you can be my roommate."

That was all I needed.

I turned back to the girl with a smile. "I am his girlfriend."

Instead of being furious, as I expected, she now looked doubtful. Her eyes appraised me, up and down, like just seeing me for the first time.

"She isn't your girlfriend," she concluded, far too confident for my liking.

"Why not?" I tried to step forward, but Will still held me in place. "I could be his girlfriend. I am his girlfriend."

"That's right," Will agreed.

"There is no way you would choose *her*,"–she nodded at me with a grimace–"over me. Can't you just make her leave?"

Through my sudden anger–she didn't need to be so rude to *me*–I heard Will mumble something into my ear about how she wasn't wrong. I turned my glare on him. He winked and then said aloud, "She isn't going anywhere. She lives here." He grabbed my bags and tossed them into the hallway. My anger vanished with them. "You've actually caught us on the day of the big move. Now, if you don't mind, we're really quite busy." He pulled me inside and slammed the door closed. I locked it for good measure.

"At least it's a downgrade!" she screamed.

I laughed, too happy to take offence.

"That was something," I said, turning to my new roommate. "Are you okay?" He looked like he needed to sit down.

"That was scary," he breathed. "Why do people think they can turn up here uninvited?" I didn't miss the way his eyes moved over me. "You can stay here until the coast is clear," he continued, turning away, "and then you can leave."

My stomach dropped.

"But you just said I could live here!" I followed him through the hallway.

"I told you before that having a girl for a roommate isn't the best idea. That statement still stands."

"That doesn't take away the fact you told me I could live here. And I have a witness–do you want me to go get her?" I moved back towards the door.

"Don't you dare!" he warned.

I folded my arms. "Then you shouldn't go back on your word. Not after what you made me do out there. I'm probably her enemy number two now. And yes, you're her number one."

He sighed and ruffled his hair. "I just don't understand why she came here. We aren't even boyfriend and girlfriend."

"Then who is she?"

"A one-night stand."

I rolled my eyes.

"What?" he asked, immediately on the defence.

"Boys and their one-night stands. I bet you deserved it."

"What's wrong with a one-night stand? And I'm not even the one who asked for it–she is!"

"It didn't seem that way to me," I observed.

"That's what's so scary. How was I to know she'd stalk me afterwards? Girls are so confusing."

"We aren't all the same, you know."

"From my experience, you are."

"Maybe you need better taste."

He turned to me with folded arms. "And you want to be my roommate?"

I cleared my throat. "Sorry. Yes, please."

He shook his head but continued to eye me speculatively, deliberating something. "Hmm," was all he said.

"Is that a hmm yes, or a hmm no?"

"I suppose you did come in handy just then," he allowed. "I don't think Alicia would have left if you hadn't been here."

"At least you remember her name."

"Oh, gee, thanks." He tapped his finger against his lip in thought. "Hmm. What if a girl could make a girl repellent...?" he continued to look thoughtful.

"I'm lost," I admitted.

"Here's the deal." He stopped the tapping and faced me, all serious. "You can be my roommate if you do for me again what you did for me out there."

It took me a second to figure out what he meant. "You want me to keep pretending to be your girlfriend if she comes back? Will she come back?" I looked over my shoulder as a shiver ran down my spine.

"I don't think so. But if another girl comes over..." he trailed off.

I didn't need him to elaborate. "How many girls do you have?" I asked, not bothering to hide my disgust.

"Hold back on the judgment. None, at present. I just seem to bring home the excessively clingy type. Don't get me wrong, I make it clear beforehand that I'm not after anything serious, but that goes out of the window when the morning hits."

"They don't leave?" I guessed.

"I don't know what it is. I even make them a brew and cook them breakfast in the morning. But they never go– they just make themselves at home instead. One girl stayed for three days. *Three. Days.*"

I laughed out loud. "Are you serious? What girl would leave when she's getting a cooked breakfast. Isn't that an invitation to stay?"

"No, it's not!"

"Then what can I do to help?"

"Just, I don't know..." he waved his hands in frustration. "Okay. If they're still here by late morning, barge in, say you're my girlfriend and demand they leave?"

I wondered if he realised how ridiculous he sounded. Still, if this was all I had to agree to... "Okay, fine," I said. "I'll do it."

"Then let's shake on it." He held out his hand. I took it, feeling a weight lift from my shoulder, but then he snatched it away again. "Wait a sec. This still doesn't solve the problem of having a girl roommate."

I sighed. "And what problem is that? Actually, it doesn't matter. We already shook on it."

"Hear me out. What happens if you end up falling for me? Or if we sleep together? I have a hard time kicking out strangers, let alone a roommate. See how it can get complicated?"

I gave him a second to admit he was joking. When he didn't, I laughed. "That is not likely. You're at more risk of falling for me than I am of you."

He looked me up and down and shook his head. "I don't

think so."

"Hey, I might not look like that sexy girl out there, but I have other things to offer."

"Like what?"

"Like..." annoyingly, I couldn't think of a single thing. Even more annoyingly, it made him laugh. "Whatever," I grumbled. "Point is, I'm at zero risk of falling for you. You've already made it known that you sleep around, and you want to use me to get rid of your one-night stands. The point is, you're a pig, and pigs are not my type."

He stared at me with his mouth slightly open. From the look in his eyes, he already regretted his decision. "Just put your bags upstairs." He waved in dismissal. "Your room is the second on the landing. But come back down again. We have some rules to lay down."

CHAPTER THREE

I was sitting in his front room, feeling strange now that I was actually here, listening to a set of rules given by a stranger.

He sat on a chair beside me. I sat on the sofa. A coffee table sat in front of us, several magazines sprawled across the surface. My eyes fell to them first. They were gaming magazines–X-box, PlayStation, Empire–and I itched to read them. Later. Right now was rule-setting time.

My eyes drifted to the sixty-inch TV before moving around the bright, open living space. They stopped on a mahogany cabinet. His taste was obviously modern, but with some elements of tradition mixed in with the new. A long, oak dining table ran the length of the room adjacent to me.

My bags had now been dumped in the bedroom upstairs. I had to remind myself that it was now *my* bedroom, however surreal that felt. It was barren compared to the rest of the house, with only a double bed and wardrobe for decoration. I would add some personality to it on payday.

The wardrobe doubled up as a mirror, so at least there

was that. I'd checked myself out in it before coming back
down and immediately regretted that action. I looked
much, much worse than I'd thought. It actually made me
laugh, given I'd pretended to be his girlfriend earlier. My
hair, tangled and matted, clung flatly against my face; the
morning air made my face red, and my blemishes looked
angrier than usual. And to top it all off, my sweats had dirt
on them.

None of this seemed to matter to him.

"Rule number one," he said, holding up his forefinger
with an intent look in his eye. "We respect each other's
privacy. I don't go into your room, and you don't go into
mine. I don't touch your stuff, and you don't touch anything
of mine."

"Fine by me," I agreed with ease.

"Rule number two," a second finger joined the first. "You
warn me before you invite anyone over. I don't want a
bunch of strangers coming round."

"Do you need to warn me before inviting anyone over?"

"No. This is my house."

I frowned. "But I'll be living here now, too. What if, I don't
know, I'm naked or something, and someone walks in?"

His mouth dropped open. Quickly closing it, he squinted
his eyes shut, shaking his head as though trying to rid
himself of a bad image. "Rule three," he forced out, opening
his eyes again. "You do not walk around the house naked.
Bedroom–fine; bathroom–fine; kitchen–not so fine."

"As long as that rule applies to you also."

He looked at me like he couldn't quite figure me out.
"Fine," he agreed. "None of us walks around the house

naked. Happy?"

"And you'll warn me before inviting people over?"

He rubbed his temples with a sigh. "Yes. Yes, I will warn you."

I smiled. "Rule four?"

"We keep out of each other's space. If I'm watching TV in here, it's me time, so don't come in. If you hear me in the kitchen, wait for me to finish. I hope I don't need to stress the same for the bathroom."

I shot him a dirty look. "I won't go into the bathroom if you're in it." I spat, and then, under my breath, "It's not like there will be anything I want to see anyway."

He heard.

"Do you want to be my roommate?"

"Could you stop threatening me with that? Yes, I want to be your roommate; but is it not better to show you how I am now rather than you figure it out down the line?"

"You have a point," he allowed.

"Sure, I can act all quiet and nice and agree to everything you say now, but I won't be able to keep that up. Just so you know, I am opinionated, a little annoying, and I prefer to say what's on my mind then and there rather than make a big deal out of it later."

He tilted his head. "You'd say you're only a little annoying?"

The question was rhetorical. I ignored him. "But I'm not an angry person. I'm cheerful, relaxed and won't give you a hard time. Knowing this, could you either accept or reject me as your roommate and stop it with the threatening?"

He let out a long, tortured groan before standing. After

pacing a few steps back and forth, he sat down again. "Okay, fine. I won't keep threatening to kick you out."

"Great. Now can we just go back to rule four–why is it that I can't be in here when you are? Can't we watch TV together?"

"No, we cannot watch TV together." He looked at me for a moment and then seemed to want to clarify something. "I don't want this turning into anything more than two people sharing a house for convenience. We aren't friends." Just for a moment, Nick flashed into my mind. Cold, Dani-hating, miserable Nick. I hoped I wasn't moving in with another one of him. "Which brings me onto rule five," he continued, erasing Nick from my mind, "you are not allowed to fall for me."

The way he said it–so self-assured–I couldn't help but shake my head at him.

"You do know that feelings are uncontrollable," I commented, just to be sure.

He seemed to take it differently. "Look, if you think you'll end up falling for me, this roommate thing isn't going to wo-"

"I said uncontrollable, not inevitable," I spat. Somebody needed to bring this boy's head back down to size. "Rest assured, it's not going to happen. Do you think girls just fall for any guy they see or something? I said it before–you're a pig, and pigs really aren't my type."

He looked like he might combust for a second, but then something shifted, and he burst out laughing. The effect was palpable–I had to bite back a smile of my own.

"You do sound assured," he said. "I actually feel

embarrassed. Okay–my bad. I'm sorry."

"What about you?" I probed.

"What about me?"

"I don't want you to fall for me, either. You should set that rule for yourself."

This time he laughed louder. "Oh, you're serious?"

"Yes. I'm quite the charmer, and you're in a lot of danger here." The danger was zero, and we both knew it. Still, it didn't seem fair to have the rule aimed only at me.

He shrugged. "Whatever makes you feel better."

"Are there any more rules?"

Thankfully, he shook his head. I sighed and looked around the room. Everything was neat and orderly. It crossed my mind to tell him that I wasn't either of those things–I was prone to messiness–but since he hadn't thought of that rule, I wouldn't provide him with it.

"I'll get my agent to send across the agreement," he continued. "You may as well send the deposit money directly to me."

Crap.

"Um, about that...," I trailed off, afraid that this might change his mind after all.

He looked at me expectantly. When I didn't say anything, he leaned forward.

"Are you about to tell me that, after all that, you can't even pay the rent?"

"I can pay the rent," I said quickly. "Just... in a couple of days." I tensed for his reaction. I could see this from his perspective, and it didn't look good. A tenant who couldn't even pay her deposit... what a joke.

"Well, do you at least have payslips or something so I can see you can pay going forward?"

Double crap.

"Um, no payslips, but I have a job offer I can show you." I watched his expression shift as he realised I didn't have a deposit or a job. "Hear me out," I pleaded before he could send me away for good. When he nodded, I explained my morning situation to him, ending with how I was waiting for the agent to send my deposit back over. "So you'll have it in a few days," I assured him. "You can ask the agent if you want. I'm pretty sure she's your agent, too, since she's the one who sent me the listing for this house. Albeit by accident."

"Accident?" he frowned.

"Well, she didn't seem keen to show me this place. She said you were fully booked for the next two weeks." Curious to see if she'd lied, I added, "Are you?"

He shook his head, still confused. "Oh..." he laughed. Seeing the confusion now on my face, he elaborated, "That's because I told her I only wanted guys."

"Of course you did." I sighed as the agent's strange behaviour suddenly made sense. "Well, she can confirm my story if you need her to."

"You don't look like much of a liar, but what do I know?" He took out his phone and dialled a number.

"Oh. You're doing it now."

"Good morning," he jumped to his feet. "This is Will Lovett calling for Olivia. Sure, I can hold." He walked the length of the room and perched on the table. My eyes followed him. "Hi, Liz." He grinned, causing me to roll my eyes. Of course, he was on a short-name basis with her. "It was good, thanks. And yours?" he laughed at something probably not funny and saw me watching. His body stiffened and shifted so I could no longer see his face. "I'm actually calling because I have something to check with you. I have a girl here, name Dani-" he spun back to me, "what's your last name?"

"Scott."

"Dani Scott." He turned away again. "She says you have her deposit money from some landlord who screwed her over–is that right? Uh-huh. Okay, great. In that case, you can cancel any viewings you have booked in. I've found my roommate."

I've found my roommate.

The words reverberated through my mind like a safety net as Will laughed into his phone.

"I guess I changed my mind," he said, eyes flashing to me. "Yes, you will still get your fee. After all, you're part of the reason why she's here. Don't apologise. Could you send the paperwork across now? Great. Bye."

"Did she just apologise for me being here?" I frowned.

He tossed his phone onto the table and smirked. "Brew?"

"I'd love one, actually. Coffee, one sugar."

He gave me the thumbs up and left the room. A second later, I heard him scuttle about in the kitchen. I put my feet up on the coffee table, out of habit, and waited.

"Rule six." His voice boomed from behind. "No feet on the coffee table."

"Sorry." I quickly took them off and folded them against the sofa. He placed the coffee down on a coaster with a look of contempt. "I'm used to doing it to annoy Nick," I explained. When that didn't seem to clear things up, I added, "He's my best friend's boyfriend. I used to live with them both, and he hates me."

"I wonder why," he muttered, pulling out a laptop from under the table. I watched as he loaded it up. After a few minutes of clicking, he walked over to the cabinet. There was a printer wedged between two shelves. Grabbing something from it, he returned with a wad of paper.

"What's that?"

"The tenancy agreement." He passed a copy to me, keeping one for himself, and then threw me a pen.

"Do I have to read this?" I skimmed through the sheets with an increasing level of disgust.

"You should always read whatever you sign your name against."

Looking up, I found him reading his own copy. I guessed I saw sense in that. Turning to the first page, I started reading. I soon yawned. Flipping through the important stuff–name, payment terms, date–I skipped to the end, signing my name with a silent prayer that I wasn't signing my life over. He could be the devil for all I knew.

"So you say you've got a job?" Will asked, still reading his own copy. "Where is it that you work?"

"I don't work there yet."

He sighed. "Where is it that you'll be starting work?"

"Bluebird."

He choked on the coffee he'd just sipped. Flecks of it splattered across my paper.

"Gross!" I complained.

"Did you just say Bluebird, as in Bluebird Gaming?" he looked at me with more interest than he'd shown before. I nodded with a grin, causing his brows to shoot up in surprise. "You're one of the new recruits?"

"I am. You're impressed, right? It's almost impossible to get a job there. The application process is worse than you can imagine. But, somehow, I managed to do it." I grinned again. "They're the biggest games developer in Europe, you know."

"You like to brag," he noted. I didn't take offence because, in this instance, he was right. "But that's strange. I would've remembered..." he trailed off. Blinking away whatever thoughts, he continued, "Good for you. So you want to develop games?"

"Yes! I really hope I'm on the design team. My dream is to be a games designer."

He laughed. "How uncanny. Mine too."

"No way!" I grinned. "Aren't you glad that I'm your roommate now? Maybe I can get you a job there now that I've got my foot in the door."

He smiled. I saw a smugness in it that I didn't understand.

"That would be *amazing*."

I narrowed my eyes. "What's that face for?"

"I'm not making a face."

"Yes, you are. You're doing it again!"

He bit against his lip and then laughed. "I'm not. Honestly, I'm just happy I have a roommate who can get me a job at Bluebird." He laughed again. "Real happy."

"You're making fun of me." I knew the signs–his smirk, his amused eyes, that annoying face. I just didn't know the reason.

He shrugged. "Whatever you say."

"You're just jealous that I have a job at Bluebird because you'd never make it through the applications," I guessed.

"Right." He stood, collecting the cups in his hand. I studied his face as he took them to the kitchen. His smile told me I was missing something.

Returning, he marched over and stopped in front of me, suddenly businessman-like. "How about this, if you do manage to get me a job at Bluebird, I will do all the housework for however long you're here. Cleaning, ironing, you name it."

I stared at him.

"You're serious?" I could hardly believe that anybody would offer to do any housework, never mind all of it. This guy either really, *really* wanted a job at Bluebird, or he was amongst those strange humans who actually enjoyed cleaning.

"I'm serious."

"Hmm." What were my chances here? While I liked a challenge, there was a high possibility that he'd be a terrible worker, so getting him a job wouldn't reflect well on me. I couldn't let this potential bad worker hinder my career.

I thought of a satisfying solution.

"How about I get you an interview?" I counter-offered. "Even an interview is hard to come by, and I won't have much influence for a while. I get you an interview, and then it's up to you from there."

"Sounds fair," he agreed, far quicker than I expected. He held out his hand. I reached for it, but then he pulled it back an inch. "If, however, you don't get me an interview..." his eyes glinted, "*you* have to do all the housework."

I sighed. Of course, there was a term. I was stupid not to expect it. Still, I liked my chances.

"It's worth the risk," I concluded, shaking his hand.

A smile played on his lips as he turned back to the agreement, signing his name with a flourish. Watching from the corner of my eye, I grabbed a pen to do the same. I could tell from his face he thought I'd fail–but I wouldn't let that happen. No way.

Once both agreements were signed, he put one in a folder and tossed the other in a drawer.

"Where is it that you work, by the way?" I asked, watching him shrug into a coat. I needed to know what I was working with.

"Oh, I'm currently unemployed."

My mouth dropped open. I quickly closed it. His unemployment didn't discourage me–it wouldn't stop me from getting him an interview. I hoped. I just hadn't expected it.

I realised that I'd been presumptuous about him. I'd thought he was someone with a good job, earning big money. It wasn't just the neatly stacked pile of expensive trainers I saw on the way in or his beautiful home–it was the way he talked and held himself. So confident.

I looked around the room again and frowned. "Are you recently unemployed?" His nod confirmed my suspicions. "You know, if you need me to pay more rent money, I don't mind. You're already massively undercharging me."

He paused on his way to the door. "You'd do that?"

Recently unemployed with a house like this? No wonder he needed a roommate. "Of course, I'd do that. And trust me–you'll be back on your feet again in no time."

His returning smile made me feel better than I could've imagined under the circumstances. "Aren't I glad you showed up this morning."

I grinned as he left to deliver the agreement to his agent.

When he returned, I sat by the island in the kitchen, making another coffee.

"Help yourself," he said, nodding to the coffee. After tossing a set of keys onto the counter, he threw another to me. "I got this cut for you."

"Thank you." I twirled it over in my hand. "I guess you can't get rid of me now," I teased. He didn't respond. "Do you want a brew?"

"I'm good."

"Cool."

Awkwardness settled around us. Seeming to notice it, he pointed at the door. "Well, I'm going to watch some TV."

I quickly finished making my coffee and followed him into the front room. He frowned when he noticed me.

"Have you forgotten the rules already? We stay out of each other's space."

"But what should I do?" I already felt bored.

"You have a strange way of talking to strangers," he observed. "Let's not forget that we only met each other today and that I have no idea what you like to do."

"I wouldn't call us strangers anymore. We're roommates."

"Lucky me." He grabbed the TV remote and threw himself onto the sofa. The sound of daytime television filled the room.

"Could I watch TV with you?" I asked.

"No."

I groaned. "Seriously, what can I do then? I don't know anyone to go out with, and there's no TV in my room."

"Do whatever you normally do on a Saturday."

"I normally watch TV."

He sighed. "Well, I'm going out later, so you can watch it then."

"Ooh, can I come?" I instantly knew that I shouldn't have asked.

He turned to look at me with despair in his eyes. "What part of we are not friends do you-"

"-Not understand," I finished for him. "Fine. It's your loss." I gave the TV one envious glance before stalking from the room.

One more thing to add to the list of things I needed to buy–a TV.

Throwing myself onto the bed, I stared at the ceiling. I soon got bored of that. I tried watching Netflix on my phone, but I needed to go downstairs when the data usage warning popped up. The light had faded outside the window, replaced with darkness. My stomach growled when I realised I hadn't eaten for a while.

"Hey, can I have the Wi-Fi password?" I directed my question at where I'd left Will, but he wasn't there anymore. Heading to the kitchen, I found him with his head stuck in a cupboard. He'd changed into a shirt and jeans and had the room smelling faintly of cologne. "John Paul Gaultier?" I guessed, breathing in the scent.

"What?" he hit his head on a shelf and winced. Rubbing it, he turned to look at me. "Yeah, how'd you know?"

"It was Nick's go-to."

"Nick, the guy you don't like?"

"The one and only."

"Huh. What a lucky coincidence." He slipped a bottle of whiskey into a carrier bag and turned to the fridge.

"You're quite annoying," I noted.

His lips tugged up as a bottle of coke joined the whiskey. Opening a drawer, he rummaged through it, pulling out a slip of paper. "Here. The Wi-F password."

"Thanks." My stomach growled as I reached out to grab it.

"Help yourself to the food," he said. His carrier bag rattled as he moved to the door. He paused, glancing back at me. "So, er, don't break anything while I'm gone. And don't forget what you said you'd do for me!"

I frowned at his retreating back. He couldn't mean what I thought he meant, right? "You're not bringing a girl home this soon, are you?" I called after him.

He shrugged, one hand twisting the handle. "It's Saturday night. Cya."

He smiled and disappeared into the night.

CHAPTER FOUR

My new roommate had a social life. Meanwhile, here I was, spending my Saturday night scavenging for food.

Will had good stock, so at least there was that. And excellent organisation. Herbs in one cupboard, pasta in another, snacks in a third. Spotting a pot noodle at the back of the snack cupboard, I grabbed it, taking a Kit Kat with me for good measure.

"Ahh," I sighed minutes later, sprawled on the sofa with the smell of noodles wafting up at me. *This is good.*

Switching on the TV, I grabbed one of his blankets and made myself comfy. I didn't move from that position until past midnight when I had to force myself to crawl groggily upstairs and into my surprisingly comfy bed.

I jolted awake sometime later by the sound of someone burgling the place. I lurched for my phone, ready to warn Holly when I heard the sound of Will's drunk, slurred voice mixed with the commotion. And then I remembered that I lived somewhere else now. Relaxing back into the pillows, I checked the time.

"You have got to be kidding me," I groaned. It was three in the morning. *Three*.

And he wasn't alone.

As the noises moved upward, I heard an unmistakably female laugh mixed in with his. His bedroom door slammed shut, and I prayed to anything and everything above that the walls were thick here.

The walls were not thick.

The walls were thin like a sheet of fragile ice.

I suffered through too many nauseating sounds before I drifted into welcome oblivion. And then I was being awoken for a second time.

Ignoring the knock on my door, I pulled the quilt above my head. He–at least I assumed it was Will–knocked again, and again, and again. "Go away!" I called when the knocking became insufferable.

"Dani," his voice came in a low, urgent whisper. "I need you to do what you said you'd do for me. This is a code red."

"Code red, my ass." I wiped the dribble from my mouth and rolled over, pulling the quilt above my head some more.

Unfortunately, it didn't block out his voice. "Hey, come on. You know what we agreed."

I wondered if I should help him since I had agreed to do it. But then I remembered the noises I'd heard during the late hours, and my helping spirit disappeared. "Go away."

"*Please*?" he sounded desperate this time. I threw a pillow at the door. "Fine," he snapped. "This makes me feel a lot better about what I've done to you."

I heard his feet march away and removed the quilt from my head. An uneasy feeling settled in my stomach. What the hell had he done to me?

I found him in the kitchen when I finally felt awake enough to drag myself out of bed. He glared at me as I entered. I smiled, but he returned his attention to the sausages he was cooking and ignored it.

"Are any of them for me?" I asked.

He turned to face me, throwing down a set of tongs as if I had indeed upset him. "I can't believe you," he hissed. "The one reason I agreed to let you live here, literally the one reason, and you refused to do it."

From his whispering, I assumed she was still in his room.

"I can help you now?" I offered.

He glowered at me. "I told her I'd make her a sandwich."

"What did I tell you about doing that?" I groaned. "You're inviting her to stay! The smell alone would make me not want to leave." I breathed in the scent of cooked sausages and felt my appetite stir.

"It's not for you," he warned, picking the tongs back up and snapping them at me. "And I wouldn't be in this situation if you helped me earlier."

My skin prickled at his tone. Taking a deep breath, I said, "You're right. I'm sorry. It's just... I really don't do well with lack of sleep, and you kept me up a lot last night." At least he had the decency to look embarrassed. "Just pass me the sandwich. I'll go deal with this."

His face brightened.

I marched upstairs with the sandwich in hand and knocked on the door. My confidence wavered as I entered the room, but she was fully clothed and looked ready to leave anyway. I smiled, a little awkward, and passed her the sandwich.

"He wants you to leave," I said. After explaining the situation to her–without lies–she was more than happy to go.

"What a jackass." She pulled on her shoes and thrust the sandwich back at me. "Do me a favour? Throw that sandwich in his damn face."

The front door shook as she slammed it.

Will appeared the second it closed.

"Is she gone?" he asked.

I considered throwing the sandwich in his face like she wanted me to. But it seemed such a waste, so I took a bite instead. "She's gone."

He sighed. "Did she say anything to you?"

"Just that you're a jackass." He frowned. "You have to admit that you are," I added, completely on her side.

"Hey, I made it perfectly clear that I just wanted a one-night stand."

"Well, she was about to leave on her own, so why the panic this morning?"

His face crumpled in distaste. "She wouldn't stop trying to cuddle me."

"Unbelievable." I moved past him.

He followed. "What's unbelievable?"

"What's unbelievable is you. God forbid a girl wanting a cuddle after just having sex."

His head tilted, eyes sparkling with amusement. "Have you ever had a one-night stand before?" he questioned. My face flushed. An automatic reaction because no, I had not. He took that as my answer. "Then let me tell you that you don't cuddle after it."

"Remind me not to have one, then."

"You like to cuddle?" he smirked.

I didn't gratify him with an answer. "I'm not helping you again," I told him instead.

His smirk disappeared. "It's what we agreed."

"Was it in the agreement I signed?" I knew the answer before I saw his face cloud over. "Then I don't need to do anything. And you can't kick me out for not doing it, either. Or so according to the government."

His face turned gloomier as he stared at me. "You're really annoying."

"So are you."

We glared at each other for one long moment, and then he stalked from the room.

I spent the rest of the day staying out of his way. I suspected he was doing the same with me because I didn't see him when I finally emerged from my room. I wasn't in the habit of staying angry, so I was over our spat the next day. But I didn't see him then, either.

This pattern continued into the following week. I started to *want* to see him–if only for some human interaction. He was obviously a social person to be out all the time. I just wished he'd invite me out, too. It would be nice to make friends.

The Sunday before I started work arrived. I removed my clothes from the drier and found his shirt mixed in with my load. It was nice. Designer. I kept hold of it.

It wasn't like he had work tomorrow anyway.

As I lugged my basket into the kitchen, I found him

standing there. It was the first time I'd seen him in days.

I twisted the basket with his stolen shirt out of view. "Hi."

"Hello." He sounded more civil than I expected. "First day at work tomorrow?"

"Yep," I shifted around him, eager to escape.

"Are you nervous?"

"A little. More excited than anything."

He grabbed an apple and wiped it. "Do you remember our bet?"

I frowned before I remembered. No wonder he caught me before my first day–he must really want a job. "I will get you an interview," I promised. And then, remembering the rest, "So be prepared to do all the cleaning."

He smiled. "Or you'll need to do it." His smile stretched into a grin. "Good luck." With that, he strolled past me with a swag in his step.

"I don't need it!" I called after him.

That night, I lay in bed thinking about how I'd succeed. All I knew was that I needed to be the one to win. I hated cleaning, so having Will do it for me was an opportunity I couldn't let slip. Determined, I flicked off the light and prepared myself for my first day.

In the morning, I had enough courtesy to tiptoe around the house so as not to wake him. My hands shook as I buttoned up the white Ralph Lauren shirt I'd borrowed–I'd give it back eventually–and I knew it was due to nerves. I threw on a blazer, hiding the extra room, and went downstairs. After wolfing down breakfast, I left the house with time to spare.

The Bluebird office looked different from the ones

surrounding it. For one thing, the people who entered weren't wearing suits. They wore casual, often colourful, clothing. I sucked in a deep breath and walked to reception. After taking my details, the receptionist passed me a security card and told me where to go. I grinned when the card granted me access. It made it real.

I exited the elevator on the eighth floor, where another receptionist greeted me.

"Um, Dani Scott, here for my first day."

"No problem," the receptionist pushed out her chair and stood. "Let me take you to the training room."

I followed her through the floor, my eyes widening as I took in my surroundings. When we stopped outside a door labelled *Beginner*, my heart rate accelerated. The nerves I held at bay all morning finally hit me. Taking a deep breath, I peeked inside. Three faces craned to look back at me. The receptionist smiled, probably used to this behaviour, and then closed the door when a moment of courage moved me inside.

I took a seat beside a boy with a friendly smile. He immediately turned to face me, holding out his hand.

"I'm Finn," he greeted.

"Dani," I smiled back, taking his hand.

He nodded to the girl sitting to his left. "This is Lily,"– a nod to his other side–"and this is Lewis. The receptionist said we'll be eight in total, and then the big dogs will come."

I frowned. "The big dogs?"

"You know, the team leaders–the people at the top. I can't wait to meet the lead designer," his eyes suddenly glinted as he rubbed his hands together.

"Who's that?"

His brows shot up. "You don't know?" When it became clear that I didn't, he continued, "He's the youngest ever in the company. He was in his early twenties when he got promoted. *And* he was the main person involved in the game that won the Game of the Year award."

"Wow." That was impressive. About as impressive as Finn's level of knowledge.

The door opened for four more people. We chatted a little, but mostly we sat in silence as we waited. Finally, somebody entered who didn't look like they were the new kid at school.

Placing a laptop at the head of the table, she sat down. Another person followed after her, leaving one chair empty.

"Where's Will?" the woman asked.

Great, I almost rolled my eyes. *Another Will.*

The man shrugged and looked at the door. "My guess is late."

She tutted and opened her laptop. After hooking it up to the projector, her eyes moved to our faces, flashing between each in quick succession.

"Hello, everyone," she smiled. "Welcome to your first day! My name is Jasmine, but you can call me Jas. I started here ten years ago as an apprentice myself, and I now lead the art department. Billy here leads up the programming. We're just waiting for our lead designer to arrive, and then we can begin. For now, why don't we start by introducing ourselves and telling an interesting fact?"

Finn volunteered first, to no one's surprise. After that, she moved anti-clockwise, meaning I came last. Luckily, the door opened before it reached my turn.

"Finally," Jasmine sighed. "Why are you always late?"

"Sorry," a male voice said. "I got held up this morning. And I'm not always late."

For a second, I thought my ears deceived me. But then I saw the newcomer's face, and my jaw dropped. I knew that face. I knew that tousle of brown hair and dimpled smile.

What I didn't know was why it was here when it should've been at home sleeping.

CHAPTER FIVE

"**H**oly sh-" I quickly covered my mouth to stop myself from cursing.

I didn't think anyone heard me. They were all too busy ogling at the lead designer. *At my roommate,* I thought with disbelief. *Who should be at home in bed.*

I watched his face as he sat, trying to figure out whether this was a prank or not. It was the only plausible explanation because Will could not work here. He just couldn't. If he did, then I'd been played. To the extreme.

First of all, he hadn't said a word to me about any of this. I remembered an earlier conversation in the front room when I'd told him I wanted to work in design, and he said the same. Well, now I felt foolish. Not only did he work in design, but he was also the *lead*.

My brows creased as I remembered something else. Isn't this the guy who told me he was unemployed? And hadn't he accepted my offer to pay more rent because of that? I glared at him, but I wasn't sure if he noticed. He seemed to be avoiding my eye.

And then there was the bet.

My stomach did a flip.

I accepted the terms because I thought there was a chance of winning, even if that chance was slim. Now I knew that there was no chance because I couldn't well get an interview for someone who already had the job.

That explained why he'd looked so smug about it–he knew I'd fail. He'd placed the bet knowing full well that I wouldn't be able to do what he asked.

How utterly brilliant.

"Where are we up to?" he asked, eyes stopping on every face but mine. I cleared my throat, hoping it'd catch his attention. He didn't budge, but I could've sworn his lips twitched in amusement.

So he wasn't as oblivious to me as he let on.

"We're in the middle of introductions," Jasmine replied.

"Ah," sitting straighter, Will flashed one of his dimpled smiles. I noticed one of the girls subconsciously run a finger through her hair. If she found him attractive, I couldn't understand why. He looked like an irritating liar to me. "I'll introduce myself, then. I'm Will, and I've been working here for about ten years. I'm the lead designer, so those placed in that department will work with me."

Not, under any circumstance, did I want to work with him. No, not *with* him, but *under* him. I cringed at the thought. Maybe he could read my mind because his lips twitched once more.

"If you don't mind me asking," Finn said, still ogling at Will, "how old are you?"

"I'm twenty-six."

An impressed murmur spread through the room. I pressed my lips together to stop myself from joining in.

He leaned back. "So, who's next?"

"I think this young lady here," Jasmine nodded at me.

Will finally looked at me, and I suddenly wanted to hide. "Oh, um," I cleared my throat. "Hello, Everyone. I'm Dani. Um, an interesting fact..." I tapped my finger against my lips as my eyes drifted back to Will. Shouldn't *he* be the one hiding? Not me? "So this technically isn't about me," I said, feeling braver. "But I recently moved in with someone. I thought this person was just your average human, but it turns out that he's actually a world-class deceiver."

Will snorted. "Sorry," he said, thumping his chest. "I have a cough. Please, Dani, continue."

"As I was saying," I moved my eyes away from him, but he may as well have been the only one in the room. "My roommate is a deceiver."

Jasmine gave me a serious look. "That's interesting. Do you mean that your roommate is a fraudster?"

"You could say that."

Maybe this wasn't the best time to call him out on it. Still, it was worth it for the look on his face.

Or it would've been worth it if my high ground didn't crumble the next second.

Will's eyes moved down to the shirt I wore, and I suddenly remembered *whose* shirt I was wearing. His. The one I'd stolen. He did a double-take, a crease forming between his brows.

Shifting in my seat, I pulled my blazer closed. His eyes moved back to my face, still with that frown. Even after

I looked away, concentrating hard on Jasmine, I could still feel his eyes on me.

"Okay," Jasmine said, "so I'm about to play you a video of a project we're working on currently. But before that, Will– could you hand out the packs?"

"Sure." Will pushed out of his chair and grabbed a pile of thick envelopes. He threw one to each of us, asking for names here and there for those he'd forgotten. Mine he threw with more force than the others.

"Thanks," I smiled in a way that I hoped looked menacing. He did flinch back, but then he threw me a pen that almost hit me in the face.

"If you could please put your name card on," Jasmine called, "it will help others in the office know who you are. And please sign your names at the end of the forms. It's the boring stuff, sorry. The blue one tells you which department you've been assigned, so you might want to look at that one first."

We all aimed straight for the blue sheet.

"Yes!" Finn fist-pumped the air before turning to grin at me. "I got design. What about you, Dani?"

I bit back my disappointment as I waved my sheet in front of him. "Art."

"Oh. So we won't be working together, then."

"There'll be a lot of cross-department working," the girl whose name I remembered as Lily chimed in. "I'm in art, too," she added, smiling at me.

I smiled back. But, before anything else could be said, Will called our attention to the front.

"Does anyone have any questions? If not, I'll get the video

started. The sooner it finishes, the sooner we can show you around and head out for a drink."

An excited murmur passed through the table.

"We're going for a drink?" Finn asked.

"It's our custom to take first years out on their first day," he answered, grabbing a remote. "Alright, is that everything?" I raised my hand. He met my eye, and I tried to suppress my irritation at his deceiving ways. *How are you here?* "Go ahead, Dani."

"Will we get the opportunity to work in other departments, or is this final?"

"Which department are you in?"

"Art."

He looked at me for a long second. Long enough that I wondered if he remembered what I'd said about my interest in design.

"There'll be an opportunity to move department after six months," he said. "But it's not guaranteed. Actually, it's not likely. I strongly advise you to give your all into the role you're assigned, even if it's not what you expected."

"Of course."

After looking at me for another second, he nodded. "Well, if that's all, I'll get the video on."

"Can I just have your signed forms first?" Jasmine interrupted. "I need to run them across to HR."

"Are you sure you're not just avoiding watching this video again?" Will muttered. She jumped to her feet and gave him a wink.

I tried to concentrate on the video like everyone else, but my eyes kept moving to peek at Will. This morning,

I'd thought he was unemployed. Now I knew that not only did he have a job, but he worked as the *lead designer* in a company I'd been dreaming about for years. I just couldn't wrap my head around it.

I realised that I'd misjudged him. Of course, that only demonstrated how good of a liar he was. Just thinking about it annoyed me. All those opportunities to tell me he worked here, and he hadn't said a word.

He caught me glaring at him and pulled a face, but I held firm. He wouldn't get away with this.

I planned to confront him after the video, but he was a step ahead of me. He escaped the room as soon as Jasmine returned.

But I knew he couldn't avoid me forever. For now, I was content with following Jasmine through the office and marvelling at it as she gave us a tour.

"Did you see that monitor?" Finn asked, pointing with enthusiasm at a gigantic screen. He behaved like a gaping child touring a chocolate factory.

So did I.

"Look at that room," I pointed at a splash of colour.

"That's the break-out room," Jasmine told us. "It's where we go if ever the stress gets too overwhelming. It holds the newest gaming consoles and games you can play. Gaming is research for us, after all."

"Is that an air hockey table?" Finn now stood on his tiptoes. I held back a laugh, resisting the urge to join him.

"Yes," Jasmine smirked before indicating a row of desks. "This is where the programming team sits. Some of you will be sitting here. Right here is where the design team sits-,"

Spotting Will at the head of the table, my skin immediately prickled. *You should be at home in bed.* He looked up as we passed, his eyes meeting mine. He diverted them before I could ask for a word.

That was fine. If not now, I would find a way to corner him later.

We moved on. After showing us where the lead producer sits, we followed Jasmine to the opposite side of the floor, where big, circular things replaced workstations.

"Those are pods," she said, following my gaze. "It's just a seat inside. They're for anyone who needs some quiet time or to take a call. This is the kitchen," she opened a door. "Take twenty minutes. I have a paper to submit, then I'll return to you."

I took a seat beside Finn and Lily.

"So," Finn said, looking at me with eyes that wanted a story, "tell us about that person you moved in with. What happened there?"

"I-" before I could think of a plausible lie, I looked toward the window. I could have sworn I'd just seen Will passing it. Alone. "I'll be back in a minute."

Outside, I spotted Will's head bobbing up above one of the pods. I called his name, but he ignored me. I wasn't willing to let him get away from me this time. "Hey, Will!" I called again.

This time he turned to face me. His eyes were impatient as he put a finger to his lips.

I glowered at him. "What's the matter, scared people will find out I know you?" I didn't think that was actually the case, but then he hurried toward me with another shush, putting a finger over my mouth. "Hey!" I mumbled into his skin.

He pulled me into one of the break-out pods and closed the door.

It was small inside. Too small. My knees brushed against his as I perched on the seat opposite.

"What's this about?" I demanded. "Do you actually care if people find out you know me?"

"That isn't it."

"Then what? You don't want to be seen with a junior? You're embarrassed by me?"

He looked offended by the suggestion. "I didn't do it for me!"

I raised a brow. "So you did it for me?"

"Look, I've been working here for a while, so I know what the people are like. Any ounce of success, and they try to find fault in it. I'm not saying everyone is like that, but if the wrong person finds out you know me-"

"I hardly do," I interrupted, wanting to get that one in there. He didn't give me a chance to get to know him.

He gave me a sour look before continuing. "If people find out we live together, you'll have a hard time here."

I didn't understand. "Why would knowing you mean I get a hard time? Are you on some kind of boycott list?"

"I'm the Lead Designer. I'm not saying that to show off," he added quickly, seeing the look on my face, "but many important decisions pass through me. Imagine an idea of yours gets selected, or you're congratulated on something; there are enough pessimistic people here who will claim your success is down to me."

I stuck my chin out. "My success is my own."

"Exactly. And I'm not arguing that. So, given how badly you wanted this job, I'm guessing you're with me on acting like we're strangers."

The strangers part was easy. We practically were that, even in the house. And he was right–I did not want a hard time, not when I'd worked so hard to get here. "Okay, fine," I said. "I'll act like I don't know you. When I see you walk by, I won't make eye contact; if I do need to talk to you, I'll address you as my senior-"

"You don't need to go that far," he smirked as though he liked that idea very much.

I struck it off the list.

"I'll come to work in the morning without you," I continued like I hadn't heard him, "and I'll go back to the house in the same way. It will be as though we never met."

"Perfect." The grin still played on his lips. I wanted to wipe it off.

"Can we please move on to the fact that you lied to me about your job?" I gritted out.

The smile vanished. "I didn't lie."

"You so did! You said, and I quote, that you're unemployed. And then you accepted my offer to pay more!" The more I thought about it, the more I wanted to stuff him into a cave with a bear.

He bit back a laugh. "You don't have to pay me any of that."

"You're damn right I don't."

He sighed. "Okay, I guess I should've told you. But can you really blame me when such a perfect opportunity arose? I was going to tell you as soon as you told me. Really. But I guess my inner child stopped me from saying it. The look on your face when I walked in before," he didn't stop the laugh this time. It rang like a bell. "Honestly, it was gold. I couldn't let a chance like that slip by. Please forgive me."

Thinking about it, I guessed I would've done the same in his position. At the very least, I would've been tempted. And I could see why it was funny. "Fine," I said. "But that bet that we made? It's off the table."

He didn't like that. "A bet is a bet."

"But you had an unfair advantage."

"Isn't that how all bets are first made?"

"I'm not doing the cleaning when you withheld information from me. I obviously would never have said I could get you an interview if I knew you already had a job here."

He smiled to himself, pleased by his scheming ways.

"Can't you just hire a cleaner?" I continued. "You're obviously well off." That made me think. Why did he need a roommate? It couldn't be for the money.

"Why do I need a cleaner when I have you?" he asked.

I glared at him. "You need to take a long, hard look at yourself," I said, getting to my feet.

"Wait," he reached out as I turned for the door.

I paused, fingers enclosing the handle. "What?"

"Were my eyes deceiving me earlier, or are you actually wearing my shirt?"

My face heated. I fastened my blazer before turning back to him. "So what if I am?"

His eyes scrutinised my face. "Are you not embarrassed

that I caught you?"

"I'd be more embarrassed if you weren't so...," I struggled for the right word as I waved my hands at him, "You."

His brows flicked up. "What's that supposed to mean?"

"It means that you're not very intimidating. Sorry."

"Huh." He contemplated what I said. "Maybe I should try harder."

"Go ahead."

We stared at each other for a long second. Realising that time was ticking, I turned again, but the flash of his shoe caught my attention.

"Are you allowed to wear trainers to work?" I asked.

"Are you telling me off?" he laughed.

Like I could. "No, I'm just wondering if it's allowed. I won't wear these horribly uncomfortable things anymore if it is." I grimaced at my loafers, already feeling a blister coming along. His eyes followed mine.

"You're allowed to wear anything here," he said, looking back at me. "Have you not seen half the office?"

A smirk crept onto my lips. If I could wear what I wanted, I no longer needed to buy workwear–I already had it at home.

Will seemed to guess the direction my mind had taken me.

"First years tend to dress smart," he warned. "So if you don't want to stand out, I suggest you refrain from wearing the stuff I see you in at the house."

He meant my baggy sweats.

"But trainers are allowed?" I asked.

"Yeah."

"And I can keep the shirt?"

"No."

With that answer, I twisted the handle and left.

CHAPTER SIX

After we finished our office tour, Jasmine showed us to our desks. The design team sat one row away from us, so I could see Will from my spot at the end. He sat at the head of the row, looking busy but probably faking it. Finn snatched the desk nearest to him.

Every workstation in this place had enough space to seat two. They also held multiple monitors as if one wasn't enough. Which, in this job, it probably wasn't.

I tested the springs of my chair before scavenging my drawers. They weren't empty. Within them, I found a laptop–still boxed–tech equipment, stationery, and other things I didn't know the name of.

The girl to my right hadn't acknowledged me yet. Too busy, I assumed, with flicking through her large pile of paperwork. I didn't want to disturb her, so I stayed quiet, observing the items littered across her desk. Unlike mine– clear except for the monitors–hers was a catastrophic mess. Beneath the paper, mugs, and wrappers, I couldn't see even a slither of dark oak.

"Chrissie?"

"Yes!" the girl's face sprang up, lightning-fast, as Jasmine appeared by her side.

"Have you had a chance to meet Dani yet?"

"Who's Dani?" she turned, blinking when she saw me. "Oh. Sorry."

"Chrissie is my assistant," Jasmine told me, putting a hand on the back of our chairs. "She's been in your shoes before, so ask her anything you need. Chrissie, you'll be Dani's mentor, so teach her everything you know." I wondered if Jasmine caught her flicker of distaste at the mention of being my mentor. "But not today," Jasmine continued, pausing from where she'd walked a few steps ahead. "Right now, we're going for drinks."

"Do I need to come?" Chrissie's eyes darted to her pile of paperwork.

"Yes, we're all going. You know who included," Jasmine winked.

I turned away as colour peppered Chrissie's cheeks, wondering who she meant by *you know who*.

I walked to the pub with Lily and Finn and learned that the latter had Will as a mentor. It had him bouncing on his feet the entire way there.

When we got to the pub, the first years crammed into one table while the older employees claimed another.

"There's a tab on the bar," Will called over to us. "Get whatever you want."

Eager for a drink, I took the first order and, with the help of Lily, brought two trays back to our table.

"Do you think that Chrissie girl has a thing for Will?" Lily whispered, indicating the other table.

I turned and immediately saw what she meant. Will and Chrissie sat next to one another, and the latter was clearly besotted by my roommate. She hung onto his every word, laughing now and then at something he said. That was my first indication. Because whatever Will said, it probably wasn't funny.

"*Oh*," I said, suddenly remembering Jasmine's not-so-subtle mention of *you know who*. "So *that's* who she meant."

Lily frowned. "What do you mean?"

Part of me wanted to share what I knew–that Chrissie *definitely* had a thing for Will–but I didn't think it was fair. Nor was it my secret to share. "It doesn't matter," I said. "They seem like they're only colleagues to me."

"Do you think so?" she tilted her head. "Maybe I stand a chance with him, then."

"Don't waste your time." As soon as I said the words, I clamped my teeth together.

"You say it as if you know him," Lily laughed.

"I don't. It's just… he looks like a player. That's all."

"Huh. He seems like one of the good ones to me."

Clearly, she wasn't a good judge of character. I wanted to warn her against trying anything with him, but I stopped myself. Telling her would only mean I'd have to back my argument, and I couldn't do that without giving away what I knew–and, more importantly, *who* I knew.

After finishing my second drink, I spotted Will at the bar. He picked up a tray, wobbling slightly from the weight of it.

The smell of sambuca made my nose wrinkle as I walked over to help him.

"Who are those for?" I asked, lifting one side of the tray.

He grinned. "Me."

A bubble of panic rose in my throat. "All of them?" I could only imagine what a drunken nightmare Will would be after these. Was it acceptable to lock him out of his own house?

He laughed as if he could read my every thought. "Don't worry, I can handle my drink."

"Or maybe you'll knock yourself clean out." And maybe I wasn't against that.

His eyes glinted as we placed the shots onto his table.

Jasmine let out a long groan. "Damn it, Will. Why do you always resort to shots?"

"Hey, Dani helped bring them over! Why do you always assume it's me?"

Jasmine turned her eyes to me. "Dani, did you buy these?"

"Nope."

She smirked, turning back to Will. "I'm not having any of them, so what will you do about that?"

"Actually." Will pushed the shots to the edge of the table with a grin. "These are for the first years."

"Sorry, what?" I stared at him, half wondering if I'd heard him right.

His smile widened. "Come on, first year. This one's for you." He passed me the one that brimmed the fullest.

It was funny that he seemed to think this was some form of punishment. A free shot? I wasn't going to say no to that.

I took it from his hand as he called the other first-years over. They came hesitantly, eyeing the shot in my hand with distrust. Those same eyes bulged when they saw the tray full of them.

"We got you a shot," Will told them, smiling like a man who took pleasure in pain.

"*You* got them a shot." Jasmine corrected. "*I* have nothing to do with this."

"Okay, *I* got you a shot. It's tradition for first-years to take one."

Somehow, I didn't think that was true.

"Um, I don't actually drink," one person said.

"Fair enough. You can sit down. Everyone else," he indicated with his finger, "grab your shot."

They did as they were told, some with a pout, some with a determined look in their eye. A few slipped away like shadows in the night. Will didn't call them back.

Nobody seemed to want to take the first shot, so I took one for the team, wrinkling my nose at the taste and then wincing as the liquid went down, burning my throat.

"Impressive," Will nodded his approval as I slammed the empty glass down.

"I told you I can handle my drink," I replied. Crap. "Before–earlier– just then, I mean."

He rolled his eyes when it became clear that everyone else was too distracted with their shots to notice my slip.

"That was horrible," Lily said, sticking her tongue out in disgust.

Finn wiped his mouth with the back of his sleeve, half the sambuca ending up on his chin. "Never again."

Three shots still remained on the table.

Will sighed, looking at them. "I can never get them to take them all."

"You know the rules," Jasmine smirked. "Any that are left need to be taken by you."

I exchanged a worried glance with Lily.

One shot was okay. Two were pushing it. Three were downright puke-inducing.

Will picked one up and gave it a gentle swirl. It disappeared in a second. "Ah," he winced and looked hard at the second glass. His fingers inched toward it, and then he looked at me. "Want two?"

The short answer was no, not really. But I couldn't bear the thought of any person taking three shots in a row, let alone the one I lived with. If I had to clean up his puke...

"Sure," I picked up a glass. His brows shot up as I gulped it down. It burned. "Water," I pleaded to anyone who cared. Lily's laugh came out like a howl. I turned my eyes on her, ready to beg on my knees if it meant I'd get water.

"Sorry. One water coming up."

"Make it two," Will choked, slamming his second glass down.

I fought back the vomit threatening to rise before meeting his eyes. He seemed to be fighting the same thing. When Lily returned, we gulped the water down simultaneously.

"Well, Will," Jasmine's eyes appraised me. "It looks like you've met your match. I'm glad you're on our team, Dani. We can never seem to beat him when it comes to drinking."

I turned a smug smile on Will. "I could match him anytime."

He raised a brow as if daring me to try.

CHAPTER SEVEN

When I got home, I fell asleep as soon as my head hit the pillow.

Will hadn't come back with me. He stayed out—the self-proclaimed life of the party.

And, once more, I was jolted awake by the sound of his antics.

"You have got to be kidding me!" I looked at the time and groaned into my pillow. The clatter from downstairs grew noisier.

A girl laughed.

I flipped over onto my back and glared up at the ceiling. *It's okay. He'll go to bed soon. And then...* nope. I swung my legs out of bed and stood.

If we were going to live together, I needed to set some ground rules of my own.

I marched down the stairs, grumpy from tiredness and a developing headache, and headed for the living room, where I found him on the couch nibbling on a girl's neck.

"*Will*," I growled. They both jumped. Good.

It took him a second to focus his eyes. When they found

my face, they narrowed.

"What's wrong with you?" he slurred. "You look grumpy."

"I *am* grumpy." I almost picked up a cushion to throw at him. "We both have work tomorrow, and *you* woke me up."

The girl quickly untangled herself. Her eyes appraised me with alarm.

"So sorry about that," Will continued, standing up with a sway. "We'll just get going, then."

The girl stood up with him, eyes still wary. She was a gorgeous brunette with envious curves, and I had no idea what she saw in Will.

"I'm sorry," she said. "I didn't know that he has a girlfriend. I'll get going."

"I'm not his girlfriend," I replied, relieved that she at least sounded semi-sober.

She frowned. "Oh?"

"I'm his roommate," I elaborated.

She did not look impressed. "He lives with a girl? *Urgh*."

My mouth dropped open as she grabbed her jacket and left the room.

I followed her. "What's wrong with a girl roommate?"

The door opened and closed with a bang, leaving my question unanswered.

"Everything," Will answered instead. I turned to see him banging into a wall on his way up the stairs. I followed behind with my arms extended, fearful he'd fall back on me like a bowling pin. Although I wasn't sure if he deserved getting caught.

He avoided me most of the next day. I didn't see him in the morning at the house, and I was surprised when he eventually turned up to work. He did look a little worse for wear. One hand blocked the light from his eyes as if it burned, while the other covered his mouth–probably to catch impending puke. I smirked as he took his seat, especially when he rubbed his temples, grimacing, and shooed an approaching Finn away before he'd even said a word.

And there was me thinking he could handle his drink.

I would have grabbed him a glass of water if we were friends. But, as it happens, he didn't want that. More fool him.

"Are you finished with that?" Chrissie's mildly demanding voice brought my attention back to her.

"I'm just finishing the last one."

So far, Chrissie hadn't tasked me with anything interesting or game-related. I'd spent all morning de-stapling an excessive amount of paper for her. I did ask her when she'd show me the software they used–which she'd said she'd do–but she just gave me a look. A look that I interpreted to say *be quiet*.

I wouldn't have minded so much if I hadn't seen Lily working on some drawings. Even Finn, who had Will and his hangover to contend with, seemed to be doing something more interesting than me.

"Once you're finished with that can you do a coffee run?" she asked.

I held back a sigh. "Do you want me to run to the kitchen or a shop?

"The kitchen will do today." She rubbed at her temples. "Make mine strong. And black."

I wondered if she'd stayed out late too. I wanted to ask her, but I got the sense she didn't want to converse with me. I finished what I was doing and asked the table if anybody else wanted a drink. This proved both a blessing and a mistake. On the one hand, at least making coffee was more fun than de-stapling paper; on the other, I was hit with an onslaught of orders. I had to write them down in case I forgot anything.

Making the drinks was easy. Getting them back to the table was another task altogether. I balanced them on a tray, wincing as coffee sloshed over the rim.

As I reached the kitchen door, tray surprisingly steady in hand, Will's face flashed through my mind. I wasn't sure why I needed to think of him at this particular moment. I shook the thought away, but he sprang straight back–rubbing his temples and wincing in pain this time.

I carried an extra glass of water as I walked back to my row of desks.

I sat the drinks down on the table.

"Coffee one sugar?" I asked.

"That's me."

I distributed the drinks out until only the water remained.

I feigned a frown. "Hmm. I made extra water." Please work. I raised my voice. "Does anybody want a glass of water?"

I held back my relief as Will's head snapped up. He nodded, a wince coming straight after it.

Before I carried it over, I quickly rummaged through my bag. My hands enclosed the packet I was after. I fiddled, popped out two paracetamols, and hid them under my sleeve.

I slid them onto his desk along with the water.

"Thank y-," he spotted the pills and blinked. His eyes moved slowly to mine. I couldn't tell if he thought I was trying to poison or help him. I gave him evils, just in case it was the former and walked back to my desk.

From the corner of my eye, I saw him pop the pills into his mouth and gulp them down.

So he knew I wasn't trying to kill him.

The rest of the day passed by mundanely. I didn't think *mundane* was a word I'd use in conjunction with Bluebird. But, after the de-stapling task, Chrissie had me scanning the documents onto the computer, and mundane was the only word for it. It took me the rest of the day to finish it, and then I had to stay behind an hour because Chrissie wouldn't let me leave until I'd done it all.

By the end of the week, I was ready to ask if I could switch mentors.

"Are you sure you can't come for a drink with us tomorrow?" Lily asked as we walked to the elevator. It was Friday, and the buzz in the office was electric.

A buzz that I didn't feel. "I'm sure. Chrissie's given me work to complete by Monday."

Both Lily and Finn's mouths dropped open. Mine did the same when she first handed me the wad of paper.

"She's given you work?" Lily sounded appalled by the idea. "But it's the weekend."

"It's good, though, right?" Finn struggled to find a reason. "Maybe it means she sees potential in you."

"If by 'potential' you mean someone who can read through a mountain of documents and check for spelling mistakes, then yeah. She sees potential."

Will slipped inside the elevator just as the door closed. He barely glanced at me before turning his back. I was used to that. Over the past week, I'd realised just how serious he was about pretending to be strangers. He never so much as smiled at me. Even if I found him sitting alone in the kitchen, I still didn't get an acknowledgement.

I ignored him now as much as he did me.

As the elevator moved down, I listened to Finn and Lily finalise their plans. A few more people entered from the lower floors, forcing Will to shuffle towards me.

"Sorry," he mumbled as his arm pressed against mine.

"No worries." I nudged it away to get mine into a more comfortable position and smiled at the look on his face.

"I take the sorry back," he hissed into my ear.

I held back a laugh as the door opened for the third time. The group on this floor took one look inside and decided to leave it.

"People must want to get home for the weekend," Finn grunted from his place squished in the corner. "Maybe next time we leave a bit later."

The door finally opened to the ground floor. We rolled out like an overpacked box of Styrofoam. Spotting Will speed-walking ahead, I quickly said to the others, "I'll see you on Monday. Have a great weekend!" And then I chased after him.

This was the first time we'd left the building together, and I wanted to see how he got home.

I wasn't stupid enough to catch up to him straight away. There were too many people from work around, and it would've looked strange if they saw us walking together. So I waited until we'd covered a few blocks first before I called out his name.

He ducked his head, and I could've sworn he released a sigh.

"Yes?" he asked, turning to face me. He looked everything like a man who'd had his patience tested.

Why did I even bother with him? "Do you want to walk home together?"

"No."

"Why not?"

"Because people might see us together. We don't know each other, remember?"

"I doubt that anyone will see us here. You know, I'm starting to think this is more for you than it is for me. You just don't want to spend any time with me. Admit it."

"Thank goodness you figured that out." He rolled his eyes, turning away again. I stuck my tongue out, thinking he'd walk ahead, but he spun back. "Do you always do that when my back is turned?" he demanded.

"Maybe."

"Makes me feel better about what I do behind yours."

I opened my mouth and closed it. I didn't want to know.

"So, do you want to walk with me then?" I didn't know why he'd turned again.

He scratched the back of his neck and looked down the street. I followed his eyes, but there was nobody around.

"Thanks for the other day," he said quietly.

I frowned. "The other day?"

"The pain relief?" He searched my face to see if I remembered.

I did–I just wasn't expecting a thank you for it four days later.

"Oh. Well, you're welcome. Thanks for trusting me and taking them."

His lips twitched. "I did wonder for a second if you were trying to kill me."

I shrugged. "There was always the chance you'd be allergic."

Now he laughed. He immediately tried to cover it up with a cough, but I'd heard it.

"There was actually something I wanted to ask you," he continued, a faint blush tinting his cheeks.

"Go on."

He sucked in a deep breath and shook his head. "No, never mind."

"Tell me!" I reached out my arm as he turned away. He saw it coming and jumped out of reach.

"It doesn't matter," he hopped away as I lurched for him.

"I hate it when people do that," I complained.

"Stop chasing me!"

I didn't listen. I jumped after him, but he was too quick for me. Gasping for air, I demanded, "What did you want to ask?"

He shrugged. "See you at home."

"What?" I stared in disbelief as he started walking. "Can't we at least walk home together? There's no one here."

"We aren't friends," he reminded me from over his

shoulder.

"Because who wants to be friends with you," I grumbled.

"Just make sure you stay at least ten feet behind me."

I stopped walking, scowling at his back as he marched ahead.

And then I realised that I was actually listening to him.

"Not a chance," I stormed forward, shortening the distance between us until finally, I could reach out and grab him if I wanted to. I smiled sweetly as I passed him, pleased by his surprise.

He could walk behind me.

I thought I'd reached the house first, but the hallway light was on when I got there. Confused, I peeked over my shoulder, but there was no sign of Will down the street. He must be lagging behind. I didn't slow down once, and if that wasn't enough, I didn't see him pass me. Served him right for-

I yelped as the front door swung open. Will grinned down at me, looking so pleased with himself we may as well have been racing for a title.

"How did you-?" I couldn't finish the question with my heart now stuck in my throat.

"Did I scare you?" he grinned.

I clutched my chest and managed to ask, "How did you get here?"

"I took a shortcut."

I looked him up and down, narrowing my eyes. "You look out of breath. Did you run?"

He seemed offended by the suggestion. "No, I did not run. And if you'd followed behind me, you would have seen the shortcut."

I barged past him. "I don't believe you."

"Hey, fair is fair." He closed the door and followed me.

I swivelled around him and headed up the stairs. "You definitely ran here!" I called before slamming my bedroom door closed.

After changing into PJs, I wiped off my make-up and brushed my hair out. The relief was instant. I hated wearing make-up–it felt suffocating–but I wasn't a girl blessed with clear skin.

Grabbing my work bag, I went downstairs, bumping into Will on his way from the kitchen. He stared at me long enough that it became rude.

"What?" I demanded.

"You look different without make-up."

If it had been anyone else, I might've blushed. But this was Will, and I didn't care what he thought. "It's called having bad skin. You should try it." I moved past him into the kitchen.

"I didn't say it was a bad thing," he said, leaning against the doorframe.

"Gee, thanks." I flicked the kettle on. While I waited for it to boil, I moved to the sink. A glance told me Will had disappeared. Good. I emptied the dishwasher and reloaded it, sighing at the dirt pile that never seemed to end.

Will and I had come to an agreement regarding the bet. Instead of doing the cleaning for twelve months, I was now on duty for two. I couldn't complain about this reduction–it was pretty generous, and he could have argued for more. But I also couldn't bring myself to enjoy doing it, either.

While Will wasn't what I'd call dirty–he at least rinsed his plates before dumping them in the sink–cleaning up after anyone wasn't something I wanted to do. I already made enough mess for the two of us.

He was reading a magazine when I took my coffee and work bag into the front room. His eyes narrowed into two daggers as soon as I entered.

"Can I at least sit at the table?" I asked, slamming my bag down. This 'no being in the same room together' rule was tiring. "I may as well move back in with Nick if this is how you'll be."

His laugh wasn't the reaction I was going for.

"Fine, you can sit at the table. Just don't talk to me."

I pulled out the chair as noisily as possible and sat, spreading the paperwork out in front of me.

"I see Chrissie's given you work to do," he observed.

"I thought you told me not to talk," I replied, picking up the first sheet.

"Suit yourself."

I glanced at him. It didn't look like he'd say anything else, so I put the paper down. "I don't think she likes me."

"What makes you think that?"

I opened my mouth, but it didn't feel right to complain about Chrissie to him. Not when he was technically her senior. I shook my head. "It doesn't matter."

"Go on," he prompted.

"I can't. It isn't right complaining to you. She'd hate me for it."

"It sounds like she already hates you."

My heart dropped. "Has she said something to you?"

"No," he laughed and sat straighter, throwing his arm over the back of the sofa. "Let me guess. Is she making you do coffee runs, stand by the printer," his eyes flashed down to the paper spread out in front of me, "and giving you work to do from home?"

"All of the above. I wouldn't mind, but it doesn't seem like she wants to teach me anything either."

"The thing with Chrissie is that she hates training people who don't deserve it."

Well, that stung. "But how does she know if I don't deserve it?"

"She doesn't... yet. That's why she's testing you."

"She's testing me?" I didn't like the sound of that.

"You have no idea how many people join Bluebird and think it'll be an easy ride," he told me. "Those people are the ones who don't take the job seriously; they always quit at the end when they realise how hard this industry is. Chrissie tries to weasel those people out early. Trust me, if you can get through a few months with her, you'll realise that you've hit the jackpot with your mentor."

I thought about it for a second and realised that it made sense. "So you're saying she's good? But I need to prove myself first." He nodded. "Alright, then." I picked the sheet up as another doubt settled in my stomach. I looked back over at him. "But what do I do if I fall behind the other first years? Finn said you've already involved him in a proposal you're working on. I'll be so far behind him if all I do is stand by the printer."

He shrugged. "That's for you to decide." I pulled a face at his not-so-helpfulness, and he elaborated. "You can learn in your own time. That's what I did. There are so many books out there, YouTube videos, wiki..."

"But I don't have a laptop." My lip pulled down at the thought of having to spend more money.

"You have a work laptop."

"I can bring that home?"

"Of course. And it has everything on it. Maya, iClone, Unity... And if you need books, I have a load in that case," he indicated a storage unit. "Help yourself."

My worry suddenly cleared. "Thank you."

"Well, that's enough talking." He turned his attention to his magazine, but I noticed his eyes flash back to my face.

"Are you sure you don't have anything else to say?" I asked.

He swivelled back to me. "That question I was going to ask earlier...,"

"Yeah?"

"Did I-" he cringed. "Did I bring a girl back the other night?"

"You don't remember?"

Pink spots appeared on his cheeks. "So I did? The only thing I remember is seeing you and your angry face."

"Yes, I was angry because you woke me up. So thanks for that."

He smiled apologetically. "I'm not used to living with someone."

"Why did you need a roommate, by the way?" I'd been curious about this ever since learning about his job. He certainly didn't need the money.

He shifted his eyes to the floor like I'd hit on something

awkward. "Extra income never hurt anyone."

I waited for him to continue. When he didn't, I scrutinized his face for a second before deciding to let it go. If he wanted to talk about it, he would.

"The girl left because she found out I was your roommate," I told him instead.

He looked up again. "Is that so?" he laughed. "You really are a girl repellent."

I smiled, surprised that he was taking it so lightly. "Just at the wrong time of the day."

"The wrong time," he agreed and stood. "In the future, maybe you don't come out to yell at me?"

My eyes followed him from the room. "Only if, in the future, you don't wake me up on a work night. Where are you going?"

"Upstairs. I'm going out. And no, you can't come," he smiled knowingly over his shoulder.

"I wasn't going to ask." For once, that was true.

I turned back to my paperwork and rolled up my sleeves, ready to work through the weekend if it meant earning Chrissie's trust.

CHAPTER EIGHT

T he worst thing about living in this house, I began to find, was the one bathroom.

I jiggled in my seat, trying to ignore my desperate need for the toilet as Will hogged the bathroom.

He was currently in the shower. From experience, I knew that he took forever. All I could do was wait for him to finish and blame myself for drinking that second coffee.

I heard the water finally shut off and raced upstairs.

"Woah." Steam followed Will from the bathroom as he emerged with a towel wrapped around his waist. He pressed his back against the wall as I barged through.

"Sorry," I breathed. "Need the toilet." I slammed the door in his face.

I could barely see a thing through the steam. Scowling, I shoved the window open. It was something Will never did himself. That fact was beginning to annoy me because, no matter his difference in opinion, his house was not immune to mould.

I was still scowling as I left the bathroom.

"What's that face for?" Will asked.

I blinked, surprised to see him still standing there.

"Did you need to listen to that?" I asked.

He pulled his face. "I left my washbag inside." He circled around me and grabbed it, waving it in my face on his way out.

"You know," I said, shoving it away, "it's a wonder you don't melt into the drain with how hot you have your showers."

"Oh yeah? I bet you have yours cold to match your personality."

"Har har." I folded my arms.

He flashed a playful smile and stepped forward. Heat emanated from his bare chest onto me, forcing me to step back.

"What's the matter?" he asked, taking another step.

I gulped. "Nothing's the matter."

"Are you sure about that?" He lowered his face so that we were at eye level.

The wall greeted my back.

"I'm sure." His eyes were green, I realised. Deep green like the rainforest. I tore mine away, trying not to think about the beauty in his as I searched frantically for something to concentrate on. A drop of water threatened to fall from his hair. I latched on to it. "I am immune to whatever charms you think you might have, William."

His lip quirked up. It was a different smile from the ones I'd seen before. It was almost... *daring*. "So, you're not tempted?" he whispered.

Don't look at his face. "No, I'm not. At all." To prove this, I pressed my hands against his chest and pushed. Big mistake. My fingers met with warm, toned skin, and I did not dare admit to myself that I liked the feel of him.

He laughed at my attempt, which barely moved him an inch, and jumped back. "I was only testing you. I'm happy to say that you passed." He shook his wet hair at me and disappeared inside his bedroom.

I stared at the closed door for a second, slightly dumbfounded. What just happened? Will had never acted like that before... And he'd needed *to test me*? Why? It wasn't like I'd ever given off vibes that I liked him. Of that, I was sure. Or... Doubt crept in. I thought back through our previous conversations and realised that Will might just be the kind of person who mistakes insults for flirting.

I couldn't be having that.

I banged on his door just as another worry settled in my brain.

"Yeah?" His voice came from the other side of his room.

"Can I speak to you?"

"I'm in the middle of getting changed."

I sucked in a deep breath. No matter how awkward, I needed to deal with this immediately. "You're not... I mean, you don't..." I struggled to get it out. After another deep breath, I forced it. "You don't fancy me, do you?"

The question was met with a deafening silence. I cringed as I waited for a response.

His door flung open. He had one arm through a sleeve of a sweater and his belt undone. He pulled the other half over his head and ruffled his hair.

"What did you just ask?"

"You heard." I didn't want to say it twice.

"You think I fancy you?" I cringed again. Hearing it from him, I realised how foolish I sounded. He came out of his bedroom and closed the door. "What makes you think that?"

I fought through the embarrassment and held firm. "Well, you sort of just came onto me a moment ago."

He shook his head. "No, that wasn't me coming onto you. Please don't think that it was."

I analysed his face. When I saw honesty in it, I relaxed. "Then what was it?"

He shrugged. "I thought it would be a good opportunity to see what you'd do."

"And what did you think I'd do?"

"I *hoped* you'd push me away."

"Which I did."

He nodded. "You did."

"So, we're good."

He nodded again. "We're good."

I pursed my lips. This was a strange conversation, and it didn't seem like either of us knew how to end it. "So I don't fancy you, and you don't fancy me," I said, feeling ridiculous. "Let's agree to be friends?"

"I don't even want that."

I narrowed my eyes. This was the Will I knew. "Fine," I turned and walked down the stairs. When I glanced back, I found his eyes still on me.

The best thing would be to erase the whole episode from my memory. It was awkward, and, I realised with surprise, I rarely ever felt that way around Will. If anything, it was a taster of what he'd mentioned about the complications between a boy and girl living together–it could get messy. I didn't want that. Not that I was ever in danger of falling for him anyway, but it only affirmed that it wouldn't work if I did. And if he ever did anything like that to me again, I decided I'd punch him squarely in the face.

He came downstairs an hour later. All awkwardness was gone, so I guessed he'd also forced it from his memory. He ignored me as he switched on the TV, stopping on a music channel.

"When are you going out?" I asked over the noise.

"Soon." He looked towards the window and got to his feet. "Ah, there's Jordan now."

He disappeared from the room. A second later, a male voice echoed through the house. "Where should I put this?"

"The kitchen will be fine."

I turned curiously as two sets of footsteps pattered through the hallway. Will came back into the room as his friend disappeared into the kitchen, but not before I caught a glimpse of his face.

"Oh my God." The words came out before I could stop them. I put my hand to my mouth.

"What's the matter with you?" Will asked.

"You didn't tell me you had anyone coming over," I whispered. *You also didn't tell me that you have cute friends!*

"Should I have told you?"

"Yes!" I lowered my voice. "Wasn't that one of the rules... to warn each other?"

"Oh." He glanced at the hallway. "Sorry. I forgot about that."

I gave him a look and leapt to my feet. Ignoring his

perplexed face, I hurried from the room, taking two steps at a time and almost falling on the stair in my haste to disappear. If I had known that Will had a cute friend–and that said cute friend was coming over–there was no way I'd have let myself be seen in my current state. And his friend wasn't only cute–he was hot. Like call-the-firefighter-this-place-is-about-to-burn hot.

Safely shut away in my room, I grabbed my make-up bag and moved to the mirror. A small part of me recognised this was ridiculous as I slathered on foundation. But then I thought of his friend again, and that voice shut off. I changed out of my sweats and pulled on some jeans. To finish the transformation, I brushed through my hair so that it wasn't just a bird's nest but a smooth, flowing sheet falling down my shoulders. After one last look at myself, I went back downstairs.

I could hear their voices coming from the front room. The music had gotten louder, and so had Will's voice. He was joking about something. I paused around the corner, flushed, and then entered before I could talk myself out of it.

The newcomer sat on the sofa facing away from me, so he didn't see me at first. I was glad about this, except it meant that Will saw me immediately. His eyes did a double-take and then narrowed as though I'd gone away as one thing and came back as something else. I tried to ignore him as I resumed my place at the table, but his eyes followed me like an assassin watching his target.

"Have you changed?" he asked.

I worked on keeping my voice neutral. "No, I've not."

He tilted his head. "I'm sure you have."

"I haven't, Will." I could feel the heat rising in my face. I tried to give him a pointed look, but my eyes fell on his friend instead. The brown-haired beauty returned my gaze with curiosity.

"Who's this?" he asked, eyes darting away to question Will. That voice was as dreamy as his face. And those muscles...

"My roommate."

His brows shot up in surprise. "You never told us your roommate is a girl." He said it like an accusation.

"I barely remember it myself," Will muttered, turning his attention away. I frowned at the back of his head, but then he spun back. "You've definitely changed. And you've put on make-up."

My mouth dropped open. *Yes, Will. I have because your friend is super cute. Isn't it obvious?* With a sigh, I lied, "Yeah, I'm going out tonight, so I got changed."

"Oh." His pacification lasted a mere second. "Where are you going?"

"Um," I looked up at the ceiling. "I'm meeting Finn and Lily from work."

I thought that was a good enough answer, but, for some reason, it made him frown. "Isn't that tomorrow?"

"How do you know that?"

"Finn invited me."

Of course, he did. "Well, you must have mixed up the dates because it's tonight."

"It's a good job that I said no then." He finally turned away.

I looked toward his friend. "I'm Dani, by the way."

"Jordan." He flashed a white-toothed smile at me.

I smiled back, ignoring the sudden thumping of my heart. "It's nice to meet you."

"Likewise." He continued smiling and then nodded toward Will. "So, what's it like living with this guy? I've always wondered."

"You've never wanted to try it yourself?"

"Not really," he laughed. I joined in and then stopped when Will turned to glare at me.

"He's not that bad," I said quickly, aware I needed to be careful here. Actually, it was true. "Give or take a few moments, and he's fairly tolerable."

"Now tolerable is a word I'd use to describe him." He punched Will playfully in the arm. Will caught it and swatted it away.

"I'd say I'm delightful."

I barked out a laugh and quickly covered my mouth. "Sorry. You're a delight."

"I'm more a delight than you," he retorted, catching my sarcasm.

I opened my mouth to respond, but Jordan beat me to it.

"I disagree. She's definitely more of a delight than you."

The compliment caught me off guard. Blushing, I turned away and busied myself with the paperwork. I heard Will mutter something like *you don't have to live with her*, but I ignored him. I was too busy trying to control myself around his friend. When I thought I could speak again, I turned back to them. He was so good-looking it wasn't fair.

"Where are you going tonight?" I asked.

"We usually hit a few bars and then end up at a club,"

Jordan answered. His eyes suddenly danced. "Hey, why don't you meet us?"

Now I wished that I was going out tonight. My heart sank when I realised I couldn't. Not that it mattered–I could tell by the look on Will's face that he wouldn't allow it.

"It's okay. We aren't going near the centre. Besides, Will doesn't like to mix work with pleasure."

He looked disappointed for a second, and then his brows shot up. "Wait a sec," his eyes dashed between us, "you two work together?"

"Yeah, she just started at Bluebird," Will said, just as I enthused,

"Yep, I just started!"

"No way." It looked like he found something amusing. "And would you say that you two are friends outside work?" He waited for an answer, which was a simultaneous *no*. He laughed. "Wow. You surprise me more and more, Will."

Will's brows furrowed. "What's that supposed to mean?"

"It doesn't matter." Jordan laughed again. I really wanted to know what he meant, too, but a glance at Will told me not to press it.

I stood. "Would you like a drink, Jordan?"

"Oh, erm... I don't want to trouble you."

"It's no trouble," I quickly assured. "I always do drink rounds. Right, Will?"

Will gave me a funny look. "No. You never make me a drink."

I gritted my teeth together. "Yes, I do. Remember."

"No, you don't. It actually annoys me because I always see you with a coffee, but you never offer me one. And you-" he squinted. "Are you winking at me?"

I stopped winking. "No." My cheeks were getting hot again. Was he trying to embarrass me? "Will, can I borrow you a sec?" I moved to the hallway. When he didn't follow, I growled, "*Please.*"

He flinched, but at least it got him to his feet. I led him into the kitchen with a smile.

A smile that disappeared as soon as the door closed.

CHAPTER NINE

"What are you playing at?" I demanded.

Will frowned, utterly confused. "I don't understand. I'm not playing at anything."

I kept my voice low but made sure my aggravation was heard. "You're trying to humiliate me."

His confusion deepened. "Now I'm seriously not following. Humiliate you? How would I do that?" He looked suddenly suspicious. "Wait a sec, are you doing that thing where you're trying to play with me?"

"I do no such thing." I hadn't realised he'd noticed that. "No, I'm talking about the fact that I'm obviously trying to impress your friend, but you keep embarrassing me at every chance you get."

He laughed. It was a short, disbelieving sound. "I haven't once tried to embarrass you. What are you-? Wait..." his eyes brightened. He twisted his head to the front room before glancing back at me. "Why are you trying to impress Jor-"

I quickly covered his mouth, terrified that he might be

overheard. "Would you at least keep your voice down?"

He frowned down at my hand and then met my eye. Slowly, the confusion seemed to clear from his face. He mumbled something that I couldn't hear. I removed my hand but kept it raised just in case.

"Do you fancy Jordan?" He marvelled.

I lowered my hand fully, relieved that he'd finally realised the magnitude of the situation and spoke in a whisper. "Well, he is fit." I laughed at my choice of word. I hadn't described a person as 'fit' since high school.

Will chuckled, probably for the same reason as me. "Fit. I'll make sure I tell him you called him that. He'll be pleased."

"Don't." My voice came out as a tremble.

He eyed me for a second and then smiled. "Don't worry. Your secret is safe with me. Then again, he probably already knows that you fancy him."

"Was I that obvious?"

He indicated a big head. "He thinks every girl fancies him."

"Oh." That was a turn-off. Quite like Will, actually. Did vanity run through their friendship group?

"But," he put a finger to his bottom lip and tilted his head. "What exactly did I do to embarrass you? Oh," he seemed to realise something. His smile turned apologetic. "You're not actually going out tonight, are you?" I shook my head. "And you got changed and put on make-up for Jordan, didn't you?" I nodded, blushing at the admission. He laughed a little. "How could I be so clueless? I'm sorry about that."

He sounded annoyed with himself.

"I actually expected you to laugh at me or something," I admitted.

He frowned. "Why would I laugh?"

I pointed out the obvious. "Your friend is way better looking than me. Like way."

"Oh, that's a point."

I reached out to punch his arm, but he jumped out of the way before I could land a hit.

"Jordan hates girls with a temper," he joked, holding his hands up when it became clear I would pounce again. "I'm kidding!"

I should've known to expect some jokes. I batted his fingers out the way as he laughed again. "Very funny, Will."

"Sorry. Jokes aside, do you want me to put in a good word for you?"

"No thanks."

"No?"

"I prefer to make an impression on my own," I told him. "That's just how I roll."

"But why when I can help you?"

Maybe he would, or maybe he'd sabotage me. "What's the use saying good things if he doesn't see them for himself?" I argued. "He'll make up his own mind in the end anyway." And I preferred not to set high expectations. It would only lead to disappointments.

He seemed satisfied by my answer. "Fair enough. I'll leave it to you, then."

"You won't tell him anything, will you?" I had a sudden image of him blabbering about it. "Not a word?" He shook his head, but it wasn't enough. "Promise?" I pressed.

"I promise."

I eyed him carefully. It wasn't like I could be sure either way, but something about Will felt trustworthy to me.

"Okay, I believe you. But out of curiosity," I tilted my head. "What good things would you say about me?"

"Hmm..." He thought hard before answering. "I actually can't think of anything good to say about you." His eyes danced. "I guess I would've had to lie."

"Oh really?"

"Yeah, really."

I tried to keep a straight face, but a laugh burst through my lips. He laughed with me.

"I feel like we're having a friendship moment here," I confessed.

His face changed from happiness to alertness in an instant. "No." He pointed his finger at me like a parent who'd caught his child swearing. "This is not friendship. We are not friends."

"I kind of feel like we are."

His brows knitted together in frustration. "No, we are not."

"We are." He was so easy to tease, and I loved it.

"Hey, it takes two people to be friends, and I don't agree with it."

"Fine, I'll be friends with myself."

He looked momentarily confused by what I said. It softened me. When he looked like this, he almost seemed adorable.

"What are you two doing in there?" Jordan's voice came from outside the door, causing us to jump in unison.

"Do you think he heard what we said?" My voice came out as a panicked whisper.

Will pressed a finger to his lips and reached around me. He pulled open the door to reveal Jordan, whose eyes flicked curiously between us.

"We were just discussing Dani's love life," Will told him. I shot him a betrayed look. He returned it with what I guessed was supposed to be a reassuring one.

"Oh yeah?" Jordan's eyes appraised me. "What about it?"

I didn't know how to answer that. "Uh..."

"It's none of your business," Will assisted, surprising me by putting his arm over my shoulder. He twisted me away, leaning close to whisper in my ear. He spoke loud enough that I knew Jordan could hear. "If that guy asks you out again tonight, call me, and I'll tell him to back off. Okay?"

"Um..." my eyes flicked to Jordan. He was leaning slightly forward as though trying to overhear. "R-right," I said. "Thanks."

Will smiled and turned back to him. "What's up?"

"We need to go." His eyes were still on me. "The others are already there."

"They always go early," Will grumbled. He stalked from the room, leaving us alone. The silence turned painful.

"So," Jordan said. "Is someone bothering you or something?"

If only Will knew what a terrible liar I am.

"Sort of," I managed to say.

He mulled that over. "Do you want them to ask you out?"

"Um..." I needed to remove *um* from my vocabulary. Will reappeared at the door, jacket folded over his arm, and saved me from the need to extend my lame answer.

"Everything okay?" He asked, eyes flicking between us.

"Fine," I answered. I turned my eyes to Jordan and smiled. "Have a good night."

"You too," he said. "And it was nice to meet you."

I watched him walk to the front door, waiting until he was outside before letting my composure break. I turned on the cold water tap and splashed my face.

"Aren't you going to wish me a good night too?"

I hadn't realised that Will was still standing there. I switched the water off and turned to face him, leaning back against the counter

"No, I don't think so. You're probably going to wake me up later anyway, so you can have a bad night."

He smirked. "Aren't you hilarious?"

"Thank you." He rolled his eyes but didn't leave. "Was that all you wanted to say to me?" I pressed.

"Actually, no. But I'm not sure I want to say it now."

"Go on," I insisted.

He checked the door before looking straight at me. "Confidence suits you better," he said.

I blinked at the sudden tenderness in his voice. "What do you mean?" He smiled but didn't elaborate. "Hey!" I called as he walked away. "What do you mean?"

He didn't stop walking, but his voice trailed back to me. "I mean, you don't need to wear make-up or change your clothes to impress someone. You can impress them without it."

It took me a second to realise that he wasn't offending me. He was... complimenting me. That felt weird–and new.

I grinned. "Thanks, friend!"

He shook his head but didn't say anything else. As the front door closed behind him, the house turned eerily quiet, and I realised that Will had a certain presence in the house that I liked.

I mulled over his words as I went back to my work.

Confidence suits you better.

I agreed with that statement. Confidence suited anyone better, and I needed to remember that. Next time, I'd let Jordan see me bare-faced and dressed in my sweats. Because what was the point if he didn't like me then?

I must have dozed off at some point because, before I knew it, the sound of the front door opening forced me from my slumber. I peeled my cheek off the table and checked the time, surprised that it was way past midnight.

"Is that you, Will?" I called.

Instead of an answer, I heard a bang. I scrambled to my feet, but Will stumbled through the door before I could make it further than the sofa, looking pleased about something.

"Look what I've got." He waved something in front of me.

"What is that?" I took a step closer, examining the bottle. What I thought was booze was actually milk–the kind people had delivered to their front door in glass bottles. "Why do you have milk?" I questioned. Out of all the things I'd brought home when drunk, milk was not one of them.

"Do you want some?" He placed the bottle on the floor with a grin, swaying slightly. "I found it on my way home."

"Where on Earth did you find milk?"

His grin widened. "On someone's doorstep."

I stared at him. He was serious. "That's not finding, Will—it's stealing!"

"No, it's not."

"Yes, it is. Someone will be waking up tomorrow morning wanting milk, but they won't have it because you took it," I scolded.

He looked thoughtful for a second. "Huh. You're right." Scooping up the milk bottle, he disappeared into the hallway.

"Where are you going?" I asked, following him.

"To return it."

A sudden coldness swept through the hallway as he opened the front door.

"Do you even remember where you found it?"

"Of course I do."

I watched him nervously as he went out into the night. Halfway down the garden, he tripped over a rock, or maybe it was thin air, and somehow managed to hold onto his balance. Torn between staying warm and helping him, I grumbled something under my breath, grabbed my coat, and followed him out. The sudden temperature change made me shiver.

"Wait for me!" I called.

"Huh?" He turned and squinted, one hand on the gate.

I locked the door. Without the light from the hallway, it was pitch black.

"Come on," he said, waving at me to hurry, even though it was him who couldn't get the latch on the gate open. "Someone will miss their milk."

I bit my lip against a smile and held back to watch him.

He stumbled down the street with his milk bottle in hand, trying and failing to walk in a straight line.

"Are you sure you know where you found it?" I asked, catching up to him. "It's freezing out here."

"It's pretty hard to forget when it's where I always get it from."

He turned into one of the neighbouring gardens. My eyes widened. *"You steal from our neighbours?"*

"It's not stealing if you put it back."

He slammed the glass down with enough force that I was surprised it didn't shatter. A light flicked on in the upper window. I hissed at Will to be quicker, covering the back of his head with my arms to hide him as an older man grimaced down at us.

"Keep your head down," I told Will as I steered him away. Becoming enemies with the neighbour probably wasn't advisable.

But Will was in a world of his own.

He swivelled his head, looking straight at the old man and waving. The curtains ragged closed, but not before I caught sight of a terrifying snarl.

My heart jolted.

"Right, let's go," I grabbed Will's hand and dragged him forward, half expecting to hear an angry call as we stalked back to the house.

Somehow, we made it back without getting chased down the street.

I turned my eyes on Will in expectation, but he stared past me, his eyes out of focus.

"Want some milk?" he asked.

I couldn't contain it any longer. A laugh burst through my lips, and once I'd started, I couldn't stop.

Through my tears, I saw Will's brows knit together. "What's so funny?"

"I–don't–know," I could barely breathe from laughing. I waved my arms around, hoping to calm myself, and took several deep breaths. "I think it's the image of you waving at the old man. Or the way you smiled as you held the milk."

His frown deepened. "Which old man?"

"Oh!" The uncontrollable fit came over me once more. I moved to the kitchen, pouring a glass of water to calm myself.

Will followed me. I turned to find him with a whisky bottle in hand, trying to pour it into a glass with the lid still on.

"Oh no, you don't." I grabbed it from him before he could do any more damage to his liver. "I'll get you a drink. You go sit down."

He left without argument. I let the water run cold and poured him a glass, buttering some bread to help with the hangover.

His eyes were closed when I brought them to him. I held back, watching him from the door. He just looked so... peaceful. Like a boy who I never wanted to see hurt.

"Are you going to bring me that?" he asked, snapping me out of it.

"Here," rushing forward, I placed the bread and water on the table.

His eyes narrowed on the water. "What is that?"

"It's..." I considered lying, telling him it was vodka or

something, but then I hated when people did that. "It's water," I confessed. "Believe me, you'll be grateful for it in the morning."

"Thank you." He reached out and gulped it down without complaint.

"The bread will help too."

His lips quirked up. "Look at you watching out for me."

"Don't get used to it," I warned.

"I won't." He ate it with surprising quickness before closing his eyes again. I found myself lingering once more.

"Well, goodnight," I said, turning quickly.

"Wait," his hand enclosed my wrist, stopping me from leaving. The hold was gentle enough that I could break free if I wanted, yet I didn't move.

"What are you doing?" I asked.

"Just stay with me for a bit. Talk or something."

"I don't want to talk."

"You always want to talk."

I made to move, but his hold fell from my wrist to my hand.

I swallowed. "I thought you didn't like being in the same room as me? It's a rule."

He closed his eyes and sank back into the pillow. "Humour me."

I didn't know what to say. When the silence dragged, he said, "Please? I don't like being alone."

I stared at him. This didn't seem like the type of thing he'd confess if he wasn't drunk, and I wondered how he must feel to be saying it now.

I caved. "Okay. I'll stay until you fall asleep." I expected him to let go of my hand, but he kept an iron-tight grip as I sat on the floor beside him. I eyed the sofa with envy, but it was too far away without breaking his hold. And sitting on Will was probably a step too far.

My back ached as I waited for Will to fall asleep. I tried to slip away more than once, but his grip would tighten, and I'd realise he wasn't asleep yet.

Reaching behind me, I managed to grab two pillows. I used one to rest on and the other as a sorry excuse of a cover. Why I did this was a mystery to me. I should just rag my hand away and go to bed.

Maybe Will revealing his vulnerable side had done something to me.

"Night," I said, falling into the pillow.

He twisted, holding my hand tighter. "N-night."

CHAPTER TEN

I awoke to find Will leering over me with a half-perplexed, half-bemused look on his face.

Sweat clung to my PJs. Not from my makeshift pillow cover–but from the blanket I now shared with him. That was enough to make me jerk my head up.

That's when I saw it.

My hand was still in Will's, except this time, *I* was the one gripping his. I peeled my fingers away, trying not to cringe as he flexed his fingers.

"Would you like to explain why you were holding my hand?" he asked politely. "Wait–would you like to explain why you're sleeping on the floor next to me? Wait–would you like to explain why we're sharing a blanket?"

"Which one do you want me to explain first?" I croaked. My throat felt so dry it burned. I swallowed hard and grimaced at the taste. Thanks to him and his 'I don't want to be alone', I hadn't been able to brush my teeth last night.

He noticed the smell at the same time as I did.

"You have bad morning breath," he observed, wrinkling his nose.

"So do you." I shuffled away, aching from head to toe.

He huffed into his hand and sniffed. "Oh, man. I stink of alcohol."

"Have you ever considered going out less?" I asked.

"Work to live and not the other way around, right?"

I tried to think of a comeback, but I couldn't argue with that. "Fair. But have you ever considered getting less plastered? I thought you could handle your drink."

"I'm not usually like that. For the past month, I've had something to celebrate. Last night it was a birthday." He rubbed his temples with a groan. "And I can handle my drink."

I raised a brow. "Steal any milk recently?"

He stared at me for a long second before pulling a face. "Please tell me I didn't."

"I can't do that."

"Damn it! I told Richard I wouldn't do that again."

"Is Richard the name of our neighbour?"

"Yes." His eyes scanned the floor and table, searching for something. "Wait," he stopped searching and looked at me, "how do you know?"

"He saw me last night when I helped you return the milk. You don't remember?"

"No." He sank back into the sofa. "I don't remember anything after a certain point. But at least he got the milk back, right? He can't hate me too much."

I raised myself onto the sofa, ignoring the protest in my muscles. "To answer your first question," I said, reverting back to them, "I was holding your hand because you wouldn't let go of mine. So thanks for that. What–you don't believe me?" He looked at me like I was a liar.

"There's not a chance. No way would I hold your hand."

I felt an urge to argue, but there was probably no use. "Right. To answer your second question: I slept next to you because you wouldn't let go of my hand. And to answer your third: I don't know why we were sharing a blanket. Maybe you woke up in the middle of the night, saw me lying there, and thought I needed extra warmth. How sweet."

"I don't believe you."

"Well, it's true." I got to my feet and stretched. Several pains shot through my body, making me wonder if I'd slept on a rock instead of a flat surface.

He noticed. "What's wrong with you?"

"Have you ever tried to sleep on a hard floor before?"

"You should have gone to bed."

I gave him a loaded look. "You have a tight grip."

His cheeks actually turned pink this time. Maybe he did believe me.

"Where're you going?" he asked, seeing me leave.

"To shower," I answered.

"I need a shower."

I stopped and turned at the door. "I'll race you for it."

He tried to stand, but, as expected, it caused him physical pain. "My head hurts too much. You go first."

Satisfied, I turned to leave. But then I remembered something he'd said the night before, and I couldn't let the opportunity slip. I turned back. "Last night, you told me you don't like to be alone," I waited for his reaction. "Why is that?"

"I said that?"

"Yes."

He cringed. "Wow. Um. I don't know why I don't like to be alone... I guess I get that way when I'm drunk."

"Is that why you held my hand?"

"I didn't hold your hand."

"And begged me to stay?"

"I didn't beg you to stay."

"Then is that why you always bring a girl home?"

He gave me a dirty look. "I don't always do that."

"So, just when you're feeling particularly lonely?" I smirked at his wordless expression. He realised that I was having him on and smiled.

"Very funny. You're very funny."

I paused again. "In all seriousness, though, is that why you wanted a roommate?" His look told me I was right, but he didn't give me a verbal answer. I didn't press it. "I'll be going for that shower," I said, wondering what ghosts from his past haunted his present. "Don't be lonely without me."

I heard a chuckle behind me and smiled. If he ever wanted to talk about it, I'd be there to listen.

For now, I desperately needed the shower.

As the warm water cleared the sweat from me, I thought of Will waking up to find us sharing a blanket and holding hands. It brought a laugh to my lips. What a fright it must've been, what with his rules.

I found him in the same position as when I'd left, except now he wore a wet towel on his forehead. I'd changed into clean clothes, but my hair was still damp and clung to my face. My skin also stung slightly from the spot cream I'd had to put on. More thanks to Will for not allowing me to take my make-up off.

Will didn't look up when I sat on the sofa beside him. My only clue that he was alive was the face he pulled as if in pain.

"I really thought the bread and water would help," I told him.

"What bread and water?"

I scowled. "It doesn't matter." Because if he couldn't remember that part of the night, he deserved to suffer.

"What are you doing in here?" he asked suddenly.

I scowled again. "Asserting my right to sit in whatever room I want."

"You can sit in here. Just not when I'm in it."

"Well, what I'm doing is for both of us, so..." I waited for him to ask what I was doing. When he didn't, I said loud enough to draw another wince, "I'm writing a food shop list. There's barely any food in, so it needs to happen. Will you help me?"

"What do you mean there's no food in?" he retorted. "I bought some not long ago."

I was infinitely glad that his eyes were closed. "I might've... eaten a lot of it."

His eyes popped open. The look he gave me made me want to turn into vapour. "I paid for all of that."

"I know. And I'll pay you back when we get paid. I promise."

"You better. Why do you need me to write a food list, anyway? Just do it yourself."

"Well, it is for the both of us, and...," I lowered my voice to a whisper, "I need to borrow some money."

"What was that?"

I couldn't bring myself to say it any louder. "I need to borrow some money."

"I still can't hear you. You'll need to raise your voice."

"I need to borrow some money!"

His lips pulled up. "I heard you the first time."

"You-" I tried to think of a word for him, but I couldn't. None were cruel enough. I settled for shaking my head. "Can I borrow some, or not?"

"Remind me again why I let you live here? I'm struggling to remember, what with you not even being able to pay for anything and eating all of my food."

"Because you wanted my help getting girls out of the house." I diverted my eyes. We both knew how well that was going.

"Yes. Like that time when you refused to help me and that other when you kicked her out *before* the morning."

"I didn't kick her out. She chose to leave."

"Well, maybe if you hadn't come down to shout at me, she wouldn't have."

"Well, maybe the real reason you let me live here is that you want my company. You don't like to be alone, remember?"

He jumped to his feet. "It's worth the pain," he said, wincing as he placed the towel back on his head. "Just to get away from you."

I watched him leave with a twinge of regret because I really did need to borrow some money. Settling on trying again later, I busied myself with the shopping list, ignoring the sound of him loitering about upstairs. He stayed up there for a while. When he finally re-emerged, he went straight to the kitchen. I grabbed the completed list and followed after him.

"About the money-" He raised a finger and held something out to me. My brows shot up when I saw the notes. "So you're not annoyed with me anymore?" I asked, taking it from him.

He shrugged. "I don't like to hold onto those feelings, and I wasn't that annoyed, to begin with. Just make sure you pay me back."

I smiled. "I will. And thanks a lot." Turning to leave, I asked over my shoulder, "Do you want to add anything to the list?"

"Wait, are you going to the shop like that?"

I blinked. His tone implied that there was something wrong with me. "Did you seriously just ask me that question?"

"It's just you're basically still in your pyjamas. I swear I saw you in those last night."

I didn't bother blushing. "Who exactly do I need to impress in a supermarket?" I bristled. "And for your information, this outfit is the epitome of shopping practicality. Don't diss it."

"Oh yeah?" he folded his arms. "How so?"

"Well, let's say there's an item on the top shelf, and it's the only item left. I want it, and the girl in a dress beside me wants it. Who do you think gets it first?" He didn't answer, so I answered for him, "I do. Because the girl beside me is too busy worrying that her dress will rise. Me, my ass isn't going to be on show, so I reach to my heart's content. Or let's say I'm at the checkout, and I forgot something. My items are being scanned; I need to be quick. What do I do?" I didn't bother waiting for an answer this time. "I make a run for it, that's what. I'm in my trainers, I'm in my joggers, I'm fast. Hence, the epitome of shopping practicality." I opened my arms to give him a clear view of my clothes to appreciate.

He stared at me for one long moment before suddenly bursting into laughter. It was a half snort, half grunt sound like he'd failed to hold it back. It sounded so funny that I laughed with him.

"Remind me to come shopping with you one time," he said, wiping a tear from his eye. "And never to question your choice of outfit."

"I'm glad you see sense in it now."

"Very practical," he agreed.

I left him chuckling to himself, pleased that I could make him laugh. Whether he wanted to admit it or not, we were on our way to becoming friends.

One hour later, friendship was the last thing on my mind as I watched Will remove the groceries and lay them on the counter.

"Five pot noodles, two tins of soup, one bag of pasta." He listed them as though reciting the Twelve Days of Christmas, and his tone did not sound impressed. "Oh, two more tins of soup, ten potato waffles, one bag of Haribo's, one box of cereal, and... milk."

That was the last of the items. He thumped the milk on the counter and stepped back, shifting his eyes to my face.

"What's the problem?" I asked innocently. Shouldn't he

be grateful? A trip to the supermarket was like doing a full-body workout. My arms still hurt from where the carrier bags dug into them.

"Is this really all you bought?" he asked.

"Yeah. What's wrong with it?"

"Oh, jeez." He covered his face with his hands and sighed. "Please tell me you got some fresh stuff. Where's the fruit and veg?"

"I didn't want to squash them with all this heavy stuff."

"Unbelievable."

"Hey, there is nothing wrong with what I bought. Who doesn't love noodles? I know you do. I've seen you eat them."

He uncovered his face to look at me. "Yeah, but I don't eat them every day. You can't really expect us to live off this processed garbage."

"This stuff got me through three years of Uni, I'll have you know. And it saved me a tonne of money."

"Are you a Uni student now?"

"No."

His eyes shifted to thoughtfulness as he continued to watch me. "Have you ever done a food shop before? Without being a Uni student, I mean?"

I had to think about that. Now that he mentioned it, I hadn't. Not fully. "Holly used to do the shopping. I just ate whatever she brought back."

"No wonder they didn't like you," he muttered.

"What was that?"

"Nothing. Right," he grabbed his coat from the back of a chair and moved to the door. "Let's go."

"Where are we going?" I followed after him.

"To show you how to do a real food shop."

I stopped. Was he serious? "I'm not walking back there again. My arms are killing me."

"We won't walk. I'll drive."

My mouth dropped open. "You *drive*?"

"Yeah. Have you not seen my car parked out front?"

I'd seen *a* car. I just assumed it was one of the neighbours. "That's yours? I had no idea. You don't seem like the driving type."

He tilted his head. "Is that an insult? Never mind, let's go."

I grabbed my coat and followed him out. As he fiddled with the keys to lock up, something occurred to me. I frowned at his back. "If you drive, why didn't you offer to drive me before?"

"I was too hungover to even think about doing this before. I can't believe I'm even doing it now."

"Oh." I followed him to his silver Mercedes and climbed into the passenger seat. "Nice car," I observed. The black leather somehow felt soft and warm. And it was meticulously clean, unlike Holly's tiny Toyota that held a year's worth of McDonald's wrappers. "It smells like a pinecone in here."

He flicked a piece of card dangling from his rear-view mirror, and I found my explanation.

The drive took as long as it did for me to walk, if not longer. I didn't think that was possible, but traffic seemed to stop us at every turn.

"Jeeze," I peered out the window as he pulled the car to a stop again. "I didn't realise traffic was so bad here. What's going on?"

"It's always like this. Why do you think I choose to walk?"

"Now I'm glad I never used my time to learn."

"You haven't got a license? How old are you again?"

"Twenty-two. I wanted to, but I could never afford it."

He glanced at me in a way that made me think he wanted to ask me more, but he decided against it. Maybe it was too personal for him.

He turned up the radio.

"What type of music do you like to listen to?" I asked, realising that I still knew little about him.

He shrugged. "I don't have a preference. I can listen to anything. Old, new, rap, pop. If I think it's good, I'll listen to it."

"Me too."

"I like this song," he added, indicating *The Cure* playing on the radio.

"So do I."

He smiled and then sighed. "Most of my friends are into Drum and Bass. I have to change the station whenever I drive them, or they'll complain." He saw my look of disgust and laughed. "Not for you? You best hope they don't force me to have another house party, then."

The car returned to silence as the traffic lights changed to green. As he switched to first gear, I thought about everything I still had to learn about his life and personality.

"Why are you staring at me?" he asked.

I blinked and looked away. "I just wondered if I'm the first girl to be in your car." I wasn't sure what made me say that, but now that I had, I supposed I did wonder about it.

"Why would you even think that?"

"Am I?"

He cleared his throat. "Yes. But that doesn't mean anything."

"But you've driven your friends around before," I pointed out.

"So?"

"So all lines point to us being friends. Just saying."

He barked out a laugh. "You're really set on being friends, aren't you? I hate disappointing you like this," he sighed, shaking his head.

"I do want to be friends with you," I admitted. "Actually, scratch that. I can probably do better."

"Oh yeah?" he quirked a brow. "I'd like to see that. It's good, anyway. I already have a lot of friends, and I wouldn't want to add a subpar one to the list."

I sighed and said with mock sadness, "I wish I had a lot of friends."

He surprised me by turning instantly concerned. "You don't have any friends?"

I shrugged and looked out the window. "I have Holly, but she hasn't even messaged me since moving out." That much was true. It'd been a little over a month and not a single message. She didn't even know I lived with Will.

"You're not just trying to guilt me into being your friend, are you?" he asked.

Despite my best efforts, my lips pulled into a smile.

"You're unbelievable," he said, pulling into the supermarket.

I waited for him to park up before I jumped out of the car and grabbed the trolley before he could. Wheeling the trolley was my favourite part of shopping because I had this game where I'd jump on the back and see how far I could fly. One time I made it all the way from the pet food aisle to checkouts. It was a personal best.

The temptation to trolley-fly now almost defeated me, but I resisted. From experience, people didn't like it when I used the trolley as a toy. Holly used to roll her eyes and walk away from me. I guessed Will would do the same, and I wasn't entirely sure he'd come back.

"Where to, Captain?" I asked.

He pointed. "To the Fruit and veg."

Will walked ahead of me like a man on a mission, striding past the promotion aisle without a glance. I walked a little slower, scanning the snacks on offer with more attention now that I knew a car would be carrying them back for me.

I caught him by the onions and waved a box of *Celebrations* in his face. "Look what I've got. Half price. Bargain."

"That's your first mistake." He dropped a bag of carrots into the trolly. "Fresh stuff first. Snacks at the end."

"Why is that?"

"Because this is the boring part. If you get snacks first, you have nothing to look forward to."

He tapped his nose knowingly before drifting toward the potato section. I followed him with an increased interest because he might just be wiser than he looked.

"So, how do you know what stuff to buy?" I asked next. "I always give up whenever I think about what meals to make. It hurts my head."

He held his phone out. "I keep a list of recipes on here. If I like a meal, it gets added. Makes things easier."

"Oh. I think I might do that."

"You should." He moved to the fruit section.

"Would you say you're a good cook?" I asked, picking out blueberries.

He gave me a look that made me feel like I'd just asked an Olympic swimmer if they thought they could swim. "Maybe–and this is a big maybe–I might just cook for you sometime, and then you can judge that for yourself."

Excited by the prospect, I followed him from the fridge aisle to the canned goods. He'd been right when he said this was the boring part. I soon lost interest and idly watched as he threw baked beans into the trolley. The worst part was seeing the trolley pile up because the heavier the trolley, the less fun it was to fly. I eyed up the empty aisle and puckered my lips at the waste of a perfect runway.

"Hey, pass me that," Will said, nudging my arm.

"Pass you what?"

"The trolley."

Had he read my mind? I released it slowly, half wondering if he would scold me for thinking about something I didn't get to do.

"Watch this," Will set off running.

My mouth dropped open.

I'd never felt this surprised as I watched Will perform the most perfect trolley fly yet.

He was halfway down the aisle before I collected myself enough to chase after him.

"No way!" I laughed. "I've wanted to do that this entire time but I thought you'd be embarrassed by me."

"Seriously? The only thing that'd embarrass me is if you didn't try it yourself." He handed over the reins. "I bet you can't get further than me."

"Challenge accepted." I wheeled the trolley around. Each step back to the starting point was taken with an unwavering determination.

That same determination wheeled me straight past where Will stood with his mouth hanging open.

I hopped down with a grin. "Don't worry about it," I said, patting his arm. "I'm like a pro at this."

A determined look settled in his eye as he twisted the trolly around. "Rematch."

As Will readied himself to go again, a snarly-faced woman dressed in uniform stepped in front of him.

"You're not allowed to do that," she said, spoiling the fun.

"Oh," Will hopped down with a smile. Something about his dimpled grin made the woman falter. "Sorry about that," he said. "It won't happen again." He wheeled the trolley away and caught my eye. I could tell he was dying to laugh and needed to fight back one of my own.

They burst out when we turned the corner.

"Has anyone ever told you that you're not allowed to use a trolley as a toy?" I asked him.

He held his chest against another laugh. "Has anyone ever told you that shopping aisles are not to be used as runways?"

The sound that escaped my mouth could only be described as a snort. It shocked me so much that I covered my mouth and stared wide-eyed at Will.

"You're a snorter?" he asked, bemused.

I considered lying, but what was the use? "I've been known to snort."

He threw his arm over my shoulder and moved us into a walk. "What an adorable trait."

CHAPTER ELEVEN

By the time we'd left the store, the sky had morphed into an inky blue colour, and the traffic had died down.

Will had some wisdom to offer for this part of the shop, too, but I already knew the gist of it–snacks in one cupboard, dairy in the fridge, and so on and so forth.

My pre-emptive knowledge meant that we had it done in no time.

"What time are you going out tonight?" I asked, leaning on the counter beside him.

He sipped his drink. "I'm not going out tonight."

"Oh."

He raised a brow at my tone. "Why do you sound disappointed?"

I didn't think he'd notice. "Well, because I wanted to watch TV tonight, but now I know you'll claim the front room, and you won't let me join you, will you?"

"You're right." Smirking, he pushed away from the counter and headed for the door.

"I see you've returned to your cold, distant self," I scowled at his back. He pretended to shiver. "Stop pretending that we aren't friends!"

I debated taking myself upstairs, but to hell with him. I was spending my night on the sofa whether he liked it or not.

He didn't look at me when I claimed my place for the night. Nor did he answer me when I asked what we were watching. That was fine. He could pretend I didn't exist all he wanted so long as he didn't kick me out.

Wordlessly, he grabbed an Xbox control from the cabinet and switched the console on. Suddenly excited, I sat up straight and crossed my legs. "What game are you playing? Can I play?"

He ignored both of my questions, but I recognised the game as soon as it loaded. *Shadows of Hell*–one of my favourites. I resisted the temptation to go full nerd mode on him as he began his campaign. Difficult when I'd already completed this game on max difficulty, unlocking 100% of the achievements. That was impressive. So impressive that I wanted to brag to him about it.

I forced myself to stay quiet, crossing both arms and legs as though it would somehow help my resistance.

"You need to collect the hidden crest," I couldn't help but tell him. "No, seriously. If you miss it now, you won't be able to come back for it and will have to kiss the achievement goodbye." He didn't listen. I clenched my hands into fists as he committed mistake after mistake. "You need to go into that cave. There's a sword you'll need for later. No, don't drop that!"

He put the controller down and glared at me. His nostrils

flared. "If you're going to stay in here with me, could you at least stay quiet?"

"I'm just helping you."

"I don't need help." He picked the control back up.

"I think you do."

He continued playing. I stayed quiet this time, even though it tore me up inside to watch him pass an artefact I knew would help him later. I couldn't hold back the groans, though. Especially when he tried to defeat a level seventy without using the right tools.

"No, no, no, *no!*" I couldn't hold it in any longer. "How many times are you going to try to kill him like that before you realise it won't work?"

"I'd like to see you do better," he griped, hitting the control panel with force as though *that* would help.

"For your information, I've completed this game on killer difficulty, so I can definitely do better."

That momentarily disarmed him. He blinked, looking at me in a new light. "Seriously?"

"Yep. One hundred per cent complete." It felt good finally saying it out loud. Even more so when I could tell he appreciated it.

Will kept his eyes on my face, and I could see the dilemma raging in his mind. To let Dani join, or to not let Dani join? He looked at the ceiling, back to my face, toward the TV, back to my face again. "So, what would you do?"

My heart soared. Finally, *finally*, he was doing the smart thing. *He was listening to me.* I shuffled forward. "First, I'd listen to me from the start." He scowled, so I quickly said, "Sorry. Joke." I wasn't joking–he really *should* have listened to me from the start–but I needed to keep him sweet now that he'd finally involved me. "Okay, so, first go back to the start of the level and collect the fallen horns you've missed. They'll help you upgrade your outfit." He did as I said and then waited for my help again. "Okay, now go to basecamp and upgrade your outfit to the flame-resistant one. It will help with the fight. Now, go get that sword from the cave I told you about earlier. You'll need it to defeat him. No, not that cave, the other one. Yeah, that's it. Grab the sword."

"What now?"

"Now you're ready."

We exchanged a fighter's nod before he made his way back to the monster. It was a hard one to defeat, I had to admit. But he had the tools to do it, and I believed in him.

Or not.

"Argh! Why. Won't. He. *Die!*" Will hammered the control with his thumb, kicking his legs in the air with an intense look of concentration.

"You're going about it the wrong way. You need to hit him when his back is turned and dodge the fire when he launches at you."

"*You* dodge the fire," he griped. "Is this right? Damn it!" He slammed the control down as he died for the third time. "This is impossible."

"Pass it here." I reached my hand out. He hesitated for a second but then passed me the control.

"I think there's a glitch in the game," he said as I took over. "So don't be upset if you die. Trust me, I'm an expert on this. There's definitely a glitch. See that? That's a glitch."

Trying my hardest to block out Will's voice, I circled

around the monster and attacked his back; when he spun around, I jumped back and changed the weapon to a bow. Will let out a surprised gasp as I switched back to a sword again, charging forward with an intent to kill. "Yes!" I yelled as the monster fell to its death. I turned to grin at Will. "There you go. Defeated."

He took the control from my hand with a slightly baffled expression. "I'm seriously impressed."

"Thank you." I pressed my back into the couch with an air of satisfaction.

"When you said you like to game, I didn't think you'd be this good."

"I love gaming. That's why I wanted to work at Bluebird."

He eyed me thoughtfully. "Wait a sec," hopping to his feet, he moved to the cabinet and rooted for something. "Here," he held out a controller to me. "Let's play co-op."

I blinked. "Are you serious?"

"Yeah."

"Awesome."

Playing co-op with Will was more fun than I could've anticipated. He had good gear, a quality I couldn't afford, and it beat playing by myself on Holly's computer. I also had to admit that he was a good player, even though I was better.

He didn't like it when I voiced that out loud.

"You have an unfair advantage," he told me. "You've completed this game before."

"Want to change the game?"

He swapped disks and came to sit beside me.

"Prepare to lose, Miss Scott."

This game was pure warfare. We chose opposite teams

so we could fight against each other, and so the bloodbath began. I cheered with joy when I shot him and cursed when he landed me with a grenade.

"What time is it?" he asked after a particularly brutal battle in which I'd barely scraped a win.

I checked my phone. "Jeeze! It's past eight. How did that happen?"

"Time flies when you're having fun." He hit pause. "Fancy a pizza?"

My stomach rumbled at the last word. "Yes."

He dialled a number. "Hey, man. Yep, it's Will. Could I order a meat feast and a- sorry, what do you want?"

"Make it two."

"Two meat feasts. No, I'm not on a date. Jeesh. Could you just order them? Thanks." He hung up.

I cocked my head. "Do you have a pizza guy?"

"Of course, I have a pizza guy. You don't?"

"No, but now I want one."

He smiled. "Another game?"

"Sure."

We played until the pizza came and then hit pause, munching in silence. It was good. So good that I decided I'd treat him to one on payday. Finishing the last bite, I wiped the grease from my hands and picked up the control.

I immediately dropped it.

"Oh crap."

Will looked over at me, the last of his pizza hovering inches from his mouth. Cheese dripped onto his box. "What's wrong?"

"Oh crap, crap, crap, crap." I pushed the pizza box aside

and raced to the dining table.

"What's wrong?" Will asked again, this time in alarm.

"What's wrong is that I forgot I have work to do!" Dread sank into the pit of my stomach as my eyes roamed over the paperwork. "How can I forget that? Look at all of this!"

Will's eyes moved slowly to the table before returning to my face. He looked at a loss for words. "Do you... want me to help?"

Flattered, I had to reject. Then, when it didn't look like he understood why, I elaborated, "You said if people at work found out we live together, they'd assume you helped me out. I don't want that to be true, even if it's something this small."

My answer seemed to both surprise and satisfy him. "As a team leader, I have to say I like your attitude. But," he continued with a sigh, "as your roommate, I have to say that it sucks."

I didn't think it was possible to laugh right now. "Right? I really don't want to work tonight." The stack of paper seemed to be mocking me.

"Can it wait until tomorrow?"

I met his eye, and our brains exchanged a silent message— *don't do it... I don't want to do it... then don't.*

"You are a bad influence, Mr Lovett."

He grinned as I launched myself onto the sofa. "At your service, Miss Scott."

My one saving thought was that even if I didn't hand it in on time, this was totally worth it.

I somehow managed to finish the work. I spent all

Sunday doing it, so that helped. As did the continuously flowing levels of caffeine that Will supplied. He could be surprisingly helpful when he wanted to be.

I was currently standing outside the office building with Lily and Finn. We would've already gone inside if not for the latter spotting Will walking in. He insisted we wait for him.

Will's eyes did a circuit of the building and lingered on me. Even from here, I could've sworn his lips pulled up into a smile. Or maybe that was the distance playing tricks on me.

Finn opened the door for him as soon as he reached us.

"After you," Will said, indicating for us to go first.

"Did you have a good weekend?" Finn asked.

The faintest of smiles touched Will's lips. "I did. You?"

"Yep. Went clubbing Saturday night. Nursed a hangover all day Sunday. What could be better?"

We entered the elevator. Somehow, I ended up standing beside Will. Finn shot me daggers, but what could I do? I didn't know how I ended up here.

I folded my arms to keep myself from brushing his hand or something equally stupid yet not totally unplausible. Was this really the guy I'd spend Saturday buying food and playing video games with? Maybe that was why I could feel a strangeness between us–an acute awareness of his presence beside me.

"Should we grab a coffee?" Lily's question broke me free from my thoughts.

I cleared my throat, keeping my eyes strictly away from the person to my left. "Count me in. And cake?"

"Isn't it a bit early for cake?"

Will shifted as I swallowed my disappointment. "Right," I said.

A glance told me he was holding back a laugh.

Resisting the urge to nudge him, I continued, "Just let me drop this bag at my desk, and I'll come." Something dawned on me then. Twisting my backpack to my front, I groaned. "Crap."

Three pairs of eyes turned to look at me. Will shot his away first. Acting, I presumed, like he didn't care. Or maybe not acting at all.

"I left my bag at home," I explained when Lily and Finn continued to frown at me.

"You have two bags?" Lily asked.

"Not usually. This one just has my work in it. I've left the one with my purse in at home." I could see it now, sitting on the table where I thought I wouldn't forget it.

"Do you want to borrow some money?" Lily asked.

I smiled at her kind offer, but I couldn't bring myself past the awkwardness to accept it. "It's fine. I'll get a coffee from the kitchen."

Will left the elevator first. Zoomed out, actually. One blink, he was there; in another, he was gone. I left Lily and Finn to get their coffee and stepped out after him.

I knew today was going to be difficult. Not only had I left my purse at home, but I'd also left my lunch. No food Dani meant grumpy Dani. But I only knew *just* how difficult it would be when I reached my desk.

Chrissie barely glanced at me as she asked, "Did you finish the work?"

I handed it to her with no small amount of pride. "All

done."

"Did you want a medal or something?"

Rude much. I didn't voice this out loud. Instead, I took a calming breath and pulled out my chair. She turned to face me.

"I need you to scan them in."

I paused halfway between sitting. "Right now?"

"Yes, right now."

"Alright, then," collecting the wad of paper, I walked to the printer.

She must be having a bad day, I told myself. *They happen.*

Halfway through scanning the paper in, someone came over to ask how long I'd be. I told them a while. When it looked like they were about to have a nervous breakdown because of this, I took the file and said I'd scan it in for them. A seemingly harmless offer.

"Why do you have those?" Chrissie asked when I returned to tell her I'd finished.

"Oh, I told Joe from programming that I'd scan them in for him since I was taking so long. I just need to drop them off in his department,"

"You work for the art department," she sniped. "Not programming."

Bad days happen. "I was just trying to help."

She folded her arms, one brow raising. "Then why don't you help us?"

I opened my mouth and closed it. And then I opened and closed it again. No words came out. Was I even breathing?

"Knock, knock," Will tapped on Chrissie's desk, obstructing my view of her. Even though he wasn't looking at me, something about his presence immediately soothed me.

I breathed again.

"Hey, Will. How was your weekend?" Chrissie didn't use her derogatory voice on him. She used her I'm-always-cheerful-and-smell-of-roses voice.

Will leaned back against her desk and folded his arms. "It was good, thanks. Yours?"

"I mostly worked." She seemed happy about that. "How's the roommate? Is he still annoying you?"

Ever so subtly, I quirked a brow. Exactly when did this boy find the time to complain about me?

Will grinned. "Oh, she's *very* annoying. But..." he shrugged. "She's growing on me."

Chrissie's spluttering disrupted any would-be-blushing. "Sh-she? Your roommate is female?"

A line formed between Will's brows. "Yes. Did I not tell you that?"

"No."

I wanted very desperately to disappear. Particularly as Chrissie's face drained of colour. I took a slow step back, but the movement brought her attention to me again. "Are you going to take those or not?" she snapped.

The harshness in her tone took away my ability to speak. Again, I opened my mouth and closed it, unable to get any words out.

"Did I hear you were taking them over to programming?" Will asked, looking at me for the first time. Something in those eyes told me that Chrissie's attitude irked him. That he was on my side. "Let me take them for you," he plucked them from my hand before I could protest and then winked when he caught my eye.

"We can't ask you to do that," Chrissie protested.

"You're not." Giving her a smile, he walked away.

My lips tugged up.

Finally taking my seat, I said to Chrissie, "What do you want me to do next?"

"Since you've scanned those in, you can shred them." Impossibly, her mood seemed to have soured further.

I did as she asked. By the time I'd finished, it was lunchtime. The office was almost empty when I returned to my desk. No sign of Chrissie, thankfully.

"Are you coming for food?" Lily asked, throwing on her scarf.

"You go ahead. I've got some things to finish."

She nodded, joining Finn by the elevator. I let out a deep sigh, ignoring the rumbling in my stomach. No money. No food. And a mentor who possibly wanted to bite my head off. No biggie.

Will got to his feet as my stomach rumbled again. I looked over as he pulled on his jacket, considering, for a moment, asking him for money. But even the thought had me shaking my head. I *could not* keep owing him money.

About twenty minutes later, I was absorbed in a game app when something dropped in front of me. I looked up in time to see Will walking to his chair. He didn't look back at me. Nor did he show any emotion as I picked up the sticky note he'd left and read:

Big Mac. Table in kitchen. Enjoy.

That's all it said.

My mouth dropped open. I glanced over at him again, but his eyes were now glued firmly on his screen.

As I raced to the kitchen, it crossed my mind that this may be a prank. I wouldn't put it past him to do that–to lift my hopes up and then drop them when they reached the top.

But there it was.

A McDonald's bag sitting in the corner of the kitchen.

And he'd got me my favourite.

I wolfed the burger down, followed by the fries, all the while comparing Will to everything good and sacred as my hunger and soul were satisfied.

I had every intention of thanking him. But he wasn't at his desk when I left the kitchen. Neither, I realised, were the other senior people. I asked Chrissie where they'd disappeared, but she only replied with 'to discuss something important'. Realising that was all I would get from her, I forgot about it until they re-emerged later in the afternoon, huddled together in the centre of the floor.

Jasmine demanded our attention. "Could you all please gather around us?" she called out.

Noise erupted as everyone unified in rolling their chairs closer. Thankfully, I could stay at my desk, but it meant I was boxed in as several people came to a stop beside me. Soon, a congress of people encircled the office leaders, resembling a small-scale ice rink.

"Okay," Jasmine continued, taking in the new crowd of faces, "now that we've got your attention, we have an announcement to make." She paused, a smile playing on her lips. "The annual *New Gamer* challenge is officially open!"

A few people hooted and cheered. I caught Lily's eye and exhaled when she seemed just as mystified as me. Will stepped forward, recapturing our attention.

"Those of you who've been with us for more than a year will know that this is for our first-year grads only," he said. "The rest of us will be voters. For first-years, this is an opportunity to show us what you're made of and to have a lot of fun. This is how it works–you'll produce an initial idea for a game and submit it. The office will vote for their favourites, and the winning contestants will develop their game. The winner of *that* will then have their game developed on a larger scale, with the potential for it to be marketed and sold."

An excited murmur spread through the room. I was amongst those murmuring. I leaned closer, eager to hear more.

"But remember," Jasmine's voice held a touch of warning, "we named this a challenge for a reason. You should only enter your name today if you're willing to put in the required hours and effort. No idea is bad, but we will be judging the terrible ones."

"Way to turn them off," Will joked.

"We'll send out a newsletter with more detail. If you want to enter, put your name and department into this box by the end of the day. We'll leave it on Will's desk." She passed the box to him, and the group dispersed, concluding the meeting for the rest of us.

I drummed my fingers against my desk while I waited for the newsletter. Finn walked over to me at one point, asking if I would enter. I said hell yes. When the email notification finally came through, I was ready and waiting to open it.

The gist was this: we had two months to think of an idea and produce a design document. And then, if we were lucky enough to win, we had four months to develop the game. The submissions were anonymous to help with fair voting, but names would be announced for the winners.

I was already decided. Scribbling my name and department down onto a piece of paper, I hopped to my feet and dropped it into the designated box, catching Will's eye as I turned away. He gave me a nod which I took to mean *good luck*.

When I returned to my desk, I waited impatiently for the day to end.

"In a rush to get home?" Chrissie asked when the clock finally hit five.

"I am," I answered, grabbing my coat and laptop. "I've got a competition to win."

CHAPTER TWELVE

An idea for a game.

An idea for a game...

I hit my head against the table and groaned. *Why* couldn't I think of anything now that I actually tried? Sure, when I wanted to sleep... that was fine. An idea would hit me then. A stroke-of-brilliance, potentially-worth-millions idea that would be gone by morning. But now? Nope. No. Nothing. My brain had decided to drain itself of creativity. Leaving not a drop.

Stubborn brain.

Will still wasn't home yet. And yes, I was waiting for him. Every time I heard a noise at the door, I'd jump up, only to slump back down when I realised I'd been fooled by the wind.

I'd made him dinner. Nothing special–I was no Michelin star chef–but my old favourite: sausage, mash, and beans. Simple, yet delicious. Something I'd pay good money for.

I needn't tell Will that I had an ulterior motive. Let him think of me as a nice, generous roommate.

Hearing the front door rattle, I pushed out of my chair,

convinced it was more than the wind this time. Will glanced at me as I sped into the hallway.

 I slowed myself into a casual stance. "You're home," I said, leaning against the wall and picking at my nails.

He pulled off his shoes. "Have you been waiting for me?"

Instead of answering, I indicated his laptop bag. "Do you want me to get that for you?"

He swerved out of the way as I made to take it from him, eyes narrowing. "What's gotten into you?"

"Nothing," I laughed. It came out horribly forced even to my ears. "Oh, and by the way, I made dinner and left some for you in the microwave."

"*Tha*-nks." He said it like he wasn't sure if he could trust me.

"Sausage, mash, and beans," I told him, swinging back on my heels. "And the mash is cheesy."

His eyes lit up, but he kept his face a cool mask. "Cheesy mash?"

"Yup."

He nodded. "Sounds good. Thank you." Moving past me, he headed for the kitchen.

"Thanks, by the way," I said, turning with him. "For the McDonald's you bought me. You didn't need to do that."

He paused with his hand outstretched. "Don't mention it."

"You're kind of nice."

A smile played on his lips as he turned to face me. "It's funny because I actually already knew that."

"Oh really?"

"Mmm. So is this why you're being weirdly nice?" he

waved a hand. "To say thanks?"

I put a hand to my heart. "I am not being weirdly nice. I'm just nice." He raised a brow, and I smiled in return, turning for the front room. "Enjoy the food. And remember who made it for you."

Returning to my position on the sofa, I pulled my laptop towards me, balancing it on my knee. I had a blank word document open. That's all I'd managed to do so far: nothing. My attempts at brainstorming were laughable.

And they continued to be so.

When Will reappeared sometime later, the document was still blank.

"Are you working?" he asked from the door.

I twisted. "I'm trying to think of a game idea for this challenge." *And failing miserably*, I chose not to add.

"Oh," Will grinned and stepped forward, taking his usual seat. "It's cool, isn't it? It's my favourite part of the grad program, even if Jasmine hates it."

"She hates it?"

He shook his head with a chuckle. "I can't tell you why. Okay, I'll tell you." He shuffled to the edge of the sofa, body facing me. "So, every year, we always get bad game designs. And when I say bad, I mean *bad*. But we can't say that to you guys because we need to say something constructive. Plus, we don't want to kill your motivation. Jasmine hates it. She's way more to the point. If she hates something, she wants to say that to you. It kills her that she can't."

I gulped. What if mine falls under the category of bad? "Submissions are anonymous, though, right?"

"Yeah, but only for voting. We see your names when the

votes are counted."

I looked at my still blank word document and gulped again. "So, Will," I spoke so quietly he probably needed to strain to hear. "Since you're my roommate and we're friends and all, could you help me out? I'm not asking you to give me the winning idea or anything," I added quickly. "I'm just asking you to point me in the right direction. That's all." And there it was. The reason for me buttering him up.

I didn't like how he stared at me. All silent and judging. Instead of gratifying me with an answer, he just tilted his head. But I could read the look in his eyes. It said: *are you serious?*

"Is that a no?" I asked.

He got to his feet and grabbed his laptop, walking silently to the dining table, where he pulled out a chair. After another long, painful second, he looked across at me.

"So are you saying you want me, a board member, to tell you, a participant, an idea for a game?"

I baulked. "Yes."

"Don't you think that would put you at an unfair advantage?"

I sighed. "Yes." And then, knowing how right he was, "I know, I know. I shouldn't have asked. It's wrong. I'm wrong."

"I'm confused." He did indeed look confused. "What happened to the girl from Saturday who didn't want my help with something so small as proofreading?–the girl who wants to win on her own?"

"That girl disappeared when her pride was on the line."

"Why's your pride on the line?"

"Because-" I felt the panic return in double force, bubbling in my throat and threatening to burst. I released it in one long breath. "Because I can't think of a stupid idea for a game, and I keep staring at a blank screen, and my game is going to suck, and everyone, including you, will laugh at me. And I'll hate it so much I won't be able to show my face again, which means I'll have to quit, and I really don't want to quit because I love this job, so I-" I sucked in a deep breath as I ran out of air, noticing how Will's mouth hung open. Then, to my surprise and annoyance, he barked out a laugh.

"Sorry, no, sorry - it's not funny," he bit down hard against his lip. "Really, I'm not laughing at you. It's just-" he laughed again. I raised a brow. "It's just the way you said it. I didn't know somebody could say so much without taking a breath."

"I'm glad my suffering amuses you," I hissed.

"Sorry. The laughter is out of my system." He opened his arms with a flourish as if to prove it. "Going back to what you said, though, why are you so worried? It's the first day. An idea isn't going to come to you on day one."

"It's not?"

"Course not. I've been doing this for years, and I still have to sift through hundreds of ideas before landing on a good one. Trust me, I have pads full of failed attempts. And no, I won't show you the pad," he added, seeing my eyes light up, "because that would be cheating. What I'm trying to say is that you can do this on your own. So don't give up on yourself so soon. You got into Bluebird, and that alone proves that you're good enough. You can do this. You will do this."

I nodded, feeling the fighter within me awaken. "I can do this."

"You can do this." He checked that I wasn't about to sink into despair again and opened his laptop.

"Are you working now?" I asked.

"Yep. I've got to approve or reject this level by Thursday, so I'm spending this week testing it."

"Ooh," I leaned forward, eager to see his screen, even though it faced away from me. "Can I help?"

He shook his head. "This isn't something a first-year can help with."

I slumped back. "I've never tested a game before. Is it as fun as it sounds?"

"No." He looked up at the ceiling. "Yes. I don't know–It's half and half."

"Why half and a half?"

He glanced at me with his finger on his lip. "Come over here. I'll show you."

"Really?" I didn't need to be asked twice. Jumping to my feet, I took the chair he'd pulled out for me.

"So," he explained. "This is the demo I received this morning. It's fun because I'm the first person who gets to play it, but it's also not fun because I have to play it with specs in mind. I can't just play like you would any normal game. I need to be constantly vigilant and on the lookout for any flaws in the design. I have to be critical. Which takes away the fun."

"I bet." I shuffled closer to the screen. "So, what kind of flaws might you find? Can I watch?"

He nodded, shuffling slightly away in a way that told me

I'd gotten close. Too close. Like invasion-of-privacy, we're-now-sharing-the-same-air kind of close.

"So," he set his avatar off at a walk. "To start, you just play as you would any game. We need to make sure we cover all ground and every base. If something doesn't feel right, or the game doesn't play as expected, we make a note. Every doubt, big or small, needs to be looked into. When someone buys a game, they don't expect it to be faulty. There, you see that?" He indicated the avatar walking into an invisible wall. "That's a glitch. We need to write it down." And so he did. I watched a crease form between his brows as he jotted down a note in that scruffy yet neat handwriting. "And here, did you see that?" I turned my attention back to his laptop. "The rock should've exploded when I shot it. That's another problem." He made another note.

"This is so cool," I breathed, eyes wide as I watched him work. "Do you think I'll be able to do this one day?" He didn't immediately answer. I turned and found him staring at me with a strange smile on his face.

"Sorry," he quickly diverted his eyes. "I just like working with people who show passion. Everyone should enjoy their job like you seem to."

"I love this job," I agreed.

"Well, there's no reason you won't be testing our games yourself one day. Bluebird encourages inter-divisional working."

"That's good to know. I like helping other teams, so I worried earlier when Chrissie told me I should only be helping the art department."

"That's-" he pressed his lips together. "That's not true.

Chrissie–she can be hard to work with. But just remember that she does know what she's doing. Keep working hard, and she'll help you."

I wondered if he only thought that way because she was helpful to *him.*

"You don't believe me?" he guessed.

I shrugged. "I'm willing to give her the benefit of the doubt."

After working for a bit longer, Will stretched out his arms. "I think I'll call it a night," he said, pushing out his chair. "Thanks for your help."

I yawned. "No problem. Thanks for showing me."

As I got to my feet, my eyes fell on the handbag I'd forgotten to take to work. I turned to Will. "Can I have your number?"

Reason being: if I ever forgot something again, I could text him and ask him to bring it. Totally reasonable. Except Will now looked at me like I'd just asked him for a kiss.

"You want my number?"

"Yes. Is that a problem?"

"Um," he scratched the back of his neck. "No offence, but I don't give my number out to girls."

I sighed. "You are kidding me, right?"

"No."

"I'm not just a girl, Will. I'm also your roommate." *And I can't believe I'm having to explain this to you.*

"But why do you want my number? You don't,"–he pulled a face–"you don't think because I've spent some time with you that I like you, do you?"

"Oh my God." I covered my ears. "You're unbelievable.

I don't like you, Will. Well, I do, but not like *that*. Stop thinking that I'm going to magically fall for you."

"Then what?" He finally seemed to express some self-doubt. At least that's what I guessed the pink blotches on his cheeks were for.

"I want your number in case of an emergency, silly. What if we needed to get in touch with each other? What if, I don't know, we run out of milk?" Bad offering. He didn't seem convinced. "Have you ever woken up to no milk before?" I fought. "It's horrific."

"I've got the solution," he clicked his fingers. "You can be on milk duty."

"Or you could just give me your number," I folded my arms.

"Nope."

"Damn it, Will." I stomped my feet. I actually stomped my feet. I wasn't even sure if I'd done that as a child. "Give it to me." He pretended to think about it for one whole second before shaking his head. I held out my hand. "Give it to me."

"I'm not giving it to you," he laughed. *Was he enjoying this?*

Right. Searching around, I looked for something to torture him with. My eyes stopped on his feet–bare except for his socks–extended across the floor. I smiled.

"What are you doing?" he asked as I moved towards him. He flinched back, but I was quicker–I lunged and grabbed one of them. "Stop it!" he yelped. "No, no, ah! It tickles! Stop!"

"Will you give me your number?" I paused so he could answer.

"No."

"Fine." I commenced the tickle attack.

"No! No! Stop! Ah! Okay! I'll give it to you!"

I stepped back. He tucked in his feet and glared at me, chest heaving.

"Here," I tossed him my phone and ignored the look of death he gave me. "You put it in."

"I can't believe it's been tickled out of me." He punched the number in with force, throwing a scowl in my direction. Maybe he imagined the phone was my face. "Done," he thrust it back to me.

I rang it just to be sure it wasn't a fake. Who knew if he could be trusted.

"Happy?" he held his phone up for me to see.

"Happy." I stored my phone away. "And now you have my number."

As I headed for the hallway, he called, "I'm not saving it! And don't you dare call me unless it's an emergency!" A pause. "And don't text me either!"

I flashed him a smile as I rounded the corner. "Night, Will."

I found Will in the kitchen when I went down to make breakfast the following morning, head bent over a bowl of cereal. He glanced up as I entered, eyes immediately on the alert. I held back a smile when I noticed him tucking his feet under the chair. How adorable.

"Good morning," I greeted.

He let his spoon fall with a clang. "Here to attack me again? What do you want this time–my Instagram handle?"

"Do you have one of those?" I reached for a bowl and

poured myself some cereal. "I'll follow you if you want."

"No, I don't want that." He stuffed a spoonful of cheerios into his mouth and continued to glare at me.

I moved to the fridge, aware that I needed to patch things up somehow. After pouring milk over my cereal, I sat opposite him, fingers twiddling with my spoon. "I'm sorry for tickling you," I said. He shifted away, eyes moving down. "It won't happen again. Will?"

He still wouldn't look at me. Instead, he gulped down the last of his milk and stood, putting his dish in the sink. Eyes ahead, he made for the door. Something red flashed in my brain as he drew nearer, every step that of a predator disguising itself as prey. *He wouldn't.*

"Wait," I jumped to my feet as a look I recognised passed over his eyes. "You don't want to do this. If you do, I'll get you back twice as bad." I hoped the warning would at least make him pause, giving me time to escape, but he continued toward me without fear. I stepped back. "Triple." Still no pause. I felt my back press against the counter and whimpered. "Please, don't."

His eyes positively gleamed as his lips curved up. "You had this coming, Scott."

I made to run, but he grabbed hold of me before I could escape, lifting me over his shoulder with surprising ease.

"No, stop!" I pleaded, laughing even though it was far from funny. "Stop! Ah!" I kicked my legs out and tried to wriggle free, but his hold was too tight. "Please- Will-"

He let go of me, setting me down by the counter. I gripped its edge with one hand and used my other to clutch my chest.

"Now," he said, taking a slow step towards me. He placed his hands on the counter at either side of me, his face so close I didn't know where to look. I settled on his lips, the ghost of a smile still playing on them, and tried to concentrate on my breathing. "We're even," he finished.

I looked up at him. "You're evil," I growled.

"Hey, come on." He stepped back and held out his hand. "We're even, right?"

I wanted to smack that peace offering away, but I knew that was just my post-tickle-trauma talking. I sighed and placed my hand in his. "We're even."

He grinned, giving my hand a squeeze. It felt surprisingly nice. Or maybe that was just more post-tickle-trauma talk. "See you at work."

"See you at work," I grumbled, watching as he disappeared into the hallway.

I rubbed my aching ribs and returned to the table, chuckling to myself. How had I landed with a roommate immature enough to perform a tickle attack? I thought I alone held that level of immaturity. And why was I smiling about it?

Because it's fun, a voice told me. *And surprising. Because Will is fun and surprising.*

I still found myself chuckling when I arrived at the office. Not even Chrissie could damper my mood. Then again, I should never underestimate her profound ability to dampen the spirits.

"I have a meeting in ten," she said, shuffling papers into her hand. "I need you to run to the coffee house and get Jasmine's usual. You wrote it down to remember, right?"

"Yes." I hadn't. And I had no idea why I'd chosen to lie. Probably because Chrissie's piercing eyes terrified me.

"Good." She turned and headed for a meeting room, and I stared, like an idiot, as the question I should've asked finally formed on my lips: *what's Jasmine's order?*

A bubble of panic rose in my throat. Ten-minutes. I had ten minutes to go out and place an order of I didn't know what. The panic doubled when I saw Jasmine heading across the office. *You did this to yourself*, I thought as I searched frantically around for someone to help.

Lily.

I rushed toward her.

"You don't happen to know what Jasmine's coffee house order is, do you?" I asked.

"No, sorry. Why don't you ask Chrissie?"

Not an option. I threw her a hurried thanks and raced to somebody else, asking the same question.

"Sorry. Haven't bought coffee for Jasmine in years."

I rolled back on the balls of my feet as both time and options ran out.

Screw it, I thought as I raced to the elevator. *I'll get her a latte. That's a safe option. So long as she isn't intolerant to milk. And I don't accidentally kill her by buying something she's allergic to.* That brought the panic back.

And then I realised it. There *was* someone I could ask. Someone whose number I'd recently tortured out of him and who undoubtedly knew Jasmine's order...

As I messaged Will, my eyes shot to where he sat, just within my view. Thankfully, he had his phone in his hand. He put it down and looked around the office, eyes searching for something. Me, I realised. When they locked on mine, he shook his head ever so slightly. Slightly, but enough for me to know his answer.

Please, I mouthed, trying to convey the urgency. He turned away, and then my phone vibrated.

Not urgent. Only text if it's urgent

Cruel roommate. Cruel, heartless, unthinkable roommate. I ran to the coffee house, thinking those words over and over. That roommate of mine. How did this *not* count as urgent? How did-

My phone buzzed.

Flat White. One-shot. One sweetener. Get Chrissie a Chai Tea Latte–thank me later.

Relief. Pure relief flooded through me as I read the text out to the barista. That roommate of mine. Not so bad after all.

I took the drinks back and handed the latte to Chrissie. Her eyes narrowed on the cup, and, for one heartbeat, I wondered if I'd been sabotaged. Maybe Will thought I deserved more revenge for the tickle attack. "What is this?" she asked. "I didn't ask for anything."

"It's a Chai Tea Latte," I answered, hesitating with one foot in the air. "Is it... alright?"

Her lips curved into a smile. An actual smile. "Thank you. How did you know I like this?"

"I think you mentioned it last time." I brushed past her and handed Jasmine her drink. She took a sip and gave me the thumbs up.

"Perfect. Thanks, Dani."

I left the room with a spring in my step. Knowing that

I should give thanks where thanks were due, I sent Will a text, looking across as he read it. My stomach did a horrible flip when I saw Finn leering over his shoulder.

Finn was the last person I wanted in on our secret.

"Who's annoying girl?" he asked, tilting his head as he leaned closer to Will's phone.

Will chuckled, his eyes on his phone. "No one in particular. Hey," his head snapped up as if just realising something. "Can you not look at my phone?"

"S-sorry." Finn stepped back, face flushing.

I sent another text, not willing to let that name go.

Annoying girl? Seriously??? Well, I hope you like being saved as pumpkin, pumpkin.

He laughed so loud it filled the entire office. Multiple heads turned his way.

"Sorry," he cleared his throat, taking a gulp of water. "Just a–funny meme."

I turned back to my work, biting my lip against an urge to laugh.

CHAPTER THIRTEEN

"Here you go," I found Will in the kitchen and passed him a wad of notes. It probably should've been painful handing over that amount of money, but it wasn't. On the contrary, it felt good finally paying him back.

Today was the last Friday of the month, which also equated to payday. I'd been so excited for this day that I'd spent most of the week distracted and impatient. To be fair, so had the other first years. The entire office, even. It seemed payday was a universal cause for celebration.

"What's this?" he asked, taking it from me.

"The money I owe you."

He raised an impressed brow, almost as if he never expected to get it back, and flicked through the notes. "You do realise you could've just wired it over, right? Internet banking is a thing."

I grinned. "I know. But there's just something so satisfying about being the one to hand it over. I also got you this," I handed him a Subway, taking a seat at the table to finish eating mine.

Shopping was exhausting, and I'd only bought one item: a gift for Will. I'd spent an hour after work searching for something when I finally found the hoodie. Green, to match his eyes. I knew I didn't really need to buy it, but I'd wanted to if only to say thanks. I just didn't know when to give it to him. Or how he'd receive it. Or whether he'd throw it away in disgust or think I had some ulterior motive like hidden love or something equally ridiculous.

I eyed him as I stored the bag with his gift under the table, finding him picking at his sub with suspicion in his eyes. "It's not poisoned, you know."

He raised his brow. "Why am I more suspicious now than I was a second ago?"

I waved a hand. "Just eat it."

He pulled out a chair opposite me. "How much do I owe you for it?" he asked, taking a bite. A blob of sauce dripped unnoticed onto his chin. I smiled.

"Don't worry about it. Call it payback for the McDonald's." I threw him a napkin. "Here. You have something on your face."

"Oh, I was saving it for later." He wiped his mouth anyway. "It's usually you who gets stuff on your face."

That was news to me. "You've never told me that before. Do you just let me go about my day with food on my face?"

"It usually disappears after a while. You lick your lips a lot," he informed me.

I kicked the hoodie further out of reach. "Next time, I'll let you go out with sauce on your face."

He smirked. "So, tell me–have you come up with an idea for your game yet?"

"No." I grimaced. "Fancy giving me one? I'm *kidding*," I rolled my eyes at the look on his face. "I will think of one. I know I will."

"That's the fighting spirit." He took another large bite of his sub as I turned mine over. "Is something wrong?" he asked, seeing the change in my mood.

I picked at the bread. "I was sort of hoping to let off some steam tonight before focussing completely on it from tomorrow. I haven't been out in... I don't know, a long time."

He eyed me carefully, probably assessing the level of sadness in my voice. "I thought you were going out tonight."

I was supposed to be. I'd had the plan in my calendar all week, which Will knew. But... "Finn and Lily cancelled," I sighed. "They're both going to this family thing in Manchester."

"And you weren't invited?"

"I think I'd be a third wheel." I gave him a knowing look, which he understood. Indeed, Lily and Finn had become best friends since starting at Bluebird. Maybe more.

"Hmm." He stared at the table for a long moment, fingers drumming against the wood. "What about that friend of yours–Holly, is she called?"

My brows shot up. "You remember her name?"

"Are you surprised that I listen?" He didn't sound offended, exactly. More amused.

A smile curved on my lips. "Sorry." I looked down. "Actually, Holly hasn't been in touch with me since I moved out. She doesn't even know I live with you."

Now he looked surprised. "She can't be much of a great friend then."

"She-" I struggled to find the right words. "She is. I mean, she's done a lot for me this past year. And she gave me a place to stay, so," I shrugged, taking another bite from my sub.

"But she made you feel like you needed to leave," he observed.

I covered my mouth and swallowed. "She never actually made me feel that way. It was more her boyfriend. But... I overheard her saying she also wanted me to move out, so I did. I hate being a burden, you know?"

He made a face that made me wonder if my memory was more painful to him than it was to me. "Listen to me," he said, shuffling forward and using his finger to accentuate his point. "A good friend isn't someone who just does you a favour and then forgets you exist–they're someone who will always be there for you and check in to make sure you're okay. I'm surprised she hasn't even texted you. That's poor."

"To be fair, I haven't texted her either."

"But you're the one who moved out. And who knows– I could have been a horrible, horrible roommate, and she would never know-"

"You are a horrible, horrible roommate," I interjected, smiling despite myself.

Unfazed by my teasing, he continued, "And so are you. That's why she wanted you to move out, obviously. But, joking aside, I bet if it had been the other way around, and she'd needed a place to stay, you would have done the same for her. And I also bet you wouldn't have made her feel like a burden–because a friend is not a burden, alright?"

"Alright." I eyed him carefully, noting the passion in his

eyes. "It sounds like your friends are lucky to have you," I said, wishing, not for the first time, I was one of them.

"Speaking of friends," he pushed out his chair, "I better hurry up and get ready, or I'll be getting an angry phone call."

"Oh, you're going out tonight?" I picked at my sandwich, trying not to sound disheartened.

He paused. "It's, um, nothing too exciting... Just a few of us meeting for a drink."

"Yeah, no, I hope you have a good night."

"I'd actually rather be staying in."

"Right? It's so cold out there, it's..." I couldn't think of anything else to say.

"It's going to be crazy," he offered. "Friday, payday... we'll be lucky to get a table anywhere."

"Exactly." Being busy made me want to go out more, but I didn't let him know that. I could already see that he was struggling. Between what, I couldn't be sure, but I guessed it had something to do with wanting to escape and feeling bad about leaving me.

He hesitated, unsure what to do with himself, so I decided to put him out of his misery.

"Honestly, it's fine, Will. I want you to have a good night. I have plenty to do here." I stood. "Starting with watching TV."

"Yeah, sure." He smiled as I passed him, but I caught it falter as I left the room.

Looking like I was having a good time was my next priority. I didn't want to put a damper on his night just because he had friends to go out with, and I didn't. So, as he went to get ready, I flicked on a comedy and prepared myself to fake-laugh whenever he came in.

I heard his footsteps coming down the stairs and barked out the worst fake laugh possible.

"So," he said, leaning against the doorframe. He tapped his fist against it, watching me with a dilemma in his eyes. "I guess I'll see you later."

"Sure." I smiled as he turned away, prepared to keep it forced in place until I heard the door close. But he took one step, scratched the back of his head, and span back.

"Do you want to come out with me?" The question came out so fast that I wasn't sure if I'd heard it right. I blinked, my mind frantically working through the probability that I *had* heard him right. That Will, the guy who regularly drew a line between us, had actually invited me out with him. "It's okay if not," he added quickly. "I know you're watching something, and it is cold out there, but-"

"Yes." My voice came out high-pitched and weird, and desperate and needy. I cleared my throat. "I mean–yes."

His lips pulled up. "You don't take long to get ready, do you?"

"I can be ready in twenty." I shot to my feet and raced past him, taking two steps at a time to prevent wasting any more precious seconds.

I didn't need to do much. After throwing on some bronzer and eyeliner, I combed through my hair, letting it fall feather-like over my shoulders. Then I changed into a cropped blouse and mom jeans and threw on my trusted trainers.

Will waited for me at the bottom of the stairs. I

launched myself down, almost decking it at the bottom. I say *almost* like I didn't fly forward and nearly faceplant the coat rack.

Will caught my elbow and steadied me. "You can't be that excited to go out with me."

"It's not with you per se," I said, straightening my cuffs, "but I am excited." It totally was with him, but I didn't need to stroke his ego.

He let his arm fall as his eyes took me in, moving over my face and hair. "You look..." he trailed off, cutting off any compliment he was about to give. Maybe he couldn't think of one.

"Cute?" I offered. "Sexy? Juicy?"

"I'm sorry–*Juicy*?"

"I don't know. The word just popped into my head." I ducked beneath him to tie a loose knot on my trainer. When I straightened, I found his hand hovering by my elbow as if he expected me to somehow deck it again.

He let it fall. "I was actually going to say *nice*, but then I realised you look the same as you always do."

"You weren't expecting some Cinderella makeover, were you?" I asked. "Even when I try to be glamorous, I fail."

"This look suits you. And let me guess, the trainers are so you can dance freely just like they're for running around a supermarket?"

"Absolutely," I hopped from one foot to the other. "Agility is key on a night out."

He rolled his eyes and placed his hands on my shoulders so he could wheel me out the door. "Let's get going before you start calling yourself succulent."

"You're hilarious."

The cold air cut straight through my blouse like a shard of ice. Shivering, I circled out of his grasp and slipped my hands under his coat, grabbing him by the shoulders instead.

"What are you doing?" he asked, frowning over his shoulder.

"Exactly what you were doing to me. Except I'm also stealing your warmth."

"Did you not think to bring a coat?" His voice didn't sound annoyed, exactly. It was reason enough to keep holding onto him–especially when he was much warmer than I'd expected. Like being tucked beneath a heated blanket.

"I'll be fine once we get there. I just didn't want to carry something bulky around all night."

It made sense to me. Will, on the other hand, seemed to get ticked off.

"No. You do not get to steal my warmth for that reason." He lurched forward with enough force that my hands slid out, exposing me to the cold. By the time I'd gotten over the shock of it, he was running around a corner.

I chased after him. "I'm sorry, Will! I won't do it again!"

He didn't slow. I feared I'd been too much of my annoying self, and he was now trying to ditch me. But then his laughter rang back to me, entwining with the wind.

He jogged back, stopped long enough to give me a wink, and raced away again.

His eyes widened when I caught up to him. "This is why I wear trainers," I laughed.

He slowed to a pace, eyes moving down to them. "I guess they have more uses than speed." His lips twitched as he met my eyes. "They're also more fun."

"Oh, *definitely*. Just be glad that I'm not wearing heels. I can't even walk in them. Unless hobbling counts as a walk." The one time I'd put on a pair to appease Holly, we'd barely made it to the taxi before I wobbled to the ground. Suffice it to say, she never made me wear them again.

"Hobbling does not count," Will said. His eyes turned curious. "Why do girls wear those things, anyway?"

"Not all girls are so woefully challenged like me. Like those artists who can actually *run* across the stage in them." I sighed, envious. "But I guess other girls wear them because the stupid part of society tells us we should. Like this one time when I was on work experience, and the male manager told me I needed to wear heels for *presentation purposes*." I stuck out my tongue in disgust.

"That's-" Will looked horrified.

"Completely unfair, right?"

"But what do heels have to do with work? What do they have to do with *anything*?"

"Exactly! But I guess you men have to wear suits, and *those* seem just as restricting."

"Blah, suits." He pulled a face. "I'm just waiting for the day when businesses realise people work better when they're treated like humans, not corporate robots."

We arrived at a club that I'd only ever seen on the outside. Although a queue stretched all the way to the street corner, the bouncer let Will straight in. I ogled before I tried to follow.

"Sorry," the bouncer stepped in front of me, big and immovable, like a giant boulder. "Can't let you in."

"Oh?" I peeked around his huge form at Will, who hadn't noticed my hold-up. "Can I just go in? That's my friend there." I pointed, but the bouncer didn't budge. My voice barely audible over the booming noise, I called, "Will?"

Thankfully, Will glanced back, eyes tightening as he saw how I shrank beneath the towering mass of the bouncer. Walking over, he positioned himself in front of me and folded his arms.

"What's the problem?" he asked. "She's with me."

The bouncer's eyes flicked between us as if he doubted our coupling. "You know the rules, Will. No trainers allowed."

Even though the situation was far from funny, I met Will's eyes and smiled.

"But I'm wearing trainers," he pointed out.

The bouncer shrugged his great, broad shoulders. "Sorry. It's the rules."

We both knew what that meant. Sure enough, when I glanced back at the line, I saw that all the girls wore heels, some in obvious discomfort.

"It's okay, Will," I said in defeat. "You go on ahead. I'm fine." I certainly wasn't about to fight for entry into a club with this kind of policy.

But Will didn't leave me. Instead, he gave my shoulder a squeeze and turned back to the bouncer. "Come on, Jez. You know I have friends inside, and we'll all leave if Dani doesn't get in."

My throat bobbed.

After a long second, the bouncer rolled his eyes and stepped aside. "It's not like I care, anyway. Just don't tell anyone it was me on duty."

Will grinned. "Thanks."

He led me down some stairs as I fidgeted with my sleeves, grabbing my hand when a crowd almost separated us. It was busy in here. And loud. And I might've been having a panic attack.

"Do your friends know I'm with you?" I asked, trying to keep my breathing steady.

"No, I don't think I told them. They won't mind, though." He glanced down at me, his grip on my hand tightening. "You're not nervous, are you?"

"Me, nervous?" I let out a laugh that sounded more hysterical than anything. "Not at all." I swallowed. "Yes. What if they don't like me?"

Will chuckled. "They're not that complex. They're out to have a good time, and so are you. What's not to like?"

He led me to a large, circular booth between the bar and dancefloor, and I counted five sitting there already. Five well-dressed, good-looking men, all with their eyes on me. One of them I recognised–Jordan–and immediately felt my face heat when I saw the surprise on his face. I looked away, my eyes falling on another boy whose eyes bulged at something further down. At Will's hand, I realised–the one still clasping mine.

He let my hand go, and I wondered if he knew he'd even been holding it. Sliding into the booth, he tapped the space beside him and immediately frowned when his eyes locked on mine. He looked over at his friends and saw what held me back.

"Would you guys stop staring at her?" he scolded, swatting their arms. "You're making her uncomfortable." Having drawn their attention to himself, he leaned back, resting his arm behind where I tentatively sat. "This is Dani," he told them. "The roommate I told you about."

I raised a questioning brow at him. *Any more complaints that I need to know about?*

He smirked, leaning close enough to whisper, "All good things, I promise."

My satisfied smile vanished when I saw how they all looked at me again. I gulped. "Hey. It's nice to meet you all."

The strange, silent atmosphere continued for another painful second. And then it was over.

"Dani!" Jordan flashed a white-toothed grin at me as the table erupted into noise. "It's good to finally see you again. This is Tae, Mike, Jack, and Dec." He pointed them out to me, but their names entered and exited my brain like an object slicing through a fog.

"There is no way I'll remember that," I laughed. When they laughed in return, my muscles finally relaxed. Beside me, I swear I saw Will relax with me.

"So you're Will's roommate, huh?" One of them leaned across the table to ask. I kicked myself for already forgetting his name. "Why has he been keeping you from us?"

"Probably saving you from my annoying personality, I assume." I turned to face Will, waiting for his response.

He chuckled. "She's right. One hour with her, and you'll wish I never brought her."

I nudged him with my elbow. "They're already so used to

you."

"If only I were annoying," he sighed dramatically.

"Oh, you have your moments," the boy with beautiful jet-black hair laughed. "I'm Tae," he kindly reminded me. "And I'm a little disappointed that Jordan got to meet you first."

"Yeah," Jordan stretched out his muscles and released a long, self-satisfied sigh. "Now we'll always have that connection. Right, Dani?"

Will kicked him beneath the table, cutting off his flirty smile. I laughed as they entered into an all-out footsy war.

"Are they always like this?" I asked Tae.

"Oh, yeah." He indicated for me to lean closer. "My bets on Will giving up first."

I glanced at the two of them practically kicking on the floor. Before the revenge tickle attack that Will enacted upon me, I might've gone with Jordan winning this thing as well. But after it... I turned back to Tae. "You're on."

Ten minutes later, I had a whiskey in front of me, specially bought by Tae. Will complained that it should've gone to him, what with the victory being his. I only saluted him and drank it in one.

It didn't take me long to realise that I liked Will's friends. What was even more miraculous was that they seemed to like me. Five strangers became five people who felt like life-long friends.

"Care for a dance?" Tae asked me after we'd all downed a shot.

I slipped my hand into his. "I thought you'd never ask."

Tae was a wild dancer, just like me. Neither of us cared what we looked like, making it all the more fun. We danced until we outreached our fitness level, and then we claimed a small, drink-covered table to catch our breath.

"So," I breathed, fanning myself with a drink mat. "How long have you known Will?"

"How long?" He looked upwards in thought. "About twelve years, I think. Since I moved here mid-high-school."

"Wow."

"Yeah." He gave me a shy, inquisitory look and shook his head. "I still can't believe you're his roommate."

"What's so hard to believe?"

"I don't know. It's just that Will..." he glanced over his shoulder, probably to check that he wasn't nearby, and lowered his voice. "Okay, don't tell him I told you this, but he is not good with girls. I mean, he's good at *getting* with them, sure, but anything after that..." he shook his head. "Seeing him laugh with you is crazy. And *holding your hand?*" His mouth dropped open. "I wasn't the only one surprised. You're the first friend of his who's a girl, can you believe that?"

"Actually, I can," I laughed. "Except, according to him, we aren't friends." I dropped my eyes to the table. "I'm only here because he felt sorry for me."

"That is definitely not true." The way he said it brought my eyes back to him. "Will wouldn't bring you to us unless he thought you'd fit in, so that tells me he likes you. *A lot.* Trust me, even in the little time I've seen the two of you together, I can tell you that for certain."

A surge of warmth shot through at the thought of Will liking me. Silly, I told myself, but- "I do really want to be friends with him," I confessed. "I know I call him annoying, but he's actually...," I paused, searching for the right words to describe Will. "Easy to be around," I went with. "And earlier today, the way he talked about you guys... he said a friend is never a burden and that you should always be there for them. I bet he's a good friend to have, right?"

Tae didn't react as I'd expected. He looked down at his hands, suddenly morbid. "He said that huh?"

"Is it a bad thing to say?"

"No, it's just..." he sighed. "Will is a better friend than you can imagine. And he's always been there for us, even when we weren't there for him." I sensed a story behind his words, but I didn't push it. He continued on his own. "Part of the reason why Will struggles to build any kind of meaningful relationship with women is because of this girl in his past. He was serious about her, and she cheated on him... with his brother."

I sucked in a gasp. Anger rose in my throat. Boiling anger that anybody could do such a thing. And to *Will*.

"I know," Tae said, reading the rage on my face. "The worst part is that none of us was there for him. I can't imagine how he got through that on his own. Me? I was busy doing my own thing and thought he was happy... so I didn't make time for his calls. But he did get through it. Somehow. But-" he ducked his head with a sigh. "He answers every single call I make without fail. I should have been there for him."

"You should," I agreed. "But life doesn't always work that way. It's good that he could be there for himself. And while you can't change the past, you can change how you are now. So I hope you answer his calls," I teased, happy to see a smile pull on his lips.

I looked over at where Will still sat laughing in our booth. He did that a lot, I realised. Laughed. I wouldn't have placed him as someone who'd had his heart broken. As I watched, his eyes moved around the club, stopping on me. He tilted his head, not breaking eye contact. I just gave him a little wave.

As he turned away, I thought I understood why he laughed. Pain is something we should learn from, not dwell in. His friends weren't there for him when he needed them, but instead of allowing it to make him bitter, he became a person who was always there for his friends. I admired that.

After a moment's thought, I pulled out my phone and messaged Holly. Because even if she hadn't checked in on me, that didn't mean I shouldn't check in on her.

A weight lifted from my shoulders as I hit send.

"Should we head back?" Tae asked.

"You go ahead," I said, tucking my phone away. "I'll come over soon."

My brain was so wrapped up thinking about Will that as I entered the bathroom, I didn't register a girl coming out of it until we banged into one another.

"I'm so sorry," I said, quickly turning.

"*Watch* where you're going, please," she snarled, barging past me.

I did a double-take. Hadn't I seen her before? But where?

I shook my head as I entered the bathroom, unable to place her. But then it hit me. I knew *exactly* who she was– and even the memory of our brief encounter was enough to send a shiver down my spine. I froze when I realised another implication. If the memory of her was enough to scare me, then...

I spun on my heel, in a hurry to find Will.

CHAPTER FOURTEEN

What would she do if she saw us here? Nothing, I told myself as I raced towards Will. She probably didn't even remember me, so I had nothing to worry about.

Will looked startled as I crashed into the booth beside him.

"We have an emergency," I told him.

"What emergency?" His eyes raked over me. Seeing no immediate threat, he glanced over my shoulder.

"That girl is here."

His eyes refocused on me. "Girl?"

"What was her name?" I shook my head. "I can't remember. But that girl who came to your house the first day we met... you know, that scary girl... when you agreed to let me live with you...,"

Comprehension flashed behind his eyes. "No."

"Yes. Have you seen her since you slammed the door in her face?" And she'd called me a downgrade, I remembered with bitterness.

He shook his head. I could see his panic developing. "No.

Where did you see her? Did she see you?"

"I don't think so." I chewed my lip, hoping she wouldn't recognise me even if she did.

"Oh, G-" the rest of Will's sentence got choked back as his eyes moved to somewhere behind me. I recognised that look. That one of pure horror. Without a second thought, I twisted my face away, catching Jordan's eyes as I chewed my bottom lip again. He tilted his head, questioning my action. I just shook mine, too afraid to speak.

A coward. That was what I was.

"Hey, Will." Yep–That was her alright. I recognised that sickly sweet voice.

Will cleared his throat. "H-hello."

"I haven't seen you out in a while."

"I've been busy."

"Are you busy now?"

Did she not remember how they'd last ended things? Will's eyes flashed to my face, and I gave him a look that warned him not to involve me. "Yes," he said. "I'm with my friends."

"You can all join us if you want. I'm with some girls–we're sat over there."

Will's eyes moved somewhere to the right, away from me. I tried to regain his attention, tried to plead with him to refuse her offer, but he wouldn't meet my eye.

"I think we'll pass," he said.

I exhaled.

"Why? It's not like you're with that girlfriend of yours."

"Girlfriend?" Will frowned in puzzlement. I kicked his shin. "Oh," he laughed, not even wincing. "She's right here."

The movement was swift. One moment, I sat beside Will. The next, I was perched on his knee with his arm sliding around my waist.

I made sure I gave Will a stern look before turning to smile at her.

"Hi," I gritted out. "Nice to see you again."

My only solace was that she did indeed look surprised. "Oh. You are here."

"Yep. And we don't want to join you, so if you could please leave."

She whispered something to her friend, who laughed in response. No doubt at my expense.

Sure enough, her friend turned to Will. "Wow. Is this seriously the girl you chose over Alicia? Great taste you've got."

I gave her a dirty look as Will's hand tensed on my thigh.

"She's better than the two of you put together," he said, sounding surprisingly sincere. "Now, will you get out of here?"

"You're killing the atmosphere," Jordan informed them.

Finally seeming to realise they weren't welcome, they left, throwing a dirty look behind them.

Tae leaned toward me. "Are you alright?"

"I'm fine," I assured him.

"I'm not." Will pulled a face. "Ga! You're so heavy, Dani." He pushed me off him with a huff that told me he'd been holding the pain in.

"Nobody asked you to put me on your knee!"

"I thought you'd love sitting on it."

"Oh, it's every girl's dream," I scoffed.

He caught my sarcasm and matched it. "Well, I'd happily let you do it again. At least I won't have to go to work with a broken leg."

I tried to hold back a laugh, but it burst from my lips. He laughed with me.

"You two are weird," Jordan observed.

"Weird is good." I took the last swig of my drink and stood. "I'm heading home. It was nice meeting you all."

"You're leaving?" The desperation in Will's voice almost made me stay.

"Yep. I've enjoyed myself enough, and I don't want to push it. Got a game to create, you know."

"You aren't going with her, are you, Will?" I could see why Jordan asked that question. Beside me, Will had gotten to his feet.

"You don't need to," I protested. "You should stay out. Enjoy yourself."

"I'm at least getting you a cab." Before I could protest further, he grabbed his coat and swept past me. I chased after him, waving a hurried goodbye at the others.

"You really don't need to," I said again. "I can get my own cab."

He didn't stop until we reached outside. There, he paused long enough to wrap his coat around my shoulders.

"Here." He looked me in the eyes as he straightened the collar. "So I don't have to carry it later," he smirked.

I looked down at the arms that drowned me. "It's so big on me."

His smirk deepened. "I had fun with you tonight."

"Just like I knew you would."

"Alright," patience at its end, he turned away and walked straight to the nearest taxi, bending to talk to the driver. I caught part of what he said as I climbed into the back. "Take my friend to that address. And make sure she gets there safe. Thank you." He turned back to me. "What are you smiling like that for?"

"Nothing." I slammed the door closed, rolling the window down enough to say, "Except that's the first time you've called me your friend," I smirked at his expression as I rolled the window back up, waving as the taxi pulled away. A glance behind told me that he was smiling.

At home, I had every intention opening my laptop to brainstorm ideas. All good intentions went out the window, and I made myself some cereal, climbing into bed instead. After gulping down the dregs of milk, I flicked the light off and stared into comforting darkness.

Tonight had been fun. I liked hanging with Will and his friends, and I hoped he'd invite me out to do it again. More importantly, Will had said, without joking, that he'd had fun with me.

I smiled and twisted onto my side. He was alright, my roommate.

Tae's words drifted toward me in the dark, and I frowned. Why did Will's girlfriend have to cheat on him? And with his *brother*? If they loved each other–fine. People fall in and out of love all the time. But they should've told Will the truth. Sure, it still would've sucked for him, but he might not have such a hard time trusting girls now if they'd been honest from the start.

That's why I hated cheaters. They were so selfish, never

thinking about the person getting hurt or how it might affect them for years after. Did they know how their betrayal still affected Will? Or were they too wrapped up in their own happiness to care?

Anger seethed through me.

I twisted to my other side, telling myself to calm down. There was no need to be angry when Will himself had gotten over it. But had he? Since living with him, I'd only ever seen him have a one-night stand. Was *that* getting over it?

Those were questions I probably wouldn't get answered. But I wanted to know he was okay. I wanted him to *be* okay. I drifted into an uneasy sleep, thinking about Will and his smile and wondering for the first time if there was pain behind it.

The following morning, I found him in the front room, nursing a hangover. By the looks of his makeshift bed, he hadn't made it to his bedroom.

"How is it you look fine when I feel like garbage?" he asked as I sat on the other sofa. He had a blanket up to his neck yet still shivered.

"It might have something to do with the oh-so-simple fact I know when to call it quits. You should learn it."

"Teach me the ways, oh Jedi Master."

I smirked. "Do you want me to get you some water? And a quilt?"

The speed at which he looked at me made me wonder how he didn't get whiplash. It did, however, make him wince. "Would you? And a pot noodle?"

"Coming right up." I stood, happy to be of help. Maybe it had something to do with the fact that I liked him more every day.

"You can get the quilt from my bed," he told me. "I give you my permission to go in."

He was breaking all of the rules.

I flicked the kettle on and worked on his pot noodle first. While it stewed, I poured the glass of water and went upstairs for his quilt, pausing outside his door. His bedroom felt forbidden to me, like the employee zone of a supermarket, so I had to brace myself as I twisted the handle and entered. I wasn't sure what I expected the inside of his room to look like, but as I walked in, I realized it was just as I expected. It was just so... him.

There weren't any flashy or expensive-looking items lying around. Everything was simple, neat, boyish–the bed black leather and hastily made, the curtains grey and blackout. He had two bedside tables: one with a lamp and several photo frames, the other with his laptop. On the right-hand side was a ginormous bookcase. I inspected it closer, finding games and notepads in place of books. Would he ever let me rummage through it?

I moved to his bed and knelt down, examining the photo frames. Most of them were of him and his friends. Smiling, I picked up the one of him and Tae. It looked like the last day of high school from the way their shirts were signed. Will looked so young, but that sunshine smile hadn't changed.

Realizing I was taking too long, I put the photo down and grabbed his quilt. It felt like a puffy soft cloud.

"Here," I said, dumping it on him when I went back down.

"You spent a good time in my room," he noted, pulling it around him.

I fought back a blush. "I had a good snoop in your drawers. Nice underwear."

His eyes shot toward me. When he saw how I smiled, he relaxed back into his quilt. "Your permission has now been revoked."

"Ever the rule giver." I passed him the noodles and water and grabbed my laptop, leaving him for the quietness of my room. After crossing my legs on the bed, I opened my blank word document.

What game did I want to play? What story would stir my emotions the most? As I thought, I pictured Will with his friends, and my mind drifted to a game with loyalty as its theme. It could work. Throw some betrayal in, and I had a story. The more I thought about it, the more the pieces fell into place.

I was so absorbed in my work, jotting down notes and creating storyboards, that I jumped when I heard a knock on my door.

"I'm going out," Will called.

What time was it? "Okay. Have fun!"

A beat. "Do you want to come with me?"

"It's-" thinking it simpler to talk face-to-face, I leapt to the door. Will stepped back, slipping his hands into his pockets as he waited for me to answer. "It's okay. Last night was enough for me. I'm fine tonight."

"Fair enough." He made to move, but then he turned back to me. "For the record, I wasn't asking because I don't think you're fine. I was asking because I want you to come."

"Oh." Wow. *Wow.* He wanted me to come. If only I didn't need to keep the momentum going... "Can we do a rain check? I've thought of an idea for my game and need to get it down."

He must have seen the enthusiasm on my face because he suddenly grinned. "Yes! I knew you'd think of something. Just don't tell me any details," he added, covering his ears. "I don't want to be biased when voting."

"Because you won't be able to stop yourself from voting for me?" I teased.

"I'm afraid I'll vote against you." Smirking, he turned away. "Work hard. I'll see you later."

"Have a good time!" As soon as he was out of view, I closed the door, already thinking about my game again.

I worked until my brain felt frazzled. No longer able to focus, I grabbed my coat and walked to a nearby café, purchasing a macaroni cheese and cup of coffee. I sat inside while I ate. Something about having an idea, however undeveloped, felt relieving, and I was happy just sitting on my own.

On my way back to the house, I craned my neck to look at the stars. They dotted the sky without a cloud in sight.

Someone was standing outside our door when I reached the gate. I paused, one hand on the handle, uncertain what made me hesitate. When the person twisted her head just enough for me to recognise her, I removed my hand and leapt back, throwing a hand over my mouth to stifle my surprise.

Peeking with the caution of an untrusting housecat, I confirmed what I'd feared: Chrissie had come to visit Will.

CHAPTER FIFTEEN

There was only one plausible explanation for Chrissie visiting Will at this time on a Saturday. She was here to confess her feelings to him.

Or she was here for a pre-arranged meet-up, but I doubted Will would invite her over without telling me. Doubted it enough that I was stuck believing the first assumption. Besides, she didn't know that he wasn't home.

Peeking again, I saw that she'd dressed up for the occasion. She wore a knee-length dress that hugged her figure, with hair curled and pinned half in a bun. She looked beautiful. So beautiful that if she confessed to Will now, I wasn't sure if he'd reject or accept the offer. I had no idea if he even liked her in that way.

I also wasn't sure why I cared to find out.

Moving as quietly as possible, I crept back until I reached Will's car, using it to hide behind. She wouldn't stay for long. She'd already tried a few knocks, and any sane person wouldn't wait for a few more.

I pulled out my phone and crouched, trying to ignore my desperate need for the toilet. Dang coffee. Jiggling, I craned my neck to listen. Another knock. Then another. Then another.

It was all I could do to suppress a groan. I scrunched my face together as my toilet need became more urgent. What option did I have but to message Will and tell him to get over here? For all I knew, Chrissie was happy to park up and camp for the night.

My message was short–I didn't have it in me to type anything long–but I hoped it conveyed the emergency of the situation. I sat on the curb, waiting, unlocking my phone just to see that he'd read my message and ignored it. What were the chances that he'd come and save me, anyway? Did I really expect that from him? He was out having a good time. He wouldn't want to return home so soon.

Chrissie stayed for another five minutes and then another ten. Just as I thought it better to get caught than wet myself beside Will's car, I saw somebody sprinting at the top of the street. I squinted. This person looked like Will, but that couldn't be right. He wouldn't run all this way just to help me.

He slowed just before he reached the garden, catching his breath, and I almost peed right there when I saw that it *was* Will. Come to save me. I waved my hands to catch his attention, but he'd already turned into the garden.

"Hey, Chrissie." That voice of his soothed every inch of me. "What are you doing here?"

"Oh, hey, Will. I... I was finalising the costume art and remembered you needed the prints for the Monday meeting. Here."

"Wow. You know you could've given me these on Monday

and saved yourself the trip?"

"I know. I just thought... better to be safe, you know."

"Well, thanks." Silence. "You haven't been here for long, have you?"

"No, not long at all."

My bladder disagreed with her.

"Great. Was there... anything else?"

"Yes. I wanted to tell you something, but... could we go inside first?"

I fought hard against a groan and squirmed to glimpse Will's reaction. All I saw was the back of his head.

"You want to come inside?" he repeated.

"If you don't mind. It's, um, cold out here. Unless your roommate will have a problem with it?"

"I–don't know where she is, actually." He turned, and I saw the agitation in his eyes. A set of keys rattled, the hallway light flicked on, and he led Chrissie inside. "Just head to the kitchen. I'll be back in a second."

Will headed back down the garden, searching behind bushes on his way.

"Dani?" he whispered, his voice low and urgent. "Dani, are you here?" I waved from my spot, and his eyes found me. "Are you alright?" he asked, crouching beside me.

"I desperately, desperately need the toilet," I jiggled.

"You should think about drinking less."

He was right. But still. "That doesn't help me now. What should I do? I can't go inside with Chrissie in there."

"Well, I'm not about to tell you to use my car as a toilet," he glanced over his shoulder. "Follow me in five minutes. I'll make sure we're in the kitchen with the door closed.

And here," he shoved out of his jacket, passing it to me. "It's freezing."

I grabbed his hand as he turned to leave. "Thank you. And thanks for coming back to help me." A small crease formed between his brows as he looked down at my hand around his. He looked up at me and stared for a long second, long enough that I removed my hand and pushed him. "Go, or I seriously will pee on your car."

He disappeared. Five minutes later, I crept inside, hoping desperately to avoid exposure. But Will kept his word. There was no sign of Chrissie as I tiptoed up the stairs. As I took the last step, I heard her ask, "Is that your roommate? Will she come in here?"

Will's answer almost made me snort. "Nah. We don't talk that much. She usually stays in her room."

I did stay in my room now if only to hide. I could not, under any circumstances, let Chrissie see me.

The one solace to my confinement was that I couldn't hear what they were saying. Sitting cross-legged on my bed, I opened up a comic. I scanned the first page, barely registering the contents, before closing it again. I looked at the door. Did I *want* to overhear?

With vigilance, I opened my door and crept onto the landing. Not to eavesdrop, I told myself. Because that would be wrong. No, this was to wash my face.

When I didn't see anyone, I tiptoed to the stairs and listened. Not eavesdrop. Just to check whether Chrissie was still here.

"The first door at the top of the stairs?" I heard her ask, voice loud as if no longer coming from the kitchen.

I spun and stubbed my toe on the door.

"Shi-," covering my mouth, I leapt into the bathroom, slamming the door behind me.

"Oh." Her voice now came from the bottom of the stairs. I held my breath, hardly daring to move despite being hidden. "I think I just saw your roommate go into it."

"She has a very small bladder," I could hear the smirk in Will's voice. "She might take a while. You should probably wait in here."

I stayed in my room after that. Thankfully, it wasn't long before I heard a knock on my door.

"She's gone," Will told me through the wood.

I followed him into the kitchen and made us a cup of coffee before sitting down opposite him. He stared at his mug without touching it, a permanent crease between his brows. As I sipped my drink, I examined that frown, trying to figure out the cause.

"So," I said, lowering my mug to the table. I curled my fingers around it, savouring the warmth. "Does Chrissie come over often?"

"What? No." He straightened in his seat, but his eyes remained on the mug, and that frown deepened. "Um, I guess a few times. To drop off work folders."

"Right." I continued watching him, wishing there was something I could do to remove that frown. "Did she say something to make you unhappy?" I probed, more curious than I cared to admit.

He looked up at me. "No. She didn't say anything, and that's my problem."

That confused me. "What do you mean?"

He inhaled deeply, the air whistling through his teeth. "I can't say," he huffed. "I want to tell you, believe me, I do. It's just personal to her."

Personal as in he knew about her crush on him? I eyed him for a second, wanting to be sure, before I said, "Does it have something to do with how she feels about you?"

His brows flicked up. "How did you know?"

"Jasmine sort of dropped a hint when I first joined." I didn't need to add that Chrissie made it obvious just by how she looked at him. "So did she just confess to you? Or has she told you before?"

"No, she's never confessed to me. And that's my problem."

"Wait, what? Then how do you know?"

"Why else would somebody bring work over to your house when you haven't asked for it, on the weekend, while dressed up?" He had a point. "And speaking of Jasmine, she also likes to drop the same hints on me every other week."

I still didn't understand something. "So, if you know she likes you, why don't you make a move? You're not waiting for her to make the first move, are you?"

His face contorted. "I don't like her like that. Part of me wants to because she's great, and I don't want to disappoint her... but I don't." He tilted his head, moving his finger around the rim of his mug. "I keep waiting for her to tell me she likes me so I can let her down gently, but she never does. Then I think she must have gotten over me, and I feel relieved, but something like today happens, and it's back to square one." He dropped his head in his hands, grabbing a fistful of hair.

I frowned, wanting to comfort but not knowing how.

"Why don't you give it a chance?" I asked, ignoring a sudden tightness in my chest. "You know, date her. You might find that you do like her."

"And what if I don't?" He lifted his head to look at me, and I saw the desperation in his eyes. The desperation for an answer. "How hurt would she be then?"

"I-" I closed my mouth. I didn't have an answer for that.

"She deserves someone who can love her completely," he continued, "and that person isn't me." Sighing, he drew a hand down his face. "If I gave it a chance, I'd only be making it worse for her later."

I hadn't thought about it like that, yet he'd clearly thought it through. Enough that it tore him up inside. But why? Wasn't he the type to have a one-night stand and not give a damn? I thought of Tae and what he'd told me about Will's ex-girlfriend, and my perspective suddenly shifted. Will had experienced heartache. Maybe he did what he did, not because he didn't trust or care enough... but because he was scared of breaking somebody else's heart.

My own suddenly ached for him.

"Will," I moved my hand across the table, but it was too long to reach him. I let it fall outstretched. "It's okay that you don't like Chrissie. She's a strong woman, and she can handle your rejection. Don't feel bad just because you can't give her the love she wants, because that's life, and she'll still find it again. Just like you will."

"Sorry–what?" His head snapped up. "*I'll* find it again?"

Oops. I pulled my hand back, regretting the slip. "Nothing," I cleared my throat, hoping my lie would save Tae from trouble. "I didn't mean anything by it."

He saw right through me. "Tae told you, didn't he?" he laughed, taking it surprisingly well. "I wondered what the two of you talked about on your table."

"He might have said something," I shrugged. "And for the record, that ex-girlfriend and brother of yours suck? They suck."

He laughed again. This one rang straight through my chest, warming me. "They do suck, don't they?"

Influenced by the joy in his voice, I joked, "They suck so bad that they deserve each other's suckiness. They definitely don't deserve someone like you."

"Someone like me?" he tilted his head. "Are you admitting to liking me, Dani?"

I smiled, pleased to see him back to his usual self. "Yes, I like you. Happy?"

His lip pulled up as silence fell. Circling the rim of his mug with his finger again, he asked, "What about you? Do you have any family members or exes who suck?"

"Well, I don't have any siblings, but my dad left when I was in high school, and my mum turned to drugs as a method of coping. So I'd say they're pretty sucky." His mouth dropped open. Realising that I may have gone information overload on him, I quickly mumbled, "I'm sorry. Sometimes I say things too easily without thinking."

After eyeing me carefully for a second, he laughed. "You do, don't you? But I like it. It makes you easy to be around–there's no fakery about you."

His description shook me a little. Easy to be around–that was just how I'd described him to Tae. "It helps that you're easy to talk to," I said.

He tapped the table with his fist. "I feel bad, though. What happened to you sucks way more than what happened to me. I'm sorry-"

"A problem is a problem," I interjected.

"I guess. Still, I feel bad…,"

"You shouldn't. And you shouldn't act any different because you feel bad for someone. It makes their circumstances a part of them when they shouldn't be. I am not my mum, and I am not my dad, and I am definitely not my crappy childhood. You are not your ex, and you are not your brother, and you are not what they did to you. So let's treat each other how we've always treated each other because *that's* who we are."

"You mean my annoying roommate?" he smirked.

I reached across the table to swat his arm, but he caught my hand with ease. His fingers circled around it with a curious expression. I didn't protest as he gently moved it back to my side of the table.

I cleared my throat. "If there's an annoying roommate here, I think we can agree that it's you."

He shook his head with a chuckle, and a smile remained on his lips. I couldn't help but notice a difference in that smile. It was as if our conversation had changed something, removed hidden walls to reveal a smile without any shadows. A smile of pure sunshine.

The sunshine dimmed as Will frowned. "What is this?" he asked, pulling something from beneath the table.

Seeing the hoodie I'd hidden from him clutched in his fingers, I cringed. "Nothing. It's just-" I sighed. "Okay, it's for you. I just wanted to thank you for, you know, letting me be your roommate. So I bought you a gift."

I waited for him to throw it at me in disgust.

"Thanks," he held it up to examine. "How did you know I like green?"

I released a breath. "I didn't. It's the colour of your eyes, so I thought it would suit you."

He quirked a brow. "You know my eye colour?"

I quirked mine. "You don't know mine?"

Leaning across the table, he peered into my eyes. "They look like mud."

"And yours look like a swamp."

We continued staring at each other. After a moment, a weird feeling surfaced, so I flicked my eyes away. He cleared his throat.

"Don't you have a competition to win?"

"Yep," I jumped to my feet and made for the door. Pausing, I felt a strange sense of comfort and happiness that I couldn't remember experiencing before.

Somehow, I knew that it had everything to do with Will.

CHAPTER SIXTEEN

I spent the next few weeks tirelessly trying to complete my game design for the work competition. That meant weeks of staying home while Will brought me randomly-timed coffees (sometimes with added doughnuts) to help me through.

I submitted the design a week ago. One week later, I was finally about to find out if it had made it to the next round. That fact terrified me.

"Dani!" Will called from the bottom of the stairs. It wasn't the first time he'd called me. "Dani, come on, or we'll be late!"

"I'm coming!" I looked in the mirror again, turning, fussing, torturing myself over the tiniest details like how my jumper looked too creased. Finally reaching my breakpoint, I threw my blazer across the room with a huff.

"Dani?" Will tapped lightly on my door. After another huff at my reflection, I tore myself away to open it. All it took was one look at me for him to sigh. "You're going to be fine," he told me for the hundredth time that week. He placed his hands on my shoulders as he said it, but I wasn't capable of feeling reassured.

"You can't know that," I said, brushing past him and heading down the stairs.

"I know you," Will answered, following behind. "And I know you'll be fine."

I wanted to believe him, but a deterrent in the form of crippling self-doubt didn't allow it. Any ounce of confidence that dared to spark within me quickly drowned beneath its will.

"Do you know if I've gotten through?" I asked, almost pleaded, as I turned on him. He just rolled his eyes as he always did at that question.

"As I've told you before, it's anonymous. We won't know until our meeting this morning the names behind the winning ideas."

"Can you tell me what ideas have got through?" I ventured. "I'll know if it's mine."

The look he gave me told me I was pushing it. He folded his arms. "You know I can't tell you that."

"Then what's the use of having you for a friend?" My lips twitched as I pulled the hood of his coat up over his eyes. He tugged it down again as I jumped out of his way.

"Wow. Is this how you treat me now? Do you want to walk to work? I'll happily let you."

I didn't need to look out the window to know I didn't want that. If it weren't the rain pelting against the side of the house, it was the cold drifting through the cracks in the windows. "You wouldn't do that to me," I said, although a break in my voice betrayed my confidence.

He opened the front door. "Unfortunately, I wouldn't. But

only if you hurry up."

Rain splattered against my now exposed face, and I twisted away, wondering if Will would allow me to pull a sicky.

"It's *freezing*," I complained.

He glanced back. "Yeah, you're going to need to wear more than that jacket of yours."

"Do you have a spare scarf I can borrow?" I liked Will's scarves. He wore those thick, woollen ones that kept the neck nice and toasty. Much better than my non-existent one.

"You seriously don't own a scarf?" he asked.

"Nope. I'm saving up to buy a new winter wardrobe. But clearly, winter isn't waiting."

With a sigh that probably ran deep, he removed the one from around his neck and wrapped it around my own. "Here," he smirked. "Now you can't say I'm useless as a friend."

I inhaled deeply, full of gratitude for more than one reason. I'd come to realise that Will had his own smell. One that tasted of honey and cedarwood and warmth, and I couldn't think of a better smell on Earth.

"Are you sniffing me?" he asked, breaking me from my stupor.

I opened my eyes to find him with his brow raised. "No."

"You are totally sniffing me, aren't you?"

My lips tugged up. "You smell good, okay?"

He rolled his eyes. "Let's go. If you're done sniffing me, that is."

He headed out. When he turned to see if I followed, the

rain had already soaked through his hair.

"You look like a drowned cat," I laughed, watching droplets fall onto his face.

"Oh yeah?" He shook his hair in my direction, sending the droplets my way. "How do you like that?"

"Stop it!" I laughed, twisting as he did it again. Circling around him, I threw up my hood and made a run for it.

"Don't fall!" he called after me.

I slowed to a pace, walking backwards as I turned to face him. "Hurry up, slowcoach. The ice has finally melted."

"That's good," he looked at the ground as he walked tentatively towards me. "I was getting sick of constantly watching out for you slipping on it."

I smirked. The only person who kept slipping on the ice was him.

Once we were safely inside his car, Will cranked up the heating. He peered out of his windscreen, up at the onslaught of rain hammering against it. "I'm dropping you off outside the office," he told me. "No fighting me this time."

"But what if people see us together?" I fought anyway.

Ever since the weather had taken a turn for the worst, Will had driven us to work. He dropped me off someplace close to the office but not so near that people would see me leaving his car. Who knew what rumours would fly around if somebody saw us together.

"Nobody will be looking," he answered, pulling away from the curb. "Besides, even if they did happen to look, which they won't, they wouldn't see anything through this sheet of water."

I supposed he was right, but that didn't stop me from fidgeting. From nerves at being seen or at the answers today would bring, I didn't know.

"What if my game hasn't made it through?" I asked, wringing my hands together in my lap.

"Don't worry," Will caught my hands with his own, soothing me. "I've seen how much effort you've put in. I've got faith in you." He gave my hands a reassuring squeeze, but his smile didn't quite reach his eyes. I wondered if he was as confident in me as he let on.

I played absentmindedly with Will's scarf as he reversed into his designated car spot. He waited for me to head inside first to avoid being seen together. Throwing my hood up, I legged it inside the building, giving Will a wave once safely beneath shelter.

I sloshed toward the elevator, the floor already soddened from those before me, and headed straight for the coat rack by Will's desk. I hung my wet jacket up on one of the stands, shook myself, and noticed a pool of water on the floor by my feet. Steady droplets splashed down from the coats already hung there.

I dropped my bag at my desk and approached Chrissie.

"Good morning," I greeted, long past expecting her to acknowledge me.

"Morning," she flipped a page in her notebook, eyes anywhere but me. "How can I help?"

"The floor by the coat stand is wet," I told her. "Can I wipe it before somebody slips?" *Before Will slips,* I didn't say out loud. Will, who was surprisingly susceptible to slippery surfaces.

"Alright. After that, will you check to see if all the printers have enough ink and paper?"

"Absolutely."

She looked up at me then. No, not at me, but at the scarf around my neck. Her head tilted. "That scarf..." she frowned. "Is that-?"

I quickly threw my hands over it, hoping she didn't recognise it as Will's. Knowing her, she probably did. "Oh, this old thing? I've had it for years. Since high school, maybe."

"Oh," she looked back at her work, dismissing me.

Will entered the office as I dried the floor around the coat stand, using tissues I'd found in the kitchen. His face was blank as he neared me, but I was used to that. We weren't friends at work.

As soon as he reached the coat stand, he shrugged out of his jacket and turned so that only I could see him.

"You do realise it's going to keep getting wet, don't you?" he said with a smirk, speaking in a low murmur. "Half the office hasn't arrived yet."

I kept my voice as low and casual as his. "You do realise I'm saving you from breaking your neck, don't you? We can't have the office knowing how clumsy you are."

"I am *not clumsy*," he gave me a stern look before throwing his coat on a hook, wetting me in the process.

"So easy to tease," I crooned.

By the time I'd finished replenishing the printers with paper and ink, Chrissie had piled up more work for me to do. None of it was related to my actual job. Another test, I presumed, before she'd finally take me seriously.

"I need you to take those to the filing room and archive them for me," she said, slamming a sticky note onto my desk. "After that, restock the tea and coffee in the kitchen," another post-it note. "Oh, and I need you to run these designs over to Ciara in programming. And the water tank outside the meeting room needs changing. And the fridge needs restocking with the juices that arrived earlier. They're in the stock room." Three additional sticky notes joined the others. I looked down at my half-covered desk and tried to keep the panic from rising.

"Got it." I grabbed the heavy boxes first and heaved them to the filing room. After finishing the archiving, I returned to my desk to pick up my next task.

Chrissie pounced on me before I even reached my chair.

"The meeting for the grad competition is beginning soon," she said, forcing another sticky note into my hand. "Those are the coffee orders for the team leaders. I need you to go get them."

"You want me to go outside?" My voice trembled.

Chrissie raised a brow. "Yes. Is that a problem?"

"Of course not." Except that it was still raining a storm out there. Seriously, Chrissie could throw a bucket of water over me, and I'd get just as wet as going out in it. I swallowed my complaints and turned, noticing Will looking over at us. Smiling faintly, I walked to the coat stand to collect my jacket.

He leaned back in his chair, eyes focused on Chrissie. "Dani doesn't need to go out for our order," he called out to her. A few people turned to look between us. "Haven't you seen the rain out there? She can make them in the kitchen."

"But you hate the office coffee," Chrissie replied, and I knew she'd send me out in an actual storm if it meant pleasing Will. "And Dani doesn't mind. Do you, Dani?"

They both looked at me. While Chrissie's eyes held a warning, Will's only held concern. My heart softened. If it were for him, then, yes, I supposed I would face a storm.

"I don't mind," I said, ignoring the concern that blazed in his eyes.

"Then you can at least take an umbrella," he reached beneath his desk and grabbed one, shoving it out to me without looking.

"Thank you," I took the umbrella from him, my fingers brushing ever so slightly against his. He shivered as if touched by ice before clenching his hand by his side. And then he stared resolutely away from me.

After shrugging into my still wet coat, I made my way down to the ground floor. I tried not to think about how most people were heading inside and not out. Or how crazy I must be for doing the opposite.

I braced myself as I pressed my palms against the door and pushed before I could convince myself to turn back.

The rain came down heavy. It thrashed against the pavement and formed puddles that would take ninja moves to avoid. The umbrella helped keep my face dry, but it did nothing for my lower half. By the time I returned to the office, coffees in hand, my feet were sloshing.

Will was now absent from his desk. Placing the umbrella back in its spot, I made my way to the meeting room. My fingers shook, and not from the cold. Behind that door, the team leaders discussed which game designs had made it through. My fate in their hands.

Releasing a steadying breath, I knocked on the door. The buzz I'd heard from outside immediately paused. Nobody said a word as I passed the coffees around. Not even Will, who seemed to be avoiding looking at me.

Bile rose in my throat. I wondered if that was a sign–that he couldn't look me in the eye because he knew I'd failed.

Placing his coffee down, I fled from the room.

Lily and Finn intercepted me as soon as I was out.

"Did you hear anything about the result?" Lily asked, gripping my arm with a feverish look in her eyes.

"No." I swallowed as I pictured Will with his eyes on the table. "They didn't say a word."

Finn's shoulders slumped. "I wish they'd hurry up and tell us already. This is killing me."

We exchanged a pathetic look before parting ways. I grabbed a handful of Chrissie's sticky notes, remembering I still had them to work through. Checking the tea and coffee levels first, I found the storage containers packed to the rim. I opened the fridge. The juice bottles Chrissie had told me to restock were already in there. Frowning, I walked over to the water tank she'd told me to change and saw it brimmed. How distracted had Chrissie been this morning? Had she realised she'd given me tasks that were already done?

Perplexed, I walked over to my desk and picked up the remaining sticky notes. I only had one task left: to take some designs over to Ciara in programming. But the folders were no longer on Chrissie's desk for me to take. Strange, because I'd definitely seen them there earlier.

Wondering if Chrissie had taken them herself–maybe I'd

taken too long at the coffee shop–I decided to check with Ciara.

She looked up from her work as I approached her desk.

"Hey," I greeted. "Has Chrissie been by with some designs for you?"

"Not Chrissie, but Will stopped by earlier with some."

I blinked. "Will?"

"Yeah," she held up a folder, and I recognised it as the one I was supposed to take. "I was surprised, too," she said, and I realised that my mouth hung open. "Will hardly ever busies himself with menial stuff like this. Says he's too important," she rolled her eyes, but there was a fondness in her tone that told me she was joking.

Everyone spoke fondly of Will.

I smiled as I walked back to my desk. Will must've done this because he felt bad for me going out in the rain, and I doubted he'd even tell me. My smile deepened as I loaded up my computer. Thanks to Will, I now had some free time, which meant I could actually teach myself something other than admin work. I played with the artwork software until the meeting room door opened. When that happened, I immediately froze.

The team leaders walked out. My eyes found Will and stayed on him. Again, he avoided looking at me, but I noticed a faint smile on his lips that dared to give me hope. My eyes flashed to Jasmine as she took her seat. Glancing at Lily and me, she smirked and switched on her computer.

Heart racing, I waited for the email to come through. The minutes ticked by torturously slow. When it finally pinged, I almost sprained my wrist in my speed to open it.

I blinked. And then I blinked again. And then I almost shrieked in surprise.

I did it.

I did it.

I did it.

I did it.

My design had made it through.

I held back a squeal of pure delight as another email pinged. Will's name appeared on my screen. His message was short and impersonal, a simple congratulations.

But when I looked up, I found the real-life Will grinning at his screen.

CHAPTER SEVENTEEN

"How should we celebrate?" Will asked, shoving out of his jacket.

I grinned. Now that we were home, I could fully express my excitement. "Shout from a rooftop? Drink champagne? Dance like nobody's watching?"

"All of the above." Will's grin stretched as wide as mine, and I wanted to hug him for it. His happiness may have equalled my own.

I kicked off my shoes. "Or we could order pizza and play some video games?"

"Yes to the video games, no to the pizza." Will gave me a peculiar smile before disappearing into the kitchen. After throwing my jacket on the rack, I followed him.

"No to pizza?" I asked. "I never thought I'd hear you say that."

Smiling, he reached beneath the table and pulled out a large gift bag decorated with balloons. "This is for you."

"You got me a gift?" My brows shot up in surprise. "Why?"

"To congratulate you on today, of course." He said it like he didn't really need a reason to buy me something. "Your idea is good, by the way. It even had me impressed."

"High praise," I smiled. "Wait a sec," I frowned at the bag before meeting his eye. "When did you buy me this?"

His eyes sparkled. "Two weeks ago. Around the time that you kept complaining to me that you're cold, actually."

"William Lovett," I put the bag on the table and folded my arms. "How long have you known?"

"Known what?"

"That my idea made it through. I thought you only found out today?"

"I did only find out today."

My confusion peaked. "Then why did you buy me this two weeks ago?"

A smile played on his lips. "Because I had faith in you, obviously."

That was sweet. So sweet that my eyes began to water. "Will-"

"Not to mention that if you didn't get through," he continued, taking on a casual tone, "I would have given it as a consolation gift."

The tear retracted. I returned to the bag, pulling out a thick, woollen coat that felt so soft in my fingers that I wanted to wear it now. Placing the bag down, I slipped my arms through the sleeves and gave Will a twirl, surprised by how well it fit. "This is beautiful," I breathed, looking down at the fabric hugging my figure. "Really, Will, thanks so much. I love it."

He exhaled. "And that isn't your only gift." He moved towards the counter, pulling out a set of pans and setting them on top of the cooker. "You're about to receive the best home-cooked meal of your life."

"A meal from Chef Will?" I couldn't hide my excitement. This was a million–no, *ten* million–times better than a pizza.

Will pulled ingredients from the cupboards. "Yep, it's you're lucky day. But I can't have you in here while I'm cooking," he added, waving toward the door. "It's too distracting."

He didn't need to tell me twice. Grinning, I threw my new coat onto the edge of the chair and dashed into the living room.

I'd finished an episode of *The Office* when Will came in with two plates in his hands. Hitting pause, I turned to face him, the smile back on my face when I saw the mass of food.

"You made that?" I inhaled the sweet fumes as they drifted towards me. "It smells delicious."

"Thanks," he placed the food before me and sat in his usual spot. "How does it taste?"

Realising he was waiting for my verdict, I speared a piece of chicken, swirled it around in the creamy sauce, and popped it into my mouth. "Mmm," I shot him an impressed look. "This is good," I mumbled. "Like, really, really good."

Pleased with himself, he settled back and faced the TV. "What are we watching?"

"Oh, sorry," I grabbed the remote and held it out to him. "You can turn it over."

"Woah, woah, woah," he looked at me as if I'd just spit in his food. "Why would I turn over *The Office*?"

I blinked. "You like it?"

"Of course, I like it. Why would you think I don't?"

Laughing, I explained, "Nick hated it. He always made me turn it off whenever he was home."

"Nick is sounding more questionable by the day," he took the remote from me and hit play.

Hearing Will's laughter while we ate made me appreciate him even more. Will, who was entirely different to Nick. And to Holly, for that matter. It made my experience living with him entirely different also. With Will, I never felt out of place or uncomfortable. I felt at ease and strangely content.

I realised I was smiling at him and tore my eyes away, shovelling food into my mouth. Big mistake. My teeth clamped down on a mushroom which, until this moment, I'd carefully avoided eating. There was a small pile on the side of my plate where I'd pushed them to the side because mushrooms and I did not get along. The story goes back to when I was in primary school, and let's just say that it didn't end well for me.

Feeling post-traumatic nausea whirling up in my stomach, I quickly spat the mushroom out, only realising the magnitude of the action after I'd done it. My eyes darted to Will, who, to my intense dismay, watched me. He looked half-horrified, half-completely-grossed-out.

My mouth hung open as we continued to stare at each other, neither of us having the words to break the silence. His expression flickered between puzzlement, disgust, puzzlement, and then back to disgust again.

Unable to take it any longer, I squeaked, "Please tell me you didn't see that."

He gave me a look that told me I was wishful thinking,

and then he put his knife and fork down. "I think I just lost my appetite."

"I'm sorry," I cringed. "I am disgusting."

"Was it something I said?" he asked. "Was it my cooking? Or," he eyed me curiously, "do you just find joy in disgusting those you eat with?"

Laughter burst through my lips. I couldn't help it. Even though I tried to hold it back, the look on Will's face was just too amusing. "I'm sorry," I said again, waving my hands in front of me. "Really, I'm sorry."

"What is it now?" Will had a frown on his face, but I noticed his lips twitch. "Do you find it funny putting people off their food?"

"No. No." Sucking in a deep breath, I tried to control myself. "It has nothing to do with you or your cooking," I assured him. "It's just, I have a history with mushrooms, and it isn't pleasant."

He stared at me. "Are you really going to leave it there? Do tell me about this past relationship of yours. What did the mushroom do?"

I forced a straight face. Whenever I'd retold this story, I'd never been on the verge of laughing. Crying from the trauma, perhaps. But never laughing. "Well," I started, wondering how I could be smiling right now, "once upon a time, a young Dani ate a tin of mushroom soup. And not long after said once upon a time, she projectile vomited it back up, splattering half of her fellow classmates."

Will tried to keep a straight face, but he failed as much as I did. Laughter burst out of him like water escaping a dam. "I'm sorry," he said, holding his hands up. "It's not funny.

Except that it is!" Laughing again, he shifted his food to the table and keeled over.

I glared at his folded form. It wasn't *that* amusing.

"Are there any other foods that make you want to puke?" he asked, still shaking. "Just in case, you know. Because I never want to witness *that* again."

"Oh, shut up." My lips twitched as he wiped a tear from his eye.

My phone buzzed, pulling my eyes away from him. I read the text. And then I read it again.

"Wow." If I'd had food in my mouth, I probably would have spat it out again.

Will leaned forward. "What is it?" Instead of answering, I held my phone out for him to see. His brows flicked up. "Holly wants to meet you tonight?"

"Seems like it." I spun my phone back, unsure why I felt so surprised. After all, I had reached out to her, and we always went out together before. We were inseparable. But it'd been so long since I last saw her that the thought of doing so now made me feel slightly queasy. "Do you think I should go?" I asked, looking back at Will.

His eyes scanned my face. "Do you want to go?"

Anxiety pummelled through my stomach. If I'd been told a year ago that I'd feel this way about seeing Holly, I wouldn't have believed it. Yet here I was, afraid to see her. But I did miss her. And if I avoided her now, I might never have that friendship again. "I should go," I sighed. Then, when his lips pressed together, I added, "I want to go. Really. It will be nice having a catch-up."

"Only if it's what you want."

I nodded. "It is. And thanks for the food. Maybe I'll cook for you next time."

"Then I'll warn you ahead of time that I don't like beansprouts. Not that I'd spit it out, but after the horror I witnessed today, who knows?"

I stuck my tongue out as I headed to the kitchen. After dumping the mushrooms into the bin where they belonged, I darted upstairs.

Thirty minutes later, I called to Will, "I'm leaving! Don't miss me too much!"

"I'll be counting down the minutes," he called back.

I made it ten steps past the garden before I debated bailing. Shivering, I glanced back at the house, yearning for the warmth of the living room.

The front door suddenly yanked open, revealing Will in the doorway. He pulled on his shoes, almost falling in his haste to get out, and rushed towards me.

"What are you-?"

"Are you trying to catch a cold?" he scolded, holding up a coat. My coat, I realised–the one he'd just gifted me. The one I'd completely forgotten about. When all I did was stare at him, he shook his head and wrapped it around my shoulders, lifting my hand to guide it through the sleeves. "Did you not want to wear it?" he asked, softly holding my fingers as he pulled back a cuff.

"I did," I looked away from his hand and sighed. "I do. I just forgot for a moment that I had it."

He released my hand to work on straightening the hood. "I'll try to not be offended by that."

I smirked. "Sorry. I just feel so nervous, and I have no idea why."

"You haven't seen her for a while. It's normal." He wasn't looking at me as he said this, too busy concentrating on my hood, but as I peered into his face, I felt the knots in my stomach loosen. "There," he said, smiling in one corner. "Now you have padding for when your distraction leads you into a lamppost."

"Like I'd ever."

He placed his hands on my shoulders and frowned. "Try to enjoy yourself tonight. And if you need me, I'm only a text message away."

I nodded. While I couldn't think why I'd need to message Will, it comforted me just knowing I could.

"Oh, and Dani?" he said as I turned away. I glanced back, finding him watching me with a solemn expression. "Please, *please*, don't walk into a lamppost."

I laughed, the knots in my stomach vanishing completely. "I think that's more of a Will risk than a Dani risk." Ignoring his look of offence, I gave him a wave and left before Holly could shout at me for being late.

We planned to meet inside a small, local bar. The bar we always came to back in our uni days, which felt so long ago now. When I arrived, I found Holly sitting in our usual spot by the window.

My smile vanished when I saw who sat beside her.

"Oh, hi, Nick," I said, taking my coat off. "You're here, too." As I pulled myself onto the stool, I tried to not look so disappointed.

"Dani," he replied, an amused little smile on his lips. "You look the same as always."

I could tell that he didn't mean this as a compliment. "As do you."

Just as I contemplated pulling an I-have-an-emergency manoeuvre to escape having to spend a single second with him, Holly leaned across the table, pulling me into a hug. "I've missed you!"

I returned the embrace, glad, at least, that she'd come. "It's been a while."

"I'm sorry that it's been so long," she apologised, leaning back again. Her lips pulled down. "We've been so busy. Nick had a promotion at work, so we've redecorated the house with the extra income. It's taken up all of our time, hasn't it?" She looked at Nick for support, who nodded. A small, bitter part of me thought she would've made the time to see me if she'd wanted to. But the same could be said for me.

"It's fine," I smiled once more. "You're not the only one who's been busy. And congratulations on the promotion," I turned my eyes on Nick, whose grin stretched wider.

"We've finally been able to renovate that old room of yours."

I heard a hidden insult in his words, but I wouldn't let it bother me. "That's great," I smiled, holding his eye. Now that I thought about it, Nick seemed to have this new, cocky air that didn't suit him. He was just the type to let a promotion get to his head. "I'll go get a drink. What're you having?"

"Allow me." I didn't protest as Nick scooted from his seat. While I didn't enjoy spending his money, I liked the thought of having a moment alone with Holly. "What do you drink?" he asked. "Is it still vodka?

"I've never drank vodka."

"Er, she'll have a whiskey," Holly's eyes flicked cautiously between us. Nick shrugged before sauntering over to the bar, flagging the barman down.

I couldn't help but give Holly a look.

"I'm sorry," she said, looking genuinely apologetic. "He wanted to come, and," she moved her hands around, struggling to come up with an excuse. "I thought it would be good for you both; you know, bury the hatchet. I know you've never really liked each other."

"It's fine," I sighed. "I'm just glad to see you again."

"So," she folded her hands on the table, her eyes sparkling. "Tell me everything. How's the new job? Is it as good as you thought it'd be?"

My mood brightened. "Bluebird is amazing. In fact, I found out today that I've made it through to the next stage of a design competition they run." Saying this made me think about the message I'd received from Will at the end of the day. I smiled to myself.

"That's great! Really, Dani, well done."

"Thanks."

She wasn't ready to move on from the conversation yet, and I found myself leaning forward to say more. I liked talking about my job. "How are your colleagues? Do they all treat you nice?"

My smile widened. "My colleagues are great." I thought about Finn and Lily briefly, but mostly my mind wandered across to the head desk by the coat stand. "Really great."

"Is that your phone ringing?"

I felt a buzz in my pocket and looked down. "It's probably

Will," I said, pulling out my phone.

"Who's Will?"

I looked up as the buzzing stopped, finding Holly staring at me in puzzlement. "Oh, I haven't told you? He's my roommate."

Her frown deepened. "You have a roommate? A *male* roommate?"

I nodded. "I moved in with him as soon as I left yours. I can't believe I didn't tell you."

"W-o-w. But," she sounded confused. "Didn't you move into a one-bed?"

"Yeah, that one didn't work out." I shook my head, glad to be on the other side of *that*.

"Wow," she said again. "Well, I'd love to meet him. Find out what he's like."

"I can invite him here?" The words rolled out a little too quickly. I hadn't realised how much I wanted him with me until that moment. And if Holly had Nick with her, why couldn't he come?

"Do you think he'll come here at such short notice?" she asked.

"I'll check." I quickly clicked on Will's name and typed out a message. *Want to come meet us? ...Please. N is here.*

He messaged back a second later. *Sure. Where are you?*

I released a sigh and texted him the address. "He's coming," I told Holly. She analysed my face, her lips tugging up at whatever she saw.

"I can't wait to meet him."

As Nick returned with our drinks, I smiled, no longer fazed about him being here.

CHAPTER EIGHTEEN

"Dani's friend is coming to meet us," Holly told Nick.

He looked at his glass in disinterest. "Oh? What's her name?"

"He's a boy."

Now his eyes flashed to my face. "You have a boyfriend?"

"He's just a friend," I said, ignoring the surprise in his voice.

"A friend," he repeated. I almost laughed at his disbelief this time. How surprising that Dani has a friend. "How interesting." Something in his voice told me he expected a lunatic to walk through the door.

I smirked at my drink. While Will was, in his own way, a lunatic, he was also an altogether impressive human. No doubt Nick wouldn't put the two of us together.

He couldn't come quick enough.

I'd always struggled to speak to Holly with Nick around, and today was no exception–with him here, words I wanted to say got stuck in my throat.

"Dani," Holly said, bringing my eyes upwards, "you're

shaking the table."

"Oh." I clamped my leg down and diverted my eyes out the window. Seeing Will circling his way around a signpost, I quickly got to my feet. "He's here!"

"Woah," Holly sounded impressed. "Dani, you didn't tell me he looks like a model."

"Does he?" I tilted my head as I watched him get closer. At work, I'd overheard enough people calling him attractive to know he had a certain appeal. But I just saw him as Will. The Will who suffered from terrible hangovers and lounged on the couch with a wet towel on his forehead. And the Will who stole milk bottles from neighbours.

"No," Nick grumbled. It took me a second to realise he'd answered my question, and I couldn't help but smirk. Yes— he hadn't expected my new 'friend' to be anything remotely like Will.

Will's eyes scanned the room as he entered the bar. When they stopped on me, we both grinned.

"There you are," he said, slipping an arm over my shoulder as he pulled me into a hug. Only Will could hug like this.

"Thank God you're here," I whispered against his neck.

"I couldn't miss the chance to meet the infamous Nick," he whispered back. Pulling away from me, he turned his smile on Holly and Nick. They both stared at him with wide eyes. "Hi," he greeted. "I'm Will, Dani's roommate and number one favourite person."

I rolled my eyes and pinched his arm, even though he was right.

Holly needed to blink multiple times before she could

respond. "Hi," she breathed. Clearing her throat, she continued in a stronger voice, "I'm Holly, and this is Nick. I'm sorry I only heard about you today."

Nick coughed as Will turned to frown at me. He still had his arm around my shoulder, and I could smell peppermint on his breath. "And here's me thinking you talk about me all the time."

"I had nothing interesting to say," I shrugged out of his arm and reclaimed my seat. Will remained standing.

"Well," he said to Holly, "I've heard a lot about you. Both of you." His eyes flashed over to Nick, who diverted his own gaze to the bar. He turned to me. "Can I get you a drink?"

"I'll have a-"

"Whiskey and diet coke, I know." He looked at Holly and Nick in turn.

Nick reluctantly met his eye. "I'll get ours," he said, pushing his chair away from the table before Will could protest.

"Perfect." With a wink at me, Will followed Nick to the bar. As they stood beside each other, I couldn't help but notice how Will had an aura that shone. While Nick stood erect and tense, Will claimed the smiles of strangers. His was a face that made people want to look at him, and it had nothing to do with his attractiveness.

"So," Holly said, drawing my attention back to her, "what's the story here?"

I downed the rest of my drink. "What story?"

"Between you and Will...," She flapped her arms in his direction. "Has something happened between the two of you? Something... *sexual*?"

"*Jeeze*, No!" I quickly glanced over my shoulder to make sure Will couldn't hear. I dropped my voice to a whisper. "It's not like that. We're just friends."

"A boy and girl can't just be friends," she dismissed. "It's been proved."

I rolled my eyes. "I'd like to see this study of yours. Besides," I shrugged, "we're proof that you can be."

"But how can you resist?" she shook her head as her eyes moved back to the bar. Her mouth hung open slightly, and I wondered what she'd do if Will ever turned his charms on *her*.

I turned to look at Will with her. He currently laughed at something the barman said, his dimples prominent even from this distance. I just knew his eyes were sparkling with that good humour that was solely his. I quickly rearranged my features as I turned back to Holly, unwilling to allow my smile to be seen by her. She'd probably misconstrue it. "He's a great guy," I said, choosing my words carefully. I didn't like badmouthing him to anyone but himself. "I'm just not sure he'd make a great boyfriend." That had been my judgement ever since the day we met. I'd learned of his heartbreak since then, but that didn't change anything. At least, I didn't think it did. "Besides," I added, shaking the thoughts away, "I don't have anything to resist. It's not like he throws himself at me."

"He hasn't tried *anything*?" The surprise in Holly's voice made me balk.

"You make it sound like he should have."

"I just thought... you know, him living with a girl... he would have tried *something*."

An unpleasant feeling trickled down my throat, causing it to dry up. I remembered the first day I'd met Will. He'd told me there was no chance he'd ever fall for me, and now I wondered if I was so completely unattractive that he wasn't even tempted.

"Do you-"

"A whiskey for you." I jumped as Will appeared beside me, cutting off whatever question of self-doubt I'd been about to ask Holly. His brows immediately creased, telling me that my every emotion was there for all to see. Not everyone–just Will and his surprisingly perceptive eyes. "Are you alright?" he asked, setting my drink down with a deepening frown.

"I'm fine," I forced a smile. Really, I was fine. Will and I had become friends, and I didn't want anything more than that. It was enough, and I couldn't allow Holly to plant warped thoughts inside my brain. Not when rule five–that we weren't allowed to fall for each other–was there to ensure things didn't get complicated between us.

I just didn't understand the weight pressing against my chest.

It was a good thing that Will found me unattractive. A good thing that he found me so utterly repulsive that he-

"Are you sure you're alright?" he asked again.

I needed to get a grip on myself. "Yep. Totally fine."

"Good." He sat beside me, eyeing me in a way that told me he didn't believe me.

I took a long gulp from my drink.

"So," Holly said, leaning towards Will. "Tell me about yourself. What is it that you do, Will?"

He nodded at me. "I work at Bluebird with this one."

"You do?" Holly's mouth gaped open. She locked eyes with me. "You both live *and* work together?"

I noticed Nick straighten in his seat. He looked interested for the first time all evening. "Ah, so you're a graduate?" he asked. That thought seemed to please him more than it should have. Remembering his recent promotion, I guessed he'd love it if Will ranked at the bottom.

"Actually," Will said, swirling his drink around his glass. "I'm one of the team leaders."

"The youngest lead at the company," I couldn't help but add, my voice brimming with pride. "And the youngest to win a Game of the Year award."

Nick's mouth gaped open. He quickly closed it, looking down at the table with a grimace. "That explains how she got the job," he muttered, so low I wasn't sure we were supposed to hear it.

Will's knuckles immediately went white around his glass. When he spoke, his voice sounded foreign to me–low and guttural and furious. "You're wrong," he said. I wondered how his glass didn't shatter. "I didn't meet Dani until after she got the job. Even since then, she's told me not to help her, and I haven't. Her success is her own."

Nick cleared his throat. I kept my eyes on Will, but I noticed movement from Holly.

"Come on, Nick," she said quietly. "That was uncalled for. Apologise to Dani."

I didn't expect to hear one from him, so I was surprised when he opened his mouth. I glanced over to see his eyes dart to Will and away again. He cleared his throat. "Fine. That was uncalled for. I'm sorry, Dani."

"It's okay." It wasn't, but I wouldn't waste time arguing with him. "Apology accepted."

Will's hand relaxed around his glass, but his eyes still blazed. I'd never seen him this way before. I wasn't sure if I'd ever even seen him angry before.

"How about a shot?" Holly said, clearly trying to diffuse the situation. She looked helplessly from me to Will, to Nick, and back to me again. "We should celebrate your win, Dani."

"That's a great idea," Will jumped to his feet with a smile that seemed forced. It made me nervous. Even more so when he glanced at Nick with flames in his eyes.

"I'll come and help you," I said, getting gingerly to my feet. I eyed him sideways as he leaned his arms against the bar. When he didn't say anything, I asked, "Are you alright?"

"That was totally uncalled for!" he kept his voice low, but I could hear the annoyance brimming beneath the surface. He ran a hand through his tousled hair and huffed. "*That explains why she got the job*," he mimicked.

"That's a good impression."

He gave me a loaded look. "That guy is a jerk. No wonder you never liked him. He's been a soul-sucker since the moment I got here." I snorted, causing his eyes to flash back to my face. He turned on me. "Tell me, Dani, do you think my being annoyed is amusing?"

"That's not it. It's-" I shook my head, trying to find the right words to explain my relief. "Really, I hate that you're annoyed, and I'm sorry about that, but it just feels so nice to have someone who understands me. I always thought I was crazy, you know–like my dislike for him was unwarranted.

And that he must be that way because I'm a bad person to live with."

"No," he disagreed. "You're a good person to live with. A little annoying, I'll admit," he smiled, remnants of his humour returning. "But in comparison to him…" he shook his head. "I don't know how you didn't make your way to me sooner."

I stared at him, taken aback by his choice of words. *Make your way to me sooner.* My throat clogged up, but Will didn't seem to realise that he'd said something so sweet. Something that made me feel like I belonged. He flagged the barman down, ordering shots like nothing out of the ordinary had been exchanged between us.

We took the shots back to our table. Holly drank hers in one, as did Will, but Nick pushed his to the side. Since I had a reason to celebrate, and I wouldn't let Nick ruin it for me, I drank his as well as mine.

After too many drink rounds, I started to feel that hazy cloud blanketing my mind, a tell-tale sign that I bordered the lines of drunk. Through the swirls and fogs, I thought I heard Will discussing my befuddled state with Holly.

"She never usually gets this drunk," he said. "But it's fine. I'll get her home safe."

"Are you sure?"

"Yeah. She'd do the same for me."

"Okay. Dani?" Holly's voice came close by my ear. "We're leaving. Will's going to take you home, okay?"

"I trust Will," I slurred. The slurring surprised me. When did I get *that* drunk?

"Good. I'll see you next time, okay?"

"Will?" I reached out my hands. Somebody grabbed hold of them, steadying me.

"I'm here."

"Should we have another shot?" I blinked multiple times until my eyes focused on the table. To my delight, four full shots still sat there, just waiting to be taken. "Ooh, two each!"

"Oh no, you don't." I felt my world spin as Will twirled me away from the table. "Those shots are mine, and I stopped taking them the moment I realised Miss I-can-handle-my-liquor was getting too drunk." He released my hands and circled around me, wheeling me out the door by my shoulders.

The cold night air whipped at my face, helping sober me up a little. But not much. I turned my face to the sky, closing my eyes, as Will made a phone call. He kept one hand on my upper arm while he spoke, almost like he feared what I'd do if he let me go.

I popped my eyes open when I heard a sigh.

"There aren't any taxis," he said, putting his phone away. "Which means we have to walk. Oh, damn it, your coat!" He turned away before spinning back to me. "Stay here. Do not move. Understood?" Only when I nodded did he turn and run back inside the bar. He returned a moment later, my coat clutched in his hands.

His worried expression relaxed. Coming over to me, he wrapped the coat around my shoulders. "Let's go."

The thought of walking fast made me want to hurl, so I moved slowly, almost sluggishly, shutting my eyes as I allowed myself to go where I willed. I swayed with every step, but the effort to walk straight wasn't worth it. Once or twice, I walked into something solid, and Will grabbed my arms to set me on the right course again. The third time, I walked straight into him.

"That's it," he sighed. "Get on."

I managed to open my eyes a slither to see him crouched before me. "Get on what?"

He tapped his shoulder. "My back, Dani. Get on my back. You can barely walk."

A part of me registered he'd probably regret this offer, just as I'd regret getting on. But the alcohol infusing my blood switched off that part that cared. I shrugged, "Okay." Will's arms wrapped around my legs as I clambered on.

"Ugh," he grunted, hoisting me up. "You're heavier than you look."

I tapped his head affectionately. "What would I do without you?"

"Spend the night sleeping in a bush, probably."

"Har, har."

"You're falling."

"Hold me."

"You need to hold me."

"Oh," I grabbed his neck.

"Don't choke me!"

He readjusted his hands around my legs to get a steadier grip before setting off into a walk.

I had a sudden urge to shake him. "*Why. Don't. You. Find. Me. Attractive!*"

He squirmed beneath me. "Ah! Dani! What are you doing?" When I didn't answer, he turned to look at me. My next urge was to squeeze his cheeks, which caused him to squirm again. "Can you please tell me what's the matter?"

"Why don't-" I shook my head, confused by my thoughts. I shouldn't be saying this to him. "I mean, why do you have so many one-night stands?" My thoughts drifted to the other part of my conversation with Holly. To when I'd said he wouldn't make a good boyfriend.

"Does it bother you that I do?" he asked.

My eyes burned. "No," I blinked a tear away. "I mean-" I shook my head again. My thoughts were all jumbled. "You have a girl roommate, you know. And she's present throughout all of your canoodlings. And it's not nice that I have to kick them out in the morning. Or that you only wanted me as your roommate because I agreed to do that." My voice broke. I sucked in air as I struggled to breathe.

Will lowered me, his grip tight and secure. He placed me gently on a bench.

"Are you going to leave me here?" I asked, blinking against the bright light of a street lamp as I searched for him. I heard a chuckling sound and twisted in its direction.

Will's face appeared before me. He crouched down, eyes levelling with mine. "Let me ask you something," he said, his voice softer than usual. "Have I brought any girls back recently?" He waited for me to answer, but I couldn't remember the last time. I shook my head. "So have I been having one-night stands?" he asked next. Again, I shook my head. His lip pulled up at the corner. "And if I remember correctly, even though you agreed to help me in the morning, you never have."

I let out a sound that was probably supposed to be a

laugh. "No. I guess I haven't." Suddenly exhausted, I drooped forward, resting my head on my knees.

Will lifted me back upright, his touch gentle and cautious. After brushing my hair from my face, he released a sigh and smiled. Even through this foggy mind, I recognised that no one had ever looked at me in this way before.

"And even if that was why I agreed to let you live with me," he continued. "It isn't the reason now." His eyes blazed with intensity. I didn't look away from them as he raised his hand. He brought it close to my face, and I leaned into it, craving his touch, but he turned away at the last moment, almost as if he second-guessed himself. "Get on," he sighed, pointing to his back again. "Somebody is in dire need of their bed."

Tired once more, I mumbled something incoherent before clambering on.

The last thing I remembered was getting lowered onto my bed.

CHAPTER NINETEEN

I didn't wake up in the morning.

I woke up sometime in the afternoon with a sore head and tender stomach.

The sunlight streaming through a crack in the curtains burned my eyes. I groaned, turning on my side and pulling the quilt up over my head. I pulled it back.

How exactly did I get here? I frowned, trying to break into the forgotten memories buried inside my brain. Did somebody bring me here? My frown deepened. When did we even leave the bar?

Something told me I might not want to remember. Still, I couldn't shake the feeling that all three questions had one interconnecting answer: Will.

With a shriek, I bolted upright, regretting it the second my head began to pound. I pressed my fingers against my temples, the image of Will still prominent in my mind. I tried to think back to what happened after we left the bar, but every fleeting image passing through my mind inflicted a severe level of cringe. I shook my head, laying down again. I'd drank many shots, that much I did remember.

And did Will give me a *piggyback*? I shook my head, faintly remembering climbing onto him.

"Why, Dani, why?" I groaned, covering my face as the cringing returned.

"Dani?" Will called from the door. "Are you up?" A sudden urge to remain silent had me freezing. I removed my hands, hardly daring to breathe. "I heard your shrieking, you know."

Panic swept through me. I scrunched my eyes closed, trying to banish the memories of last night as they forced themselves onto the surface.

I'd said things. Things that should not have been said. Embarrassing things like asking Will why he didn't find me attractive. "I'm not up!" I choked, wishing for a hole to appear and bury me ten thousand feet beneath the earth.

"Can I come in?" he tapped on the door, but I could not face him right now. "I have something for you," he continued. When I didn't answer, he turned the handle, waiting for me to protest. He entered slowly. I flung the quilt back up over my head before he had the chance to see me. "Bad hangover?" he assumed.

Wondering why he wasn't mocking me, I slowly removed the quilt, stopping with it just below my eyes. Could it be that it was all in my head? Will wasn't looking at me like I'd done or said anything embarrassing. He was looking at me like my behaviour confused him. "Quite bad," I answered, not yet daring to believe it.

"Here," he held up a glass of water and pain relief tablets for me to see before placing them on my table. "Come down when you're feeling better."

Huh. I removed the quilt as the door closed, staring at the ceiling as I allowed last night's memories to resurface. My brain went hazy after a certain point in the night, which led me to believe that I'd made most of it up. Or dreamt it. Because if I had said all of that stuff to Will... he would've mentioned it. But he hadn't.

After I'd washed the remnants of last night away in the shower, I went downstairs. Will sat at the dining table and hardly spared me a glance as he worked on his laptop.

"Hey," he said, eyes on his screen. "There's a spare sandwich going in the kitchen. If you can stomach it, that is."

"Thanks."

Still wary that I'd said something embarrassing, still terrified that he'd mention it, I edged slowly backwards. Only when I'd eaten the sandwich and washed my dishes–all without Will saying a word–did I finally relax.

"Have you got any plans tonight?" I asked, licking ice cream off the back of my spoon.

Will leaned back into a stretch, stopping with his hands folded behind his head. "Yep. I'm meeting the guys out." He looked at his watch. "I'm meeting them soon, actually."

My eyes lit up. I hadn't seen Will's friends for a few weeks, and it was always a fun night going out with them. "Can I come?"

He shook his head. "Not today."

"Why not?" my voice was too whiney for my liking.

"Aren't you too hungover to go?" he asked, one brow raised.

I fought against nausea in my stomach. "I'm fine,

actually. Besides, it's celebration weekend for me." When that didn't get him to change his mind, I asked, "So, can I come?"

Closing the lid of his laptop, Will got to his feet. "I've seen what celebration Dani is like, and she's not coming with me."

I puckered my lips as he picked up his laptop and left the room. In a way, I supposed it was a good thing if I stayed in. I was far too much of a liability yesterday to risk becoming one again.

When Will came back into the room, he looked ready to leave. I watched as he picked his keys up from the table, waiting for him to say something to me. Eventually, he turned a smirk my way. "Enjoy your recovery."

"Enjoy your night."

I thought he'd head straight out, but he stopped at the door, turning to look at me. "By the way," he said, tilting his head as if curious about something. "Does the thought of me not finding you attractive bother you?"

A sudden, fierce blush crept up the back of my neck. I fought it back, but the effort was futile. I focused on keeping my voice calm. "Not at all."

"Really?" he raised a brow. "Because that's not what you were saying last night."

I gulped. "What did I say?" The blush reached my cheeks. I resisted the urge to close my eyes and pretend I was someplace else. *It wasn't a dream.*

"You just got angry all-a-sudden, asking me why I don't find you attractive. And then you got annoyed because of the girls I *no longer* bring over."

I covered my face with my hands, distraught that it hadn't been a drunken nightmare. "Please ignore drunk Dani. She doesn't know what she's talking about."

"Because you remember the rules-"

"Yes, I remember the rules, Will," I huffed. Removing my hands, I saw that both his brows were now raised. "I'm still in no danger of falling for you," I almost spat. "I just want us to be friends." The present me knew that with certainty. Past me... I didn't know what she'd been thinking.

"Me too," Will tapped the door with his fist, his expression shifting into something I didn't understand. "Okay, well, I'll see you later."

He disappeared from the doorway, leaving an empty hallway in his place. I leaned back with a sigh. Now I really wanted to go out. If I stayed at home, all I'd do is overthink. And I couldn't allow that. Shaking my head, I grabbed my phone and pinged a message to Holly, asking if she was free for a drink. She replied in the negative. Too hungover. Sending the same message to Lily, I crossed all fingers and toes.

Meet us at Queens at 7!!! Me and Finn will be there!!!!

I huffed out a breath. Queens was a bar not far from the office. It was also a bar that Will refused to go to–too many rowdy drunks looking for a fight, according to him–so I knew there was no risk of bumping into him there. Perfect, in that sense.

I confirmed my attendance with Lily and then busied myself with whatever work I could find in the hours until then. At first, I started with housework–small, menial jobs like wiping the kitchen sides. Until I remembered I'd made it through the first challenge at work, meaning I could now start developing my game. I dropped the cloth I'd been using to clean with and grabbed my laptop.

A few hours later, I found Lily and Finn in the back corner of the bar. They weren't alone, either. As I weaved through the tables, I spotted a third person sitting with them. A boy with light, curly hair.

"You're here!" Lily enclosed me in a hug when I reached them. I smiled at Finn before sliding into the seat beside the unidentified male.

"I'm so glad you two were doing something," I said, flinging my new coat over the chair. "I'd be so bored otherwise."

"It's good to finally see you outside work," Finn said. He nodded at the stranger. "This is my cousin, Jacob."

I turned to face him. Up close, I supposed he did resemble Finn somewhat. He had a youthful face, blue eyes, and a smile that probably got him out of trouble as much as it got him in it. "I'm Dani," I greeted.

"Nice to meet you," he held out his hand for me to shake. I clasped it, and our smiles instantly faltered. A mutual understanding that shaking hands was strange in a social context.

"I'll just take that back," I laughed, retracting my hand.

"Yeah, sorry," he shook his head. "What an embarrassing introduction."

"It's fine," I could see a blush forming on his cheek and thought it an endearing trait. "When did handshakes go out of fashion, anyway?"

He laughed. "Should we make it our mission to bring

handshaking back?"

"Let's do it." I extended my hand again. He took it with another laugh, his warm fingers wrapping around mine in a strong grip.

"Aw, you two look so cute together!" Lily said, completely ruining the moment. I retracted my hand and turned my eyes on her as Jacob scratched the back of his ear.

"The only cute one here is Dani," he said.

Lily choked on her drink as heat crept up the back of my neck. I quickly got to my feet. "Drinks, anyone?"

As I brought a tray back to our table, I realised that drinks were a bad idea for me. My nose wrinkled at the smell, and my suddenly fragile stomach churned in revolt.

I covered my mouth and pushed the tray far away from me. "I don't think I can drink."

"What's wrong?" Finn asked. "You look like you're going to throw up."

"I went out last night. I thought I was fine, but-" I twisted away as a heave came along. If I vomited, I only hoped that I could spare Jacob.

When I knew I could trust myself not to vomit, I turned back to them. "I'm sorry about this. I'm not usually a party wrecker."

Finn shook his head. "It's fine. Here, I'll drink this for you."

As Finn gulped down my recently bought drink–in surprisingly few gulps–I turned my neck to look at Jacob, who'd walked over to the bar. He said a few words to the barmaid, grabbed a drink, and returned it to our table.

"Here," he said, placing it in front of me. It was water, I

realised with a sense of gratitude. "I hope you feel better."

"Thank you," I kept my eyes on his face as he smiled, surprised by the act of kindness. And it *was* a kind thing to do, considering I never even asked him for it.

The water helped ease my nausea. It also made me realise that I didn't need to drink alcohol to be here. I enjoyed myself remaining sober, watching the madness unfold before me as Lily and Finn's giddiness levels increased with every drink consumed. Their voices blurred into one noise— a buzz I had no idea how to interpret. I stopped trying and talked to Jacob instead. He became more talkative the more he drank, although he never quite reached the level of the other two.

Finn's fists came crashing down on the table. "Let's go to a club!"

When the others nodded, I decided then and there that it was probably a good time for me to go home.

As we walked outside, I thought of Will. I wondered if he'd be home and found myself hoping I'd walk through the door and find him there. Maybe we could order pizza.

"It's a shame you aren't coming with us," Jacob said, stepping beside me. I tried to stop thinking about Will and focus on him instead. "I think you'd have a good night."

"I think so, too," I nodded toward Finn, who'd stopped on the pavement to dance, and chuckled. When Lily tried to join him, they both tumbled to the ground in a heap. "On second thought," I added, "maybe I'd end up babysitting."

"Listen, I-"

"Dani?"

I stopped walking as my favourite voice coated my ears.

I frowned, wondering if it was all in my head. But no. As I turned to my side, I found Will standing a few feet away from me. Seeing him made me feel multiple things at once–giddiness, excitement, unexplainable nerves. Jordan and Tae weren't far behind him. Both had their arms slung over a girl, making me wonder why Will wasn't coupled up with them. He stood alone.

"What are you doing here?" he asked. His eyes moved to Jacob, and I saw confusion settle in them.

But now wasn't the time to explain.

"Oh, hi, Will," I said, nodding pointedly at Finn, who, by some miracle, hadn't seen or heard him yet. "I'm here with some work colleagues. It's good to see you out of work."

Confusion remained on his face, but it was only for a second because he spotted Finn approaching us the next. Realisation–and presumably regret–crossed over his features.

"Will!" Finn dived forward, pulling him into a hug I swear he wouldn't have dared do without the alcohol. "Lily, look! Will from work is here! Dani, look! Will from work is here!"

"I can see," I met Will's eye and held back a laugh. He definitely regretted stopping me now.

"Is that-?" Jordan's smiling face appeared in front of me, and I froze. One mention of my name, any indication that he knew me, and mine and Will's ruse might well be over. "It is you! How are you, D-?" he let out a shout as Will yanked him back. Furious, he said, "Hey, I was just trying to say hi to D-" Will gave him a shove and a very deliberate look. Jordan's eyes flicked between us, finally understanding.

"Where are you guys headed?" Will asked, releasing

Jordan from his clutches. The latter stepped silently back.

"We're going to the club," Finn answered, still ecstatic at bumping into Will. "Hey, why don't you join us?"

"I, um," Will's eyes flashed to my face and away again. I wanted to tell him that I wouldn't be joining, but I doubted he'd agree to it, anyway. He'd never- "Yeah, I think we will."

I stared wide-eyed. Suddenly, I had a fierce desire to stay out. But I couldn't. Not when I'd already told the others that I was leaving. They'd probably assume that I'd changed my mind for Will–which would be true.

"You guys enjoy yourselves," I said, cringing when Will turned his full attention to me. I could see the betrayal behind his eyes. I wanted to apologise, but what could I say in front of the others?

"You're leaving?" he asked. Thank goodness the others were intoxicated, or they might've picked up on the disappointment that pierced my heart.

I nodded, keeping my eyes only on him. "Yes. But I'll see you at-" *home*, is what I almost said. "Work. I'll see you at work. All of you." Waving at the others, I turned and found Jacob staring at Will. He moved his eyes to me.

"Let me walk you to the taxi," he said. I didn't protest as he stepped beside me. "Do you know him?" he asked when we were out of earshot.

"Who?"

He indicated behind us. "That guy. It seemed like... you knew each other."

I turned, finding the group walking away. Will walked alone, the only one looking back at us. I smiled as our eyes met, and he gave me a small wave, turning away again. He ducked his head, not bothering to keep up with the others.

"Only from work," I said, turning back to Jacob.

"Oh." We walked in silence for the rest of the journey. When we reached a taxi, Jacob opened the rear door for me, leaning his arm against it as I climbed inside. "So, listen," he said. "I know this is kind of, er..." he searched for the right word. "*Premature.* But do you want to go out with me sometime?"

I blinked. "Like on a date?"

He chuckled. "Yeah, I guess like on a date."

I couldn't remember the last time I'd been asked out on a date, which told me it'd been a while ago. Nobody wanted to date the girl who loved gaming more than she did dressing up. Not that it bothered me–I liked how I was, and screw anyone who tried to change that. But it did make me freeze up at his question.

"It's okay if not," he said quickly, looking mortified by my silence.

It snapped me out of it. "No. I'd love to go on a date with you." Maybe. I wasn't sure. But perhaps it'd be nice going out on a date again, and I couldn't think of a reason to say no.

"Great!" He reached into his pocket. "Should we exchange numbers?"

"Sure." A quick look at my phone told me I'd had multiple messages from Will. I swiped them away, holding back my curiosity, before passing my phone over to Jacob, taking his in turn.

"Well, then," he stuffed his phone away. "I guess I'll be in touch." Closing the door, he gave me a wave before walking away.

After giving my instructions to the driver, I leaned back, opening up the messages from Will. He'd sent me multiple in a row, and I smiled as I read through them.

Message one: *how's the hangover?*

Message two: *I hope your lack of response doesn't mean you're dead. I don't want to find a Dani corpse when I get home.*

Message three: *Do you want me to bring anything back? I'll come home if you want me to.*

Message four (sent ten minutes ago): *I miss you. Is that weird?*

My smile deepened.

Lifting my phone, I typed a reply.

Definitely weird. Or not. I've sort of missed you too. And does the offer still stand? If so, I'll have a burger. Or you will find a Dani corpse when you get home.

He messaged back a few minutes later.

"Sort of" miss me??? Nah. I need more than that. Otherwise, no burger for you. Just a bag of carrot sticks.

I laughed out loud, and that's when it hit me. *The thought of Will thinking about me made me giddy.*

I jolted, flipping my phone into the air.

I shouldn't be smiling because of Will.

I should be smiling because I'd just agreed to go out on a date.

CHAPTER TWENTY

My looming date arrived quicker than I anticipated.

Too quick.

While I'd been happy thinking about it as something I'd do in the distant future, the thought of doing it now—*today* —was unbearable.

Jacob had messaged me a week after we exchanged numbers. At first, I thought he was ghosting me, so I was surprised when the message came through at work. Lily and Finn didn't know about it, thank goodness. I couldn't handle that amount of pressure.

We were meeting up with each other for drinks. That much, at least, I could handle. It wasn't like he was taking me out for a meal at a fancy restaurant or anything. No need to prepare for anything overly romantic. Still... I hadn't been on a date in so long that I couldn't help but freak out a little.

"I thought you were excited?" Will asked, turning to look at me.

I stopped pacing and met his eye. He had his feet on the

table, something I was never allowed to do myself. Walking over, I nudged them onto the floor and sat beside him, folding my arms.

"I am excited."

He scooted away, allowing me space. "Then why do you look like you need an inhaler?"

"I don't," I shook my hands, but it did nothing to calm my nerves. So I sucked in a deep breath, pausing midway to glance at Will.

He raised a brow. "Really? You don't need me to find you an inhaler?"

I hit his shoulder. "Stop it! You're not helping me."

"Okay, okay. I'm sorry." He twisted to face me. "So why are you so nervous?"

I shook my head. "I know that I said I'm excited because I haven't been on a date in so long, but that's also why I'm nervous. I don't know how to go on a date. What if I do something embarrassing?"

"Then you do something embarrassing," he shrugged like it was that simple. When I didn't look convinced, he added, "What I'm saying is, if he doesn't like you for doing something 'embarrassing', then he doesn't deserve you in the first place. Didn't you tell me something like that once?"

I nodded. "You're right. I'm right. If he doesn't like me for my flaws, he'll never truly like me."

"And how could he not like you for being you, right?" his words were so quiet that I wasn't even sure if I'd heard them right. I gave him a quizzical look, but his expression quickly cleared. He swatted me from the sofa. "Go get ready. Nobody likes to be left waiting."

Will was surprisingly cooperative today. When I'd first told him about this date, he hadn't been happy. Actually, he'd claimed that Jacob was the worst of men. Something about how he behaved after I'd gone home–eyeing up every girl that passed, shamelessly flirting. He'd also failed to tell anyone about our agreed date, which he thought was strange. Especially if he liked me. But I'd insisted that none of that mattered. We weren't a couple, and I wasn't *that* into him. Will became less bothered after that.

I bought a new dress for the date. It wasn't something I usually wore–for one thing, it was a dress. But I decided I wanted to wear something nice, especially when I rarely ever had a reason to do that.

The dress wasn't revealing, but it did hug my figure. So much so that I felt self-conscious as I made my way down to Will to show him.

"So," I edged my way into the room. "How do I look?"

He turned away from the TV to look at me. His eyes were unfocused at first, and then something shifted.

I rubbed my arm. "Is the dress bad?"

"No, no." He jumped to his feet, moving toward me with that same look on his face. A look that made me divert my eyes to the floor. "You look nice. Pretty."

I still couldn't look him in the eye. "Are you sure it's alright?"

His thumb and forefinger enclosed my chin. Gently, he lifted my face, and I saw that he now frowned as he examined whatever emotion I displayed on it.

"I'm sure. But you also look... not yourself."

"What do you mean?"

"You look uncomfortable, Dani."

I smirked. "That obvious?" And if I felt this uncomfortable in front of Will, I could only imagine how I'd feel in front of Jacob and a bunch of strangers at a bar. "It's just this dress, it's so..." I tried to stretch it to demonstrate. "Restrictive."

"And we both know how you hate wearing restrictive clothing," Will nodded. "You prefer something you can dance freely in, right?"

"Yes." I looked down at the dress, seriously considering ripping it off. Why had I even bothered buying it? "I just thought I should dress up because it's a date, you know? Isn't that what most people do?"

"You aren't most people," he answered. "*You* aren't afraid to wear what you want. And so you shouldn't be. Wear whatever makes you comfortable, Dani. You alone are enough."

I looked at him hopefully, a sudden vision flashing before my eyes. I imagined myself out of the dress and in a sweater paired with jeans. That version of me seemed much more at ease than the one currently squeezed into what may as well be a suction dress.

"Screw it," I turned for the hallway. "I alone am enough!"

I heard him chuckle as I leapt up the stairs.

After throwing the dress on my bedroom floor and kicking it for good measure, I combed through my wardrobe, picking out something a little more me.

I returned to Will a much happier version of myself.

"So," I said, giving him a twirl. "How do I look now?"

He smiled. "Nice. Pretty. More like yourself."

"I'm not really suited for dresses, am I?" A jeans kind of girl through and through, even if it sometimes bothered me that I couldn't pull off the glamorous look.

"That's not what I meant," Will disagreed. "You suit dresses as much as the next person. It's that look on your face that's more like yourself. The confidence. It's just as sexy as wearing a dress," he twisted his face away, flicking the TV channel over.

I stared at the back of his head, wondering if I'd heard that right. Did he just... call me *sexy*? No. He hadn't meant that. He called confidence sexy, not me. Confidence.

"Well, I, um...," My face burned. "I best get going. See you later?"

He kept his back to me as he answered, but I noticed a strange, unidentifiable note in his voice. "I'm out on a date."

"A date?" We'd been talking about mine all morning, yet he failed to mention his?

He nodded, his back still to me. "It's nothing serious. I just... wanted to be busy today."

My good mood somewhat deflated, but I couldn't think of a plausible reason. Will never went out on dates. This was progress for him, right?

"Okay, well, I hope you enjoy yourself."

When he didn't turn or say anything else to me, I left the room, pushing Will and his date from my mind as I tried to focus on my own.

I was on time, but I arrived at the bar before Jacob. Thanking my earlier self for changing out of the dress, I ordered a drink and slid into a two-seater by the window, checking my phone. He hadn't messaged me to say that he was running late.

Just as I experienced simultaneous panic and relief that he might've bailed on the date, he entered the bar. He wore a simple jumper and jeans, making me double glad that I'd changed out of the dress.

He didn't apologise for being late. He just gave me one nod and walked straight up to the bar, ordering two drinks. I watched as he downed one and then the other.

"Are you alright?" I asked when he came over. Surely it wasn't normal downing two drinks like that.

He set his third drink down on the table. "I'm fine. Are you good?"

Had he undergone some sort of personality change? I couldn't put my finger on it, but he seemed different. Colder.

After ten minutes of stale conversation, I excused myself for the bathroom. I didn't really need it, but I needed to get away. This was going horribly. I now understood why Will disapproved of him. Over the past ten minutes, it hadn't escaped my notice that his eyes checked out every woman who neared our table. Fine before the date, not so fine now. In general, totally not fine and totally sleazy.

When I returned from the bathroom, I found him talking to one of the barmaids, leaning forward like a spy divulging a secret. Something told me to hold back. Listen. I couldn't explain what it was, but it was enough to make me pause a few feet away, zoning in on their conversation.

"Aren't you here on a date?" the barmaid asked. She sounded unimpressed, much to my respect.

Jacob raised a brow. "Do you really think I'd date her? No. She's just a... friend of a friend."

It felt like I'd been slapped across the face. Twice.

I didn't want to hear more, but I couldn't move.

"It didn't seem that way to me," the barmaid said, folding her arms. My respect for her increased.

"Do you really think I'd date someone that unattractive?" Jacob scoffed. His voice dropped to a whisper. "You're much more my type."

Whatever self-confidence I had abandoned me then. It left me empty and deflated–like a shard had pierced my heart. It's funny how a comment so fleeting can shatter somebody's self-esteem so effectively. *Someone that unattractive.* Tears welled in my eyes. The emptiness I felt quickly filled with pain and humiliation. But I couldn't, wouldn't, cry here. Not in front of him.

You alone are enough.

With Will's words firmly in my mind, I walked to Jacob, stopping directly in front of him. He looked visibly shaken by my reappearance but not at all remorseful. Regretting getting caught and not the action.

"Unattractive?" I said, picking up my drink. "Friend of a friend?" Jacob flinched back, but I wasn't about to waste a whiskey on him. I drank it in one and slammed it down, looking him straight in the eye. "We will never be friends, and there is nothing more unattractive than a personality like yours."

I walked out of the bar, feeling momentarily untouchable. My bravado crumbled once alone. I leaned back against the wall, sucking in a deep breath as I closed my eyes. The tears returned. Stupid, I knew. But what did that matter? However confident I felt, words like that, said by my *date*, would always hurt. Right now, they made me want to be someone who suited dresses. Someone pretty. Someone who kept the eyes of their date on them and not another woman.

Wiping my eyes with a sniff, I pulled out my phone. The only thing I really wanted right now was comforting words from Will. If I heard his voice–if I *saw* him–I knew everything would be better.

I sent him a text, asking if he was free.

He rang me a few seconds later.

"Dani?" he said. "Is everything alright?"

I closed my eyes, allowing his voice to comfort me. "Everything's fine," I lied, although my voice betrayed me. I swallowed, hoping to clear the lump from my throat. "I'm okay."

A beat silence, and then Will said, "Come meet me. I'll send you the address."

He hung up before I could answer, not that I would reject, and sent me his location pinned on a map.

It didn't take long to get there, and the walk helped calm me down. As I entered the pub, I searched through the sea of faces for a sign of him. He was in the back corner. I could just see his distressed eyes focussing on the floor.

When he saw me, he leapt to his feet.

"What happened?" he asked, scanning every inch of me as though to check for harm. It wasn't my outsides that hurt.

I opened my mouth to tell him, but I couldn't trust my voice. A sob would likely replace any word I tried to say. Will understood. Wordlessly, he took hold of my hand and guided me to his table. A pretty girl sat there already, and I remembered with a pang that he was here on a date. *Stupid, stupid, Dani. How could you forget?*

Will didn't introduce us. Instead, he pulled me into the seat beside him, stroking my arm.

"What happened?" he asked again, his voice so gentle it almost opened the floodgate.

I looked across at the girl. "I'm sorry for the interruption," I said. When she didn't respond, I moved my eyes back to Will. "I forgot you were on a date."

"It's fine," he consoled, but his date made a noise that told me it wasn't. If Will heard, he didn't let it show. "Tell me," he said, leaning closer. "What's made you this upset? Did he do something to you?" Anger flashed across his face, and the saltwater in my eyes escaped.

I rubbed the tears away in frustration. Really, I didn't know why I was crying again. I was better now. Hurt, sure, but not enough to warrant this response.

But Will was here. And he cared. And having someone care this much made me want to curl up and cocoon myself in his arms.

He cleared his throat. "Um, Chloe?" he asked, moving his eyes across the table. "Do you mind getting us some drinks? As you can see, my friend is upset. Please get whatever you want and water for my friend."

"A whiskey," I choked. "I want a whiskey."

"A whiskey," Will clarified. Chloe didn't seem too pleased as she took his card from his outstretched hand, but Will had already turned back to me.

"You shouldn't have let me come here when you're on a

date," I tried to chastise. It came out as a sob. "I don't think she'll be impressed."

"How could I not?" he defended. "You sounded so upset on the phone." His eyes turned soft as he looked me over again. "Why are you upset?"

"For a stupid reason," I dabbed my cheeks with the sleeve of my jumper. "He said- he said-" I cut off, unable to speak as the tears started streaming again. I shook my head, feeling utterly pathetic by my reaction.

Will brushed my hair from my face and leaned closer, holding me steady in his hands. "Dani, I want to help you, but I can't do that unless you tell me what happened. Alright?"

I nodded as I met his eye. Something in the swirling depths of his steadied me.

"Okay," I sucked in a calming breath. "Well, I was happy, you know, about going on a date. Happy that somebody wanted to go out with me. But when I returned from the toilet, I overheard Jacob telling a girl it wasn't a date. And that he wouldn't go out with someone this unattractive." I sniffed. I'd managed to keep my voice steady throughout the speech, but it wavered toward the end.

Will stared at me. His expression was empty, giving me no clue what he thought.

"Pathetic, right?" I said, feeling my embarrassment return. "It's stupid. Not enough for me to come here and ruin your date."

He continued to stare at me, his expression shifting from calm, to angry, to outraged.

"*He said that?*" Before I could stop him, Will jumped to

his feet. The movement was so quick and forceful that it knocked several glasses over.

"Will," I gasped, pulling him back down.

"Where is he? I'm going to kill him." He made to move. With my hand still on his arm, I yanked him back.

"*Please?*" I pleaded. "What use would it be? He's already said it. We can't turn back time."

"No, but it will make me feel better." He tugged against my grip, but I held firm.

"How about you make *me* feel better?" I questioned. "I'm the one who's upset."

He met my eye. Something passed behind his own, and then he sat down with a sigh, rubbing his face. "I'm sorry," he said. "I don't know what happened there. I just saw red."

"Is everything alright here?" We both looked up to see Chloe by the edge of the table, watching us. She placed a glass of water before me, her eyes on Will. I noted that she hadn't bought herself a drink.

Will's eyes flicked between us, clearly conflicted. He stopped with his gaze on Chloe. "Actually, it's not. My friend is upset. Do you mind if we call it a night?"

"Will-" I tried to protest, but he squeezed my hand, eyes still on Chloe.

"Fine," she said, giving me a weird look as she grabbed her jacket. She tossed his card on the table and turned without another word.

"I don't think I'll be seeing her again," Will sighed. He didn't seem to mind that fact as he pushed my whiskey glass toward me, taking a sip from his.

I stared at my glass, no longer wanting a drink. Now that

Will had calmed down, my sadness returned like we were a part of some weird, reverse cycle. Never okay at the same time.

"Why did he say that?" I asked quietly. "Am I really that unattractive?"

"Hey, hey," Will's hands cupped my face. "Don't say that. He said it because he's a jerk. Nothing more, nothing less. He really doesn't deserve you." As his thumbs brushed the newly formed tears from my cheeks, I relaxed.

"Thanks," I sniffed. "And I'm sorry for ruining your date."

"You didn't." He wrapped his hand around mine, pulling me into a standing position. "Now tell me where you left him."

CHAPTER TWENTY-ONE

"Will, let's not do this," I tugged his arm. But, of course, he was too strong for me to achieve anything more than slowing him down.

We were outside now. The bar where I'd interfered on his date was almost out of sight. Will made his way to a small park, paying no mind to me and my pulling. He was concentrating too hard on his goal of finding Jacob.

"Will," I said again, pulling harder this time.

"I'm not going to do anything, Dani," he said, still looking ahead. "I'm just going to have a quiet word with him."

"But it will be so embarrassing," I complained. I didn't have a brother, but I guessed this would be like having an older one who tells people off for picking on you at school. "Can't we just forget his existence? *Please?*"

He groaned. "Fine, fine." He brushed my hand off his arm and shoved his own into his pocket, turning his eyes up at the sky. I looked up with him. It was a beautiful day, without a cloud in sight. I hadn't noticed this before. He heaved a sigh that told me he really had given in and looked down at me.

"It's still early," he said. "Can I at least take you out for the day so that you don't think about it?"

I nodded, thinking we probably both needed the distraction. Besides, a day out with Will sounded like the very thing I needed. "Where should we go?"

"I have somewhere in mind."

After following Will through the park, I realised we were headed toward the embankment. Bodies bustled from all directions, but we didn't pay them any mind. We strolled along the pathway at our own pace, occasionally looking out at the river.

Every now and then, I caught Will looking at me. But he didn't say anything, so neither did I.

We continued along. I wondered if he had a plan from here, but I didn't mind either way. I felt at peace just walking and being here.

"You aren't afraid of heights, are you?" he asked suddenly.

I blinked up at him. "Um, don't you know I'm not afraid of anything?"

He smirked. "We'll see about that."

He sped up his walk, forcing me to chase after him.

"Hey, wait for me!" I called, which only caused him to move faster. He started running. "*Will Lovett,*" I didn't think he expected me to run so fast. I caught up to him, jumping on his back so he couldn't run away again. He lurched forward with a grunt.

"You're really something else, you know that?" he looked back at me with a frown. I stuck my tongue out, still glued to him. Rather than lowering me down, he hoisted me up into a piggyback.

"Hey, you can let me down now," I said, tapping his shoulder. He didn't budge. Instead, his grip tightened. "Seriously, Will, I can be lowered."

Now he turned to look at me with an evil grin. "Buckle up, Scott."

I yelped as he set off into a sprint. And then I laughed. Laughed so hard I thought I'd never stop.

In the end, I didn't need to tell Will to put me down again. He did it of his own accord.

"Time out," he gasped, stopping with his hands on his knees. He sucked in two deep breaths as I slid away from him. "I really wish I hadn't run like that."

I laughed and crouched in front of his buckled form. "Come on. It's my turn." He looked at me in confusion, so I indicated for him to climb onto my back.

He shrugged. "It's your death wish."

As he attempted to climb on, I quickly realised that I wasn't strong enough to carry his weight. I grunted, trying with all my might to lift him, but all I achieved was tipping him over. He crashed to the floor and immediately glared up at me from his new place by my feet.

"Oops," I said. "Sorry."

"Oh, now you're getting it." He lurched to his feet, grabbing me before I had the chance to escape.

I laughed as he picked me up, throwing me over his shoulder like I was a sack of potatoes. Building, road, and sky blurred into one as he spun us in a circle, making my head dizzy. "Time out! Time out!" I choked.

He lowered me, entwining his fingers in mine. "Come on,"

he said, setting off at a pace, "I want to get there before the sun sets."

I looked down at his hand in mine with a frown. He'd never held my hand before. Did he do it by mistake, momentary confusing me for one of his flings? "Why are you holding my hand?" I asked. I examined his face, expecting him to blush and drop it, but all he did was hold it tighter.

"My hands are cold, and yours are warm." He shrugged before stuffing our entwined fingers into his coat pocket. "Don't worry," he smiled at me. "This is strictly platonic."

I would have objected, but it felt too nice. In a platonic kind of way.

"So where are you taking me?" I asked.

He pointed with his free hand. My eyes followed, stopping on the terrifyingly tall London Eye.

My stomach did a summersault.

"What's the matter?" Will smirked as I turned my panicked eyes on him. "I thought you weren't afraid?"

"I'm not." My voice cracked in betrayal. I cleared my throat. "I can't wait to be four hundred feet up in the air. How fun."

"Four-hundred and forty-three feet, actually."

I glared at his unhelpful correction. "Even more fun."

"Come on. You'll enjoy it." With my hand still entwined with his, he propelled us forward.

I guessed I had no option but to do this–unless I admitted to Will that I *was* afraid of heights. And I wasn't about to do that. In a way, I supposed I was glad about this. A part of me had always wanted to try out the big wheel. I'd just never had anybody to try it out with.

After purchasing a ticket, we waited in line and then climbed into one of the capsules. Will went straight to the bench in the middle, patting the space beside him. I walked tentatively over, taking the seat as I looked around at the three-sixty glass window.

"This isn't so bad," I said. "I can do this."

He laughed. "We haven't even moved yet."

I gripped the edge of the bench as the wheel set into motion, causing Will's laugh to pick up in volume.

"Come on, Dani. It's not that bad. We're perfectly safe."

"And trapped," I muttered. I looked down at the panelled floor as Will walked around the capsule. I had no idea how he could do that. Nor did I understand how he could stand so close to the glass window and peer down. When we got high enough–almost to the top–I scrunched my eyes closed, feeling slightly sick.

I sensed Will sit back down beside me. "Open your eyes," he whispered. His warm breath brushed against my ear, sending a shiver through me.

"No." I kept them firmly closed.

"Come on," he tempted. "Are you really going to let your fear control you?"

How could he possibly know to say that to me? Slowly, and after bracing myself, I opened my eyes, aiming them straight at the floor.

"You can do better than that," he complained. I shot him a glare, which he returned with a look of disappointment. "Well, since you've got this far, look over there," he turned, pointing out the window.

I did as he said, more to get it over with than to be brave, and my eyes were not prepared for the beauty they saw. I gasped, much to Will's delight, and scrambled to my feet for a better look.

The sun was just setting, and I now understood why Will wanted to get here before it'd set fully. The clouds that scattered the sky were colourful, with coral pinks, peachy oranges, and deep purples. The sun laid low and cast a shimmering golden glow stretching across the river.

"This is beautiful," I turned to face Will, wanting to see his reaction, but he wasn't looking at the sunset. He was looking at me. Butterflies fluttered around my stomach like they were on a wheel of their own. When he didn't move his eyes away, I asked, "What's that look for?"

"What look?"

"You're- you're looking at me funny."

"Am I?" he closed his eyes with a playful smile. "That better?"

I exhaled. Sometimes–and it was getting more frequent by the day–being with Will gave me a funny feeling. Almost like... I was more than a friend to him, and he was more than a friend to me. But that certainly wasn't the case, and it was a dangerous thought to allow. The last thing I was in danger of was having Will fall for me. Hadn't he been adamant that it would never happen? More importantly, wasn't I *nothing* like the girls he usually went for? I turned to look out the window, feeling ridiculous for thinking about it.

Moving my eyes down to the dazzling lights below, I realised just how high up we were. My stomach whirled.

"I think I'm going to puke," I said, covering my mouth.

Will chuckled and walked over to me, placing two steadying hands on my shoulders. "Come on," he sighed, leading me back to the bench. "I don't want to be stuck in here with the smell of your puke."

I sat down, feeling better for it. Eventually, as the capsule moved us back toward the safety of the ground, my lips pulled up. "I'm glad I did this," I said, turning my smile on Will. "Even though it's been terrifying, I'm glad I did it."

He smiled back. It was a half teasing, half satisfied smile. "Look at you, conquering your fears."

"Don't tell anyone I have any," I warned, earning me an eye roll.

When we climbed out of the capsule, I took a second to appreciate being back on solid ground again. Will walked ahead, but I paused to glance back, moving my eyes to the top of the wheel. I could hardly believe we were all the way up there just a few minutes ago.

"Do you want to go back on?" I heard Will ask.

"Nope," I shook my head firmly, turning my eyes away before he could drag me back.

As we walked along the riverside, Will scooped up my hand again, and that fluttering in my stomach returned. I looked away, hoping he wouldn't see the colour rising on my face.

"Should we get food?" I asked, wanting to break the silence. It somehow made Will's hand in mine burn like I was holding hot metal.

"I know of the most amazing chippy van," he replied. His voice told me our handholding didn't affect him as it did me. Well, if that was the case, I refused to be affected.

"There's a chippy van?" I quirked a brow, waiting for him to give me the glorious details.

"Only if you're in on the lucrative location," he winked.

Beyond curious, I followed him away from the river and down a side street. Soon, the smell of fried potato wafted toward me. I spotted the van at the end of the road and pulled Will into a faster pace, suddenly ravenous.

"What can I get you both?" the lady behind the counter asked. Before I could do anything more than scan the menu, she said, "We're doing a couples special today if you're interested."

My eyes darted to her face. I wondered why she would make such an assumption when I remembered we were holding hands. *It's platonic*, I wanted to tell her. I almost did, but then Will stepped forward.

"What's the special?" he asked. I gave him a look, but he just squeezed my hand, stuffing it back into the warmth of his pocket.

"An extra-large cone for the price of a small."

"Well, I'm sold. Dani?" he looked down at me with a questioning smile. I couldn't help but frown back. "We'll take it," he said, turning away, unfazed by my puzzlement.

As we walked away, Will held the cone of chips. I didn't say anything until we were out of earshot from the van, and then I turned my questioning eyes on him.

"What was that?" I demanded. "We- we aren't a couple."

"It's basically a free cone of chips, Dani. You've pretended to be my girlfriend for much less."

I felt a bizarre mix of relief and disappointment, followed

by a whole lot of stupidity at what I'd been thinking. Why *did* I keep thinking Will had an ulterior motive? Had I actually believed for a single second that he thought of us as a couple?

"Good shout," I mumbled, turning my eyes to the floor.

Still, he didn't let go of my hand as we walked, not even after we were out of sight of the van. It was still tucked safely away in his pocket. I didn't try to take it back, either, because I couldn't deny that it felt nice to have someone's hand to hold. And Will's hand was warm, friendly. It didn't need to be weird.

"Oh, before I forget," he said as he took the cone back from me. We had to take it in turns so that the other could eat. "It's my annual birthday party on Friday-"

"When's your birthday?" I interrupted in a panic. Now that I thought about it, I had no idea. Had I missed it?

He gave me a funny look. "It's tomorrow. Don't tell me you haven't got me anything." He must've seen the horror on my face because he laughed. "I'm kidding! It's on Friday, coincidentally."

I should've known better than to think I'd missed it. Will was probably the type of person who announced his birthdays by wearing a badge on his chest. After giving his hand a vigorous squeeze for panicking me, I asked, "So what about this annual party of yours? Am I invited?"

"Of course, you're invited. But I have to warn you, it might not be enjoyable. Jordan forces me to have one every year because it's a while before the next birthday. It can get loud, and people stay late. And the music is..." he gave me a look of advanced apology.

"Not to my taste?" I guessed.

"Nor is it to mine," he shook his head as though to banish the sound from it. "But I'm massively outnumbered when it comes to song requests, so…,"

"But I'm invited?" I asked again.

"I'm not about to kick you out of your own home, am I? Besides, you're my friend, and I want you there."

"Friend," I smiled, but I wasn't sure I felt it. "Well, friend, I'll make sure it's a good party for you."

He grinned. "Then maybe I'll actually enjoy it this year."

CHAPTER TWENTY-TWO

I'd been right about Will announcing his birthday.

When I came downstairs on Friday morning, I saw him not only with a badge on his chest but with a gigantic birthday balloon floating by his side.

I nodded at the balloon. "Did you buy that yourself?"

"Huh?" He turned away from his cereal to look up at it. "That? No. Tae had it sent to me in a box."

I smirked and carefully readjusted the present I'd hidden behind my back. "Happy birthday," I said, sliding it across the table to him.

"A jumper," he held it in front of him and examined it.

I twisted my hands together. In truth, I had no idea what to buy him. I sucked at choosing presents. But I thought if I bought him an item of clothing, he could wear it for his party. Or exchange it, if that's what he preferred.

"Sorry if you don't like it," I said, pulling out a chair. "Gift buying isn't one of my skills." I leaned my chin on my hand as I waited for his verdict.

"And here's me thinking you're skilled at everything," he smirked. "No, I like it. I'll wear it right now, actually." He stood, pulling off his current jumper without warning. I flicked my eyes away, suddenly hot, and resisted the urge to move them back. "There," he said. "What do you think?"

Safe knowing that he was clothed again, I moved my eyes back. "It suits you," I said. It did. The thick, grey fabric looked better on him than I'd allowed myself to imagine. "Maybe I'm skilled at gift buying after all."

"Thanks for buying it for me. Are you almost ready to set off?"

"I'm not going in with you today." He looked at me in confusion, so I elaborated. "Half the office is probably waiting outside to sing you happy birthday as you walk in. Finn definitely is." All week, it's all Finn had been talking about. He treated Will's birthday as if it were his own.

"You're probably right," Will agreed. He pushed his chair from the table, taking his breakfast bowl to the sink. "Well, I guess I'll see you at work."

"Travel safe, birthday boy."

I made sure I was at least ten minutes behind Will before setting off myself. While there wasn't anybody singing happy birthday upon my arrival, there was an elaborate display of celebration surrounding Will at his desk. Balloons, banners, birthday confetti–you name it.

I hung my coat on the rack and tried not to laugh as I passed him.

"Good, Dani, you're here." Chrissie looked up at me from a ginormous pile of paperwork. Lifting it up, she dropped it on my desk. "I need you to do something for me."

I sucked in a deep breath. While I was used to menial tasks like scanning and shredding, I still needed to mentally prepare myself for them. "How can I help?"

"These are the memos we've been given from the design team. They detail everything we need to know about the game's armour and weaponry. I need you to create 2D illustrations for them. Once approved, you can use our software to create 3D models."

My eyes lit up. "I can really do that?"

"Yes. If you think you're up to it, that is...,"

"I am!" Had Chrissie finally seen potential in me? I bit my lip against the huge grin threatening to take place. It would probably make me seem psychotic. "You can count on me."

"Good. The deadline isn't as tight with this one, which is why I-" she cut off, distracted by something behind me.

Following her eyes, I saw Will passing by our row of desks.

"Happy birthday, Will!" she called out to him.

He paused, moving his attention over to us. As he looked at Chrissie, I thought I saw a flicker of pain behind his eyes, and I felt a sense of pity for them both. For Will, because he wanted to let Chrissie down gently but hadn't been given the opportunity, and for Chrissie, because her crush on Will was clearly enormous.

"Thanks, Chrissie. I hear there's cake in the kitchen, so I'm just going to..." he pointed over his shoulder and turned.

"That's a nice jumper you're wearing," she said, pausing him again.

Will's eyes flashed infinitesimally to me. He smiled. "Thanks. I got it from someone important." With that, he set off walking again, disappearing inside the kitchen.

A smile crept onto my lips.

"Coffee?" I asked, just as Chrissie said,

"Cake?"

We both paused on our way up from our seats, staring at each other.

"I'll get the coffee if you get the cake," I half-joked.

Chrissie didn't seem to find it funny. We set off for the kitchen, with Chrissie walking slightly behind me. I tried not to feel awkward about it, even if I did feel as though she didn't want to walk by my side.

I reached the kitchen first. As always, Will's presence evaporated any awkwardness I felt. I smiled when I saw him sitting by the counter, and he grinned in return.

"Coffee?" he asked, reaching for the pot.

I opened my mouth to answer, but Chrissie beat me to it.

"No, I'll have a tea. You know I avoid drinking the coffee from this kitchen whenever possible." She broke away from me and took the empty seat beside him.

His hands froze on the coffee pot. A slight crease formed between his brows as he pushed it away, grabbing the teapot instead.

"How's your day, Chrissie?" he asked.

I felt a sudden rush of envy as I watched him turn his attention to her. I wanted to be the one sitting with Will and speaking to him. Yet here Chrissie was, chatting like *she* was the friend here, not me. I understood why we kept our friendship hidden from work, but it was starting to bother me.

I realised the unreasonableness of my jealousy and moved to the other side of the counter, pouring some coffee into my mug. As Chrissie and Will's voices filled the room, I peeked across at them, wondering if Will also wanted to be sitting with me.

Turning my attention away from them, I grabbed the kettle. It took me a second to realise that the sugar pot was missing. I searched around, spotting it beside Will. Before I could reach for it, he slid it across to me, his eyes never leaving Chrissie.

I smiled to myself.

I left the kitchen and returned to my desk, feeling somewhat deflated. I really did crave a word from Will. But at least I'd get to see him at home. With that cheerful thought, I sat at my desk and picked up one of the specs to read through. My phone pinged a minute later. A text from Will. I looked around, but he wasn't back from the kitchen yet.

Just me in the kitchen now. Fancy another drink?

I'd barely touched my coffee, but I raced back to the kitchen without a second to waste. Before I entered, I paused to collect myself. This desperation could not be witnessed by anyone, least of all Will.

"Hey," I breathed, seeing him sitting there alone. That jumper really did look good on him. "How's your birthday so far?"

He smiled at me. "Good, except I have a deadline to meet by the end of the day and a party to think about after I leave."

"Ah, the party." I sat down next to him, happy to be able to. "Can I help with the deadline?"

He shook his head. "It would probably take me longer to explain it than if I did it myself. But thanks." He tucked a lock of my hair behind my ear before letting his hand fall. "How's your morning?"

I released a shaky breath. "Good. Chrissie's actually given me some artwork to do."

"Oh?" He raised an impressed brow. "For our space game?"

I grinned. "Yep! Seems like she's finally seeing my potential."

He smiled. "I knew she would eventually."

I opened my mouth to say more, but a noise distracted me. Both our eyes flashed over to the door as the handle started moving.

"Will, I forgot to ask-" Chrissie's head poked through the door, followed by her entire body. I quickly jumped to my feet and moved to the other side of the counter. "Dani," she blinked. "Why are you back in here?"

"I'm just making a coffee," I said, showing her my mug.

Her eyes narrowed. "Didn't you just make one?"

"I'm... a bit tired today."

Will barely covered up a laugh.

"First years shouldn't be spending this much time in the kitchen making drinks," Chrissie lectured, folding her arms. "They should be spending it working. Wouldn't you agree, Will?"

Will was trying to hold himself together, but Chrissie didn't seem to realise that. His whole body shook from the effort not to laugh.

"Absolutely," he managed to say before biting his lip and staring up at the ceiling.

"This is my last one," I promised her. I shot Will a look of betrayal.

"Make sure it is." She left without asking Will whatever question she'd forgotten to ask.

I made sure I was glued to my desk after that. I really did want to do well with the illustrations. No, better than well. I wanted them to be spectacular. I was going to be busy over the next month or so–I still had my game to design on top of everything else–but I was willing to put in the effort.

By the time the clock struck the end of the day, I was pleased with my progress. I packed some specs to work on at home and left for the elevator with what seemed like half the office. It was always that way on a Friday.

I was the first one home. Will had to stay behind to meet his deadline, leaving me in charge of prepping the house for the party. I tidied, cleaned, and hid all expensive items away.

I'd just finished showering when Will knocked on the bathroom door.

"Dani, are you almost done?" he asked. He sounded panicked–like he'd run out of time. "I can't believe I only have an hour left before people start to arrive."

"I'm done," wrapping the towel around me, I opened the door. Will stood so close that I almost walked into him.

"Oh, er, sorry-" his hands hovered around my shoulders as his eyes struggled with where to focus. He clenched his fingers into balls, dropping them by his side.

"Are you alright?" I peered into his face, which looked all flustered. "Did you run here or something?"

"What?" his head snapped up. His eyes met mine briefly before moving to the side.

"Your face," I frowned. "It's all... red."

"It's, er... I'm... Never mind," he shook his head before darting past me, slamming the door behind him.

"Alright, then." Shrugging off Will's strange behaviour, I entered my bedroom. I'd already been warned that many people would be showing up tonight, and I wanted to look semi-decent. I changed into a t-shirt and cargo pants–comfort came first at home–before putting on makeup.

The only thing left now was to wait.

"Here," Will passed me a drink before sliding into the chair beside me.

"Thank you," I held the glass out to him. "Cheers?"

"Cheers."

We clinked our glasses as the doorbell rang.

"And so the fun begins," Will gave me a look before leaving to answer the door.

Soon, the house was full of half-drunk strangers. I knew a few of the faces, like Jordan and Tae. But the rest were a mystery.

I stayed by the wall, too uncomfortable to converse with drunk strangers who became drunker by the second. Every now and then, Will's eyes would flash over to me, almost as if he were checking to see if I was alright. I'd give him a small wave, hoping it would satisfy him.

In truth, this wasn't my kind of party. But he'd warned me of that, so I couldn't complain. And it hadn't escaped my notice that most people here were girls. In fact, I'd wager that eighty per cent of the attendees were female. I pointed this out to Tae when he came over to my place by the wall.

He laughed. "Yeah, would you believe that Jordan was in charge of the invite list?"

"Ah, now it makes sense." I took a sip of my drink. "Remind me again, is it Jordan's party or Will's?"

"For argument's sake, let's call it Will's." He leaned in closer, put his hand over his mouth, and whispered, "But it's definitely Jordan's."

I laughed, making eye contact with Will from his place at the dining table.

"So, how are you holding up?" Tae continued.

I moved my eyes away from Will to give him a quizzical look. "What do you mean?"

"You don't seem to be enjoying yourself all that much."

"Is it that obvious?" I smiled down at the floor. "I'm trying to enjoy myself. But house parties…," I shook my head. "They aren't really my thing."

"That's fair enough. They aren't my thing, either. I prefer clubs, or preferably someplace with easy access to a taxi. But I, like you, am here for Will." He downed the rest of his drink. "Do you want another?"

Seeing that he was pointing to my glass, I shook my head. "I'm good, thanks."

The more I witnessed people getting drunk around me, the less I wanted to be that way myself. They were all so *loud*. Mingled in with the terrible music, I was getting a headache.

When Tae left, Will came to give me company.

"How is my least favourite person here?" he asked, sliding into the spot Tae had occupied.

I looked over both shoulders. "Sorry, who are you talking to? I think you'll find I'm your *favourite*."

He grinned. "Seriously, how are you holding up? Does this

party suck, or what?"

I didn't want to put a damper on his birthday. "This party doesn't suck. Look at everyone. They're having a great time."

"But are *you*?" He gave me a knowing look. When I didn't answer, he took my drink from me. "Come join in. Kate and Maria want to play a game of confessions."

"Okay, *now* the party sucks."

"Don't be a spoilsport," he nodded at the table. "They're setting up to play now." When I didn't say anything, he rolled his eyes. "It's my birthday, so you have to play." He pulled me away from the wall, plonking me in the space beside him.

"Ready?" Jordan asked.

Will gave me a wink. "We're ready."

CHAPTER TWENTY-THREE

O ne of the girls leaned forward and smiled at him.
She had a lovely smile and a face to match. "You're
the birthday boy, Will. You should go first."

"And I bet you have just the question for him, don't you,
Kate?" Jordan flashed her a flirty smile.

She smirked. "As a matter of fact, I do." She leaned back,
her strikingly blue eyes focused on Will. "So, Will, if you
were stuck on a desert island and had to choose one person
here to be stuck with, who would you choose, and why?"

"Easy, Dani." He shrugged his shoulders like the question
couldn't have been simpler to answer.

I wasn't the only one to look at him in surprise.

"W-why is that?" Kate asked. I wondered if she'd wanted
him to say her name.

"Because I don't think there'd be a dull day with Dani
around." He turned his smile on me, and, for one wild
moment, my mind went into a frenzy.

"Dani," Jordan said, snapping me out of it. "It's your turn.
Ask anything to anyone."

"Um," I looked around the table, but I only knew three

names. And I wasn't about to ask Kate. "Jordan... what's the most compromising situation you've ever found yourself in?"

"Oh, that's a good one." He shook his head as Will let out a satisfied laugh.

"You can always take a shot if you don't want to answer," Will grinned.

Jordan shot him a glare before looking up in thought. "Hmm. The most compromising situation... Got it," he slammed his hands on the table. "The time my mum walked in on me while I was looking at pictures of naked women."

"*Lies*," Will coughed into his hand.

Jordan shot him another glare. After a second, he shook his head and downed the shot.

"That bad, huh?" I grinned.

"Will," Jordan turned a menacing smile his way. "Will, Will, Will."

"Give it your best shot," Will dared.

"Which girl do you want to kiss the most at this table? And I know you want to kiss one girl," he gave him a wink that went completely over my head. Who did Will want to kiss?

Whoever it was caused his face to burn bright as a tomato. That surprised me. Usually, Will was full of confidence. I didn't think a question like this would bother him.

"Come on, Will," Jordan said, clearly enjoying himself. "Answer or take a shot."

As Will eyed up the shot glass, Kate flicked a lock of her golden hair over her shoulder. It caught his attention.

"Kate," he answered immediately. "My answer is Kate."

I shouldn't have been surprised. Nor should I have felt the pang of disappointment in my gut.

After a few more rounds of questioning, I managed to eradicate myself and hid away in the kitchen. It was quieter in here. While the music still boomed, it was nowhere near the level as in the front room.

So... Will had a thing for Kate. I mused over this as I poured myself a drink, leaning back against the kitchen counter to take a sip. The door swung open, drowning me with noise again.

"Oh, it's you." I relaxed back against the counter as Will walked in.

"Are you hiding away in here?"

I laughed. "Maybe. It's getting pretty rowdy in there."

"I thought you liked rowdy."

"That depends on who I'm getting rowdy with."

He raised his brow and leant on the counter beside me. "Is this not your crowd?"

"Not really," I confessed. "You are–obviously. And Tae and Jordan. But everyone else... I don't know." I couldn't articulate why I felt like I didn't belong.

Will ducked his head. "I sort of saw this coming when I heard who Jordan invited. I'm sorry."

"No, no. It's your birthday. You shouldn't have to think about me when you invite people."

"But you're my roommate. And my friend."

"I'm great, honestly. They aren't that bad; it's just...,"

"They aren't your crowd."

I smiled. "They aren't my crowd. And the music is pretty

terrible too."

He laughed. "Well then," he put his cup on the side and took mine from my hands. "How about we bring the party in here?"

"What...?"

He pulled out his phone and started typing something. It took a few seconds before I heard the music. When I did, I felt my cheeks pull up into a grin.

"This is more you're style, right?" He grinned in return.

"Oh yeah."

He grabbed my hands and pulled me to the middle of the floor. We danced seriously for a minute, swaying from side to side, but then he started pulling out weird moves, and I couldn't help but join in.

"You're a good dancer," I laughed, watching as he did some bizarre worm dance with his arms. I tried to copy him and failed, so I turned it into the robot instead.

"Nice." He nodded in appreciation and copied me. His robot morphed into the big fish dance. I couldn't help but laugh at the sight of him doing that. I knew I must look equally ridiculous because he also laughed at me.

When the song ended, we were both in stitches.

"That was fun," I said, wiping a tear from my eye as we returned to our drinks.

"It's the most fun I've had all night," he admitted.

"Really? Your highlight wasn't a game of confessions?"

He rolled his eyes at my tone of voice. "Don't tell me you don't like confessions."

I held my hands up. "I just didn't realise I was at a children's party."

"Hey, a game of confessions is a brilliant way to get two people together."

"Oh yeah?"

"Think about it," he put his drink down, using his hands to accentuate his point. "If someone's too scared to make the first move, they can just say a name during the game, and the ball is rolling. Many couples were made that way." He picked his drink back up, nodding knowingly.

"A lot of marriages too?"

"Oh yeah. And divorces."

I smiled. "I just think you should have the guts to make the first move anyway. I don't need that game."

"Oh yeah? Didn't you once tell me that you liked Jordan? Why don't you go make the first move?"

It didn't look like he thought I would do it. For that reason alone, I placed my cup down and stepped forward, determined to prove him wrong.

"Oh, no, you don't," he caught hold of my shoulders and pulled me back.

"What, you don't think I'll do it?"

"No. I think you definitely will. I'm just saving you from the rejection."

"Like he'd reject me." I met his eye and bit back a laugh because we both knew that I probably *would* get rejected. "Seriously, though," I sighed, "if it were just you and me here, I'd enjoy this party much more." Did I seriously just admit that? I looked down at the floor, embarrassed by my openness.

"Why don't you pretend it is just you and me, then?" Will asked.

I liked that idea, although how I could ignore that heavy drum and bass noise... "What is that, by the way?" I asked, nodding at his drink. I could smell it from here, and it smelt delicious–like syrup.

He looked down at his cup and smiled with pride. "*This* is my special concoction. Only I know how to make it, and only I get to drink it," he took a sip to prove his point.

"Wow. It must taste good."

"Oh, believe me, it does." He kept his eyes on his cup, thoughtful, and then held it out to me. "Here."

"But I thought only you get to drink it?"

"I can make an exception."

Flattered, I took the cup from his hands and sipped it. "Wow. This is amazing," I looked at him in surprise. "What is in that?" I licked my lips. They tasted like rum and honey and spiced cinnamon.

Will touched his nose. "My secret recipe."

"You're seriously not going to tell me? Can you at least make me one?"

"If I do, you'll be the first to ever receive one."

"Well, now I want it even more."

He grinned. "One 'Will's Special Concoction' coming right up."

"What's a 'Will's Special Concoction'?"

We both looked toward the door as Kate entered. She leaned against the doorframe, smiling a perfect smile.

Will looked back at me. "It's nothing."

"Well," Kate continued, "I'd love to try one."

Will scratched the back of his head as she advanced into the room. I wondered what he was doing. She was obviously into him, so why wasn't he showing any interest back?

"I've only got enough left to make one," he said. "Sorry."

"Oh." Kate frowned. Like me, she probably wondered why Will was being so distant. She saw me looking and turned swiftly away. "Maybe next time, then."

"Yeah, maybe."

She grabbed a bottle of cider and left the room. I waited for the door to fully close before I turned on him.

"Will, what was that about?"

He took a sip of his drink. "What was what about?"

"She is so into you."

"Who?"

I flapped my arms toward the door. "That girl. Kate. I thought you were into her?"

He frowned like *I* was the one saying something crazy. "Why would you think that?"

"Because you said you wanted to kiss her," I reminded him. "During that game of Confessions."

He was silent for a second, and then a peculiar look passed over his eyes. "Oh, right. Yeah. Her."

"I mean, I can't blame you. She is totally gorgeous."

He smiled. "She is, but she doesn't know it."

My brows furrowed. Kate definitely knew she was gorgeous... I'd seen her checking herself out at least three times. I was about to point this out when he spoke before me.

"I best re-join the party. Come back in when you're ready."

He left.

I guessed that meant I wasn't getting my drink.

I looked around the kitchen, trying to ignore the mess,

and yawned. I could go back to the party... or I could get into my PJs and climb into bed. That thought comforted me too much to ignore. And it was probably better for Will if I went up anyway since I no longer felt in the partying mood. Decided, I turned my back on the messy kitchen and snuck upstairs, closing the door to my bedroom with a sigh of relief.

"Oh, this is much better," I sighed, stretching out on the bed. After laying there for a minute, I moved to my wardrobe. I knew I had a pink, fluffy onesie somewhere because Holly made sure I packed it. And I wanted fluffy right now.

After searching for a minute, I found the onesie at the bottom. I spotted the kitten ears first. Pulling it out, I moved to my dresser and searched for a face mask.

I had four minutes left of wearing the mask when somebody knocked on my door.

I slammed my body against it in case they tried to enter. "Who is it?" I called, trying not to freak out.

"It's me!"

"Will?" I opened the door an inch to find him standing there, his eyes on the floor. He pushed against the door, forcing me to open it wider, and strode into my room.

"What's the matter?" I asked, spotting the annoyed look on his face.

"Why did you le-," he cut off, finally looking at me. His eyes moved silently over my face and clothes for too long a second. He laughed once, as though he couldn't believe what he saw, and then laughed for longer.

"What's so funny?" I asked, moving to the mirror.

"Oh." Yup, this would do it.

Will doubled over in a fit of laughter. "You–look–unbelievably–attractive!"

I had to give it to him–I did look comical. My mask had dried into a bright blue colour, my hair resembled a pineapple, and my pyjamas… pink with kitten ears–what more could I say?

"Okay," I allowed. "It is funny. But, come on, it's not that funny. Hey!" I swatted his arm.

Will no longer made a sound, but his body shook uncontrollably. He fell face-first onto the bed, laughing into my pillow.

"Would you stop?" I fought back a laugh of my own. "Stop it before I start. Laughing will ruin my mask." I touched my cheeks, already feeling it cracking.

One more look at Will's silent, shaking form, and the mask cracked around my mouth and eyes. Laughter burst from my lips as I fell onto the bed beside him.

We laughed for so long that my stomach hurt. When I thought I could stop, one look at Will started me off all over again. I seemed to have the same effect on him.

"It hurts," he breathed, putting an arm around me. "We need to stop."

After what felt like an eternity, we finally calmed down. I looked to the side, finding Will so close to me that I could see my reflection through his eyes.

"What a monster," I breathed, but I was no longer in danger of laughing. A new kind of emotion was seeping through me. I placed my hand against my stomach, feeling a strange fluttering inside.

Will didn't say anything, but he continued to look at me. Being this close to him... it made me vividly aware of our breathing. Our chests moved up and down, deep and unsteady.

Will's arm tensed around me, and for a moment, I thought he'd pull me closer. The warmth of his skin felt like fire on mine. I tried to look away, tried to break whatever spell his touch had me under, but the intensity in his eyes locked mine into place.

My breath caught.

I felt an ache between my legs. An ache I never expected to feel. Desire swirled in my stomach, wanting Will closer.

His hand lifted, hesitated. With a slight frown, almost as if he wasn't sure what compelled him, he moved it toward me, stopping with it cupping my cheek.

I didn't breathe.

He turned to face me, and I did the same. He moved closer, and so did I–until our bodies were almost flush.

That's when his expression shifted.

He pulled away suddenly, clearing his throat. "I best leave before you set me off again."

And just like that, his arm was gone. Leaving me cold and strangely empty. He moved to the door. I watched as his fingers hesitated on the handle, almost as if he didn't want to leave. But he twisted it open, and he was gone.

CHAPTER TWENTY-FOUR

When I went downstairs the next morning, I expected to find each room in a mess. I prepared myself for a few party lingerers: either those who needed a place to crash or had drunk themselves to sleep. I even half-expected to find the party still going.

What I did not expect was to see downstairs looking spotless.

I poked my head into the front room, finding everything in order. Not a body in sight. Next, I moved into the kitchen, stopping short when I saw Will inside.

He stood by the cooker. I roamed my eyes around the room, surprised by how tidy it was. The only evidence of last night was a stuffed trash bag by the utility door.

"Where is everyone?" I asked.

"Oh, you're up," Will glanced over his shoulder before returning his attention to whatever he was cooking. "Everyone left. I kicked them out before it got too late. Did you sleep well?"

"Surprisingly, yes." I stared at his back, unsure what to do with myself. "Did anybody stay over?" I asked.

"Nope. I could not be bothered having anyone to deal with this morning."

"Oh," I moved closer to him. The smell of egg and bacon drifted toward me. "You know, you could have waited for me before you cleaned. I feel bad that you've done it all on your own."

"I didn't do it on my own. Tae helped me." He must've sensed my oncoming question because he added, "He stayed behind when everyone left. We did most of this last night."

"Aren't you hungover?" It baffled me how he was up and moving, the picture of health.

"I drank water and ate bread before I went to bed, just how someone taught me." I could hear the smile in his voice, and I realised that he *did* remember me doing that for him. "Are you hungry?"

"Always."

He plated up two omelettes and took the seat opposite me. We ate in silence. I wasn't sure about him, but something stopped me from saying anything. I peeked at his face, remembering how close it had been to mine last night on the bed–remembering the feeling of having his arm around me, how it warmed my skin like sitting by a fire. How his eyes burned into mine, how I wanted to be closer...

I looked down at my plate, suddenly hot.

"Do you-" I had to clear my throat. "Do you remember being in my room last night?"

He laughed suddenly, causing my eyes to shoot back up. "Yeah, I remember. You looked so funny," he shook his head with another chuckle.

I forked a piece of egg and played with it, swirling it around the edges of my plate. Is that the only part he remembered... the laughter? He didn't seem to be blushing like me a few moments ago. But I'd been sure I'd seen something in his eyes last night. A look that told me he may or may not have wanted to kiss me. And how he'd hesitated at the door...

"Is that all you remember?" I probed, not quite sure why I pushed it.

He tilted his head. "Are you trying to tell me we did something? Did you take advantage of me, Scott?"

"Jeeze, no!" I shook my head with ferocity. "How could you even say that?"

Of course, last night didn't have the same effect on Will as it did on me. How could I forget that he did stuff like that all the time? No, he did *way* more than put his arm around someone and stare into their eyes. How stupid of me to think he'd felt something.

But wasn't it good if Will hadn't felt a spark? We were friends, and that's how it should be. This roommate arrangement worked off of friendship. Besides, I was so not his type.

I looked up, finding Will smiling at me with a tender look in his eye.

"Are you finished?" he asked, indicating my plate.

I stuffed a final bite into my mouth and swallowed. "Yes. Thank you."

He came around the table to collect my plate from me, his fingers brushing against mine as he reached for it. The same warmth I'd felt last night rushed through my fingers, a weird electricity that left a tingling sensation in more parts than the one he touched.

Will quickly moved his hand away and cleared his throat. "Um, I'm going out for a bit."

"Oh, really?" I forced myself to sound normal. "Where?"

"I'm just in the mood for a walk," he dropped the dishes into the sink and left the room.

I watched the door close behind him and wondered what caused the abrupt change. And what was this strange feeling creeping back into my stomach about? I knew that it was probably all in my head, but still. Every time I convinced myself there was nothing weird going on, Will did something to make me second guess it.

I shoved the thought from my mind.

After washing the dishes–Will had tidied up, after all. It was the least he deserved–I went back to my bedroom. I didn't do anything there except stare into the mirror.

I slapped my hands against my cheeks. "Get a grip of yourself, Dani. Will does not like you like that." Another slap. "And even if he did, you cannot allow it. It would ruin everything, and you'll end up back at Holly and Nick's house. Is that what you want?" Another slap. "That's what I thought. The two of you are friends, and that's how it should be. You both agreed that feelings would complicate things. And remember when he said that he'd never fall for you? *Get. It. Out. Of. Your Head.*"

Thinking my cheeks had taken enough of a hit, I stopped the self-talk and went to the living room. Will came bounding in not long after.

"Do you want to go to the cinema?" he asked.

That was abrupt. "The cinema?"

"Yeah, the cinema." He paced back and forth before me, agitated by something.

"Um, is there anything good on?"

"I think there's this, er, romantic comedy thing that people have been raving about."

A romantic comedy? I opened my mouth to say something, but only a splutter came out.

Will stopped pacing and looked over at me, our eyes meeting for the first time. My hand automatically moved to my stomach as that weird feeling returned.

Was this a... date? *No.* I gave myself a mental shake. *This is just like any other outing with Will. There's nothing* date-like *about it.* "Okay," I said. "Just let me, um, get ready."

He exhaled. "Good. Yeah. You, um, get ready." He scratched the back of his head and turned away from me.

This was weird, right? *No. Not weird,* I thought as I raced upstairs. *This is not a date. Not a date.* I took the last steps two at once, tripping over my feet at the top.

"Are you alright?" Will called as I thudded to the floor. He appeared at the bottom of the stairway.

"I'm fine!" I waved my hand behind my back before jumping up and rushing into my bedroom.

Not a date. Not a date. I paced up and down as I tried to stop myself from freaking out. *This is not a date!*

I stopped in front of my dressing table and clutched the edges. "This is not a date, Dani," I told myself into the mirror. "You two are friends, and that's how it should be."

Resolved that this wasn't a date, I returned to Will in my usual attire. With my hair scraped back, I hadn't bothered to put on any makeup. Let that be a statement.

Will, on the other hand, had switched into a shirt. I tried not to read too much into that. Or wonder if *that* was a statement in itself. It wasn't totally abnormal for him to wear a shirt. He wore them for many occasions. Didn't he?

"What time's the movie at?" I asked.

He jumped at the sound of my voice. "Er," pulling up his sleeve, he checked his watch. "If we leave now, I think we'll make the next showing."

"Okay," I swung back on my heels.

"Are you alright?" he asked as he got to his feet. "You seem nervous."

As he swung on his jacket, I realised he didn't seem nervous at all. Whatever had him agitated before clearly no longer bothered him.

See, I told myself. *Not a date.*

"I'm fine." I relaxed now that I knew Will wasn't viewing this as a date. We were just two friends hanging out, that was all.

We arrived at the movies with some time to spare. Will lined up for popcorn while I went to purchase the tickets. Since my line was shorter than his, I waited for him by the entrance.

"I've got popcorn," he said as he re-joined me, "and chocolates." He held up the food haul in both hands for me to see.

"Perfect," I snatched the chocolate bag from him.

"Hey, those are going in the middle."

I smiled over my shoulder before showing the theatre attendant our tickets.

I'd chosen two seats near the back, in the middle. As we walked up the steps, I noted that there weren't many people here with us. At first, I thought this a good thing. An empty movie theatre? Yes, please. But then it dawned on me that the emptier the theatre, the more alone I was with Will. That shouldn't have mattered, except, for some reason, it made my heart beat faster. It didn't help that the people here were all couples. Not the platonic kind of couple, either. The kissing kind.

I shuffled into my designated seat, grateful for the space separating me from Will.

"It's dead in here," he whispered, popping a handful of popcorn into his mouth before sitting beside me.

Again, he showed no signs of nerves. It reassured me that this was *not* a date.

"What, are you sad that there's no one here to throw popcorn at?" I whispered back.

He rolled his eyes. "I'm not as childish as you might think."

I turned away just as something hit me in the face. Spotting a popcorn rolling down the floor, I spun back to Will.

"Hey! Did you just-?"

"Shh," he put a finger to his lips and nodded at the screen. "Trailers are on. They're my favourite part."

When the movie started, I tried to enjoy it. There were some comedic parts, but mostly it was cheesy and predictable. Not the type of move that I'd usually go for. I was surprised that Will had gone for it. He didn't seem to be enjoying it at all–if he wasn't yawning, he was slapping his cheeks to try and stay awake. Now and then, he'd whisper an observation into my ear, and I'd laugh.

"If they like each other so much, why don't they admit it?" He'd say. Or, "Isn't miscommunication the most annoying trope in movies? If they were just honest with each other, none of this mess would've happened."

I had to agree with him there. Nothing frustrated me more than someone saying what they thought the other wanted to hear instead of being honest with themselves.

About halfway through the movie, I realised that I'd eaten most of the chocolates. Putting the bag in the middle– and hoping Will wouldn't chastise me for hogging them later–I reached for the popcorn.

My fingers brushed against Will's. I probably should've pulled my hand away or laughed it off, but instead, my fingers froze into place. It didn't escape my notice that Will's did the same. I stared resolutely at the screen, not paying any attention to what happened, and tried to steady my breathing. But my heart rate quickened as if Will's touch was a shot of adrenaline. I felt it course through me, starting at my fingertips and moving to someplace deep within.

And then Will's finger curled around mine. He kept it like that for a second, but then he moved across to another finger, tracing patterns up and down before locking our hands into place.

That was too much for me to handle. Feeling a strange current in the air, I quickly swiped my hand away, grabbing a handful of popcorn as a guise. After popping it into my mouth, I curled my hands into my lap and leaned to the side. I hoped the added distance would somehow evaporate whatever force this was that deluded me into thinking I wanted to be closer.

For the rest of the movie, it took every ounce of my effort to concentrate on what was happening. Even that wasn't enough. Actors appeared on screen who I didn't recognise, and conversations took place that didn't make sense. I was so painfully aware of Will's presence that it felt as if only he and I existed in the theatre. We were alone, and that intimacy made me crave something I never expected to want.

Will's hand now rested on the armrest, palm faced upwards. I eyed it for a second before twisting my body away, trying again to concentrate on the movie. My eyes wandered back to it every other minute as if by some pull that I was too weak to fight. His hand still rested there, palm upward. I wondered if he kept it there because he wanted me to hold it. But why would I do that?

Then I remembered our day in London when he'd held my hand in a strictly platonic manner. Wouldn't it be that way now? And it'd been nice having his hand to hold. So why not again?

I moved my hand to the armrest, stopping at its edge. I wasn't daring enough to go straight in with the handholding, platonic or not. When bravery returned to me, I slowly moved my hand closer to his, chickening out at the last second. But as I moved my hand back to my side, Will's caught it.

I looked down, watching as our fingers entwined together. As he moved our hands closer to the middle, I met his eye. All he did was smile, yet the butterflies in my stomach went wild. I wondered if Will could hear them flapping their wings about in there. Blushing, I turned my eyes back to the screen.

When the movie ended, Will released my hand so that he could collect our rubbish. I stretched my fingers, not quite liking the empty feeling, and stood.

"So, what did you think?" he asked.

I realised he was talking about the movie, but I had no idea what it'd been about, never mind what I thought.

"Um… it was good." I hoped he didn't need more detail than that. "What did you think?"

"It was alright," he smiled, leading us out of the theatre.

The butterflies were still having a party in my stomach, but something felt… off. I couldn't put my finger on why I felt so unsettled.

When we were outside, walking side-by-side, I realised what it was.

The butterflies weren't due to excitement anymore. They were now due to fear.

I was scared that something was changing between Will and me, terrified that our relationship was redirecting its course to a place we couldn't return from. How stupid of me to think that holding hands inside a dark movie theatre was something friends do. How silly of me to have put my hand there to start.

Did I believe Will had feelings for me? No, absolutely not. But that's what made it so scary. I didn't understand why he was doing these things. I didn't even know if *he* understood why he did them. I only knew one thing: we'd both get hurt if I allowed myself to fall for him.

Isn't that what he'd said from the start? *Don't fall for me. Things will get complicated.* Except it was so much more than that now. I knew we would've gotten over the awkwardness if we'd hooked up in the first weeks. But since then, Will had become my best friend. I didn't think I'd be able to get over losing him.

Somehow, we made it home. I was too caught up in my thoughts to register where I was walking, so I was surprised when our garden gate appeared before me. Will entered first. As I followed him into the house, I realised he hadn't said a word the entire walk home either. I peeked at his face, curious, and saw that his brows were knitted together as if in deep thought.

I hung my coat up, still carefully watching him. He seemed to be untying his shoelace, except he looked too absentminded for even that task. "Do you want a drink?" I asked.

He blinked up at me. "Hmm?"

"Do you- want a drink?"

"Yeah, er, I'll-" he shook his head. "Actually, I'm fine. I need to take a walk." Jumping to his feet, he moved passed me and headed out the door.

I watched him disappear in confusion. Had I upset him somehow?

No, I didn't think I'd done anything wrong. Ignoring the uneasy feeling settling in my stomach, I slowly walked upstairs. I didn't want to think about why Will might need to go for a walk. I didn't want to think about what played so heavily on his mind or if it was connected to him holding my hand. Sucking in a deep breath, I sat on the edge of my bed. I was there for a while, just staring at the floor when Will appeared in the doorway.

"Hey," he breathed. "Can I talk to you for a minute?"

I moved my eyes over his face, taking in his bright, agitated expression. Taking a second to calm a sudden onslaught of nerves, I nodded and followed him downstairs.

CHAPTER TWENTY-FIVE

We were standing in the hallway. I wasn't sure why we'd chosen here to talk, but I wondered if Will's nerves prevented him from moving further. He seemed anxious, which, in turn, made me feel the same way. I rubbed at my arms as I waited for him to speak, wondering where to place my eyes.

We stood across from each other. Considering the narrowness of the hallway, we weren't that far apart. I could reach out and touch him if I wanted to. This didn't help. I could see the stress in Will's eyes and almost hear the thoughts whirling around in his brain. Part of me wanted to run, but I forced myself to stay glued in place. I had to listen to whatever he had to say.

"So," Will said, exhaling a deep breath. "Wow, this is harder than I thought." He scratched the back of his head and looked down at the floor.

"What, are you breaking up with me or something?" I joked. It probably wasn't the most appropriate joke to make, but it helped ease the tension.

Will's lips twitched. "To do that, we'd need to be dating.

Which brings me to my point," he sucked in another deep breath, and then his voice turned suddenly ardent. "Dani, I don't know if this will come as a huge surprise or if I'm an idiot for saying it, but I have to tell you. I love-"

"Don't." The word came out before I could stop it. Unable to hold Will's eyes, I looked down at the floor, curling into myself. "Don't," I said again. I knew what he was about to say, and it was about to change everything.

"I love you," he finished.

I couldn't explain the effect these three words had on me. I felt impossibly happy and terrified at the same time. Closing my eyes, I tried to sort through my jumbled emotions and make some kind of sense of it all.

"I love you, too," I said eventually, swallowing as I re-met his eyes. "You're my best friend. Of course, I love you."

"No," he shook his head. "I don't love you as a friend, Dani. I love you as more than that." His eyes bore into mine, burning with an intensity that almost melted me.

For a moment, I allowed myself to imagine what it'd be like to be with Will in that way, to hold him, kiss him, and be kissed by him. I realised that I wanted that. Realised it with a sudden fierceness that almost knocked me off my feet. But there was also this other vision that couldn't be ignored.

I couldn't forget how Will was with girls. Since I'd known him, all I'd ever seen was him having one-night stands or flings. Or nothing. Because he didn't commit to a relationship. Yes, I knew he'd had his heart broken previously, and he struggled to trust it to anyone else. But how on earth was I any different?

Suddenly, another vision forced its way into my mind. I

pictured the moment which would inevitably arrive when Will realised that he no longer wanted to be with me. Either he'd get bored, decide he just wanted it to be another fling, or he'd realise that I wasn't all that much. Whatever the reason, we'd eventually break up. Would our friendship survive that?

"Please don't do this," I whimpered.

"Why not?"

"Because you don't date girls, Will!" My voice came out louder than I expected, but I was frustrated. He was ruining *everything*. "You don't," I continued, calmer but still upset. "You just have a fling and then move on to the next because God forbid you catch any feelings. I know you've been hurt before, and I get it. But what makes *me* any different? Who's to say you won't get afraid and push me away? What happens then?" I searched his eyes, in desperate need of an answer.

"That won't happen," he said quietly.

"But how do you know that?"

"Because it's you!" He closed the distance between us in one swift, sudden movement, lowering his forehead until it leant against mine. His eyes burned with a fire that I could *feel*–deep in my soul. "Was I afraid when I realised how I felt about you? Yes. But it's *you*. The one person I could never allow myself to hurt." He leaned back. "Believe me, Dani, I've thought this through. Can I walk away from you? No. Will I push you away? Absolutely not. Can I go on pretending that I'm not crazy in love with you? Tried that and failed." He exhaled slowly. "So, I'm afraid I do have to do this."

We stared at each other for an unfathomable length

of time. When Will swept his thumb across my cheek, I realised, with surprise, that I was crying.

"What are these for?" he asked with a frown. Even if I knew the answer, I didn't think I could trust my voice. "Listen," he moved his hand back to my shoulder, his voice serious again. "Before I met you, I couldn't imagine getting into another relationship or settling down. I can admit that. But that's because I hadn't met *you*," he gave me a gentle, loving squeeze. It nearly broke me. "Not only have you become my closest friend, but you're also this person that I can't stop thinking about. I look forward to seeing you in the morning; I hate it when you're not home; breakfast somehow tastes better when I eat it with you, and when you go to your room at night, all I want to do is join you. And that's not to have sex with you," he added quickly, seeing the look on my face. "But to be with you for longer." He sucked in a steadying breath. "I guess what I'm trying to say is that, somewhere down the line, I fell in love with you, and now I do want all that."

A silence settled over us. I could tell he was waiting for me to say something, but my brain had turned mushy. I couldn't think anything through the wall of nothing.

"Dani?" he asked nervously. "Are you going to say anything?"

I still hadn't found my voice as I struggled to process everything he'd said. Will was *in love* with me? *Me?* That was far deeper than anything I'd ever expected to hear from him. I just couldn't fathom it.

"I'm sorry if this is too soon," Will's words rolled out quickly. He seemed to be getting more nervous by the second. "But how do you feel about me? Do you see me as more than a friend?"

The truth was that I didn't know how I felt. Not really. Will was special to me–that much I did know. But I hadn't allowed myself to develop that kind of feeling for him, or, if I started to, I'd shove it someplace deep down, terrified by it. How was I supposed to know if what I felt was love? This was too soon. I was too on the spot. I couldn't possibly answer that kind of question right here, right now, with Will waiting.

But I didn't want to hurt him.

"I don't know," I answered carefully. "I don't know how I feel about you." Pain flashed across Will's face. I hated seeing it. Everything was changing, and it was out of my control. "I'm sorry," I choked, the panic rising. Tears blurred my vision as I searched frantically for the right words to say. "It's just... when I moved in, you told me not to fall for you, so I didn't allow it. I don't want to lose you." My voice broke at the end.

"Hey, hey," Will moved closer. He wrapped his arms around me, pulling me into an embrace. "You'll never lose me. Don't think I won't still be your friend because you don't feel the same way. It's my fault for being a jerk at the start. I did this to myself." He stroked my hair soothingly. "Nothing needs to change. If you need me as a friend, I'll be your friend. And if you decide you want something more, I'll be that, too. I can wait."

"But that isn't fair on you," I mumbled with my face nestled against his chest. "What if I never see you as more than a friend?"

I felt him smirk into my hair. "We'll see about that."

I pulled away enough to see that smug look in his eye. "Okay, now you're just being cocky."

"Not cocky," he disagreed. "Just confident."

"Do you think you can conquer me or something?" Will flinched, and I immediately regretted saying it.

"I'm not trying to conquer you," he said. "If I've learnt anything, it's that I've never felt anything close to this before. It doesn't matter to me if you like me back. Sure, I'd prefer it, but what matters is that you're happy. Believe me, if I was trying to conquer you, I would have done it already."

That last sentence ruined it.

"You know," I said, raising a brow, "you almost had me then."

He chuckled. "Damn it."

"And I know exactly how I feel. Tired. I'm going to bed." I spun towards the stairs, but he caught my hand, stopping me from escaping.

"Wait."

I looked down at the hand gently holding mine and fought back the butterflies. Those damned butterflies. "What?" I asked, refusing to meet his eye.

"Do you have to go to bed now? We could watch a movie?"

"Night, Will." I pulled away and fled up the stairs, in desperate need of thinking time. "And stop wishing you could join me!" I called once I reached the top.

"I confess my feelings to her, and she teases me," I heard him mutter. The living room door closed a few seconds later.

The next day, I awoke without having thought about it. Each time I tried to think about Will's confession or assess my feelings about it, a sudden wave of embarrassment hit me and made me scrunch my eyes closed.

So, when I eventually mustered up the courage to go downstairs, I still wasn't ready to see him.

Hearing the TV in the living room, I paused outside the door. My fingers hovered above the handle, but I was too cowardly to twist it. This was going to be awkward. This was going to be painful. How could I possibly face him?

"Good morning."

I jumped at the sound of Will's voice, which didn't come from the room I expected, but from beside me.

"G-good morning," I stuttered, pressing myself against the wall. Why did I have to sound so freaked out when *he* seemed fine? *He* didn't seem to be embarrassed at all.

He had a hot drink in his hand. With a grin, he moved toward me, annoyingly unfazed by my presence. Weren't people who confessed their love supposed to feel *some* embarrassment?

I moved back as he opened the door, and then I followed him into the living room.

"What are your plans today?" he asked, taking his seat on the sofa as I lingered by the door.

"Oh, you know, this and that." I pretended to examine my nails.

"This and that, huh? Can I be included in this and that, or are you too busy?"

"Definitely too busy," I nodded, although it was an outrageous lie.

"Really?" The way he said it told me he saw right through me. I peeked to find him with his brow raised, looking at me like I amused him. "What are you so busy with?"

"I have a date," I lied. *Why would you tell him* that *lie?* "I don't have a date," I quickly confessed. "I have no idea why I said that."

He let out a laugh. "Relax, Dani. There's no need to be so awkward. If you have a date, you have a date."

I blinked. "Is that all?" I wasn't sure what I'd expected. Maybe a little more devastation? Wasn't he supposed to be at least a little bit sad if I were going on a date?

"What do you mean?" he asked.

My surprise made the words roll out. "No 'please don't go on a date,' 'please stay with me,' 'I'm in love with you?'"

His lips twitched. "Do you want me to say that?"

"No."

"I will if you want me to."

"I don't."

He laughed and jumped to his feet. "Stop acting weird, Scott. I've told you I like you, so I'm good now. And I've also told you that you don't need to like me back, so you can go on dates if you want. We're good." He kissed my forehead and circled around me, leaving the room.

"Sure thing, Lovett," I mumbled, but I didn't think he heard it.

I walked to the middle of the room and realised I had no idea what I was doing. Disgruntled, I went back into the hallway and grabbed my coat.

"I'm off out," I called.

"Have fun."

I didn't know where I was going, but I walked down the street feeling like I needed to go somewhere. What I really wanted was to talk to someone. My first choice would be Will, but I couldn't speak to him about this. Not when it was *about* him.

I guessed that left Holly.

I headed to her house, arriving at her doorstep unannounced.

"What are you doing here?" she asked, opening the door in her PJs.

I bounced on the balls of my feet. "Can I come in?" I asked. "I really need some advice."

Clueless, Holly moved aside and let me past. She walked silently behind me as I made my way to her kitchen, only talking after she'd closed the door.

"So what advice can I help you with? And why did you need to come all the way out here for it?"

"Where's Nick?" I needed to know this information before divulging my important and super-secretive news.

"He's in the front room watching football."

Some things never changed. I pulled out a chair and sat down. "I need your help, Holly. I'm in a predicament."

She immediately stood up straight, hand flying to her throat. "What's wrong?"

"Nothing's... wrong," I said, trying to figure out how best to explain it to her.

Sitting beside me, she grabbed my hand. "It's okay. Whatever it is, you can tell me."

I took a moment to appreciate still having her in my life. "It's just…," I sighed, hardly believing what I was about to tell her. "Will confessed that he's in love with me."

Her mouth dropped open. "*What*?"

"I know! He told me last night, and I have no idea what to do about it. Everything feels so weird."

"And you're surprised by it?"

I frowned. They weren't the words I expected to hear from her. "What do you mean?"

"It's so obvious he's in love with you. I saw that when I met him. It actually took him longer than I thought to tell you… Oh, come on, Dani," her voice turned exasperated. "Don't tell me you didn't know?"

"It came as a huge surprise! I'm telling you that he's in love with me, Holly. *In. Love.*"

"It's deep," she agreed. "But not surprising."

I jumped to my feet. "Now I really, *really* don't know what to do." I paced the floor. "He's asked me how I feel in return, but I don't know how I feel. Do I feel the same way back? I mean, I *do* love him, of course. But I'm not sure it's the way he wants. What the hell do I do about that? If we give this a go, what if it goes wrong? *I don't date!* I-" I heard a giggle coming from Holly and paused. I had to watch her for a second to be sure I'd heard it right. "This is not a laughing matter, Holly," I said, swatting her arm.

"Of course, you're in love with him!" She giggled again. "I can't believe you're actually questioning it!"

"Excuse me?"

"Think about it," she pulled me back into the seat beside her. "Aren't you always doing stuff together? Don't you talk about him when you're not? Don't you worry about him?"

"Yes, but I worry about you, too." My phone buzzed. I looked down, seeing Will's name flash on my screen. The smile crept onto my lips involuntarily. I quickly wiped it away, but she'd already seen it.

"Who's that?" she asked, smiling in the smuggest of ways.

"Oh, you know," I hedged. "A person."

"A person whose name begins in *W*?"

"Okay, fine. But that doesn't prove anything."

"It proves *everything*. Do you smile when *I* text you? Do you miss *me* when *I'm* not around?"

"I'm not in love with Will!" I stressed. "I'm not, okay? I'm..." I looked up at the ceiling as a strange thought occurred to me. It felt like a current had come to sweep me from one place to another. A place of comfort for something unknown. This new place scared me, but as I got closer, I saw its beauty, and I wanted to reach out and touch it.

For a long time, I'd told myself that Will was just a friend. But that was because, deep down, I never believed we could be anything more. And I was okay with that. I was okay with just being his friend because even that was the best thing I'd ever experienced. But now, knowing what I knew about his feelings toward me, I couldn't deny it any longer.

At some point, I'd fallen in love with him.

"Oh my God," I put my hand over my mouth, my cheeks burning at this newfound realisation. "I think I am in love with him."

Holly laughed. "And the penny drops!"

I pushed out of my chair, jumping to my feet again.

"Why do you look so crimson?" Holly asked. "It's only

Will."

"But he's not just Will anymore! He's- he's-" I shook my head as the panic built up. "He's the Will who I'm suddenly imagining myself kissing. He's the Will whose hand I want to hold and whose arms I want around me. He's the Will who I don't just love but am actually in love with! Oh my goodness," I began pacing the room, using my hands to fan myself as though I were a computer overloading. "I'm freaking out over here. I. Am. Freaking. Out."

"Dani, calm down," Holly grabbed hold of me, pulling me to a stop. "You are okay. There's no reason to freak out."

I didn't believe her.

"Oh no, no, no, no, no. What am I going to do? What am I going to say to him?" I met Holly's eye, desperate for an answer.

"Relax," she said, speaking in the calm, authoritative tone of someone used to freak-outs. "He's already confessed to you, hasn't he?" I nodded. "So, he's done the hard part. All you need to do is tell him you feel the same way. You can do that, can't you?"

Thinking about Will, probably still at home, gave me enough courage to nod. I knew that my lack of reciprocation didn't seem to bother him, and, in a way, it probably didn't– but there had to be some part of him that felt wounded by my response. But he didn't need to feel wounded–because I *did* feel the same way. "I need to go," I said, bolting to the door. "Thank you so much for listening to me. I'll keep you updated!" Feeling the urge to hurry, I raced out, bumping into Nick on my way to the exit.

"Hi, Nick! Bye Nick!" I zoomed past him, unfazed by his

displeasure with my presence.

Once outside, I didn't slow my pace. If Will felt even the tiniest bit hurt right now, I needed to fix it. Fast.

And the only way to do that was to tell him how I felt.

CHAPTER TWENTY-SIX

All I could do was stare at the front door.

Where had my courage gone? Where was the Dani who wanted to stop Will from hurting?

She'd been defeated. Defeated by gut-wrenching nerves, the kind I'd never felt before. Not even in the run-up to an exam. They twisted in my stomach, wiping clean whatever brief courage I'd managed to find back at Holly's house. I wanted to run and hide. I did not want to walk through that door and confess to Will that I was in love with him. That thought made me want to pack my bags and leave the country.

Get a grip of yourself, I thought fiercely. *Or would you prefer never to tell him?*

I sucked in a deep breath, which did nothing to calm my nerves, and reached for the handle. It started to twist before I'd even touched it. I frowned, wondering how that was possible, and then saw Will on his way out.

I jumped back as he appeared in the doorway. *Yes, I would prefer never to tell him!*

"Oh, hey," he said, stepping out. "You're back?"

"Yep." I looked at a nearby bush, unable to meet his eye. My heart suddenly thumped. "Heading somewhere?"

"Yeah, I told Tae I'd help him pick out a suit because I thought you wouldn't get back for a while. Should I stay?"

"No, no. You should go!" I met his eye for the first time. Mine were wide with panic, and it didn't go amiss.

"Is everything alright?" he frowned.

"Everything's great," I edged past him toward the door, hoping to disappear inside. He turned with me. "Why wouldn't it be?"

"I don't know... you just seem weird." His frown deepened. "This isn't because I told you I'm in love with you, is it?" he asked, his eyes remaining locked on mine. "Because I told you it doesn't matter if you don't feel the same way. It doesn't need to be weird."

"Pfft," I waved my hand like I couldn't be less affected. In truth, my stomach whirled with butterflies at hearing him say *I'm in love with you* again. He made it seem so easy. "It isn't weird," I continued, my voice sounding horribly false. "I'm just... in desperate need of the toilet."

His lips pressed into a line. After a second of silence, I realised he was holding back a laugh. "Alright," he said, successfully keeping the laughter at bay. "You do what you need to do. I'll see you later."

He turned away, leaving me to cringe both internally and externally. "Bye."

With Will gone, I had no one to stop me from freaking out. At least with him here, I would've tried to hold it back, although I probably would've failed miserably. I raced upstairs to my bedroom, pacing the floor as if it were a new habit of mine.

How had he done it? How had he told me so easily that he was in love with me when I couldn't seem to get a single word of it out?

But you have to tell him, I reminded myself. *You have to because otherwise, it isn't fair.*

As I waited for him to get home, I told myself, over and over, that I could do this. I absolutely *could* tell Will that his feelings were mutual. Of course, I could. Because if he could say it to me, why not I to him?

Hearing him in the kitchen, I entered tentatively. "So," I began, wondering how best to broach the topic of being in love. "Did Tae find a suit?" Yep, that ought to do it. The perfect opener for telling someone you love them.

"Oh, yeah," he glanced over his shoulder at me before returning to pouring himself a drink. "It's nice. Nice enough that I was convinced into buying one for myself."

"*You* bought a suit?" I eyed the bag on the counter, trying not to picture Will in a well-fitted suit. Or think about how his muscles would look in it.

"Yup. I'm probably never going to wear it, but who knows?"

I nodded even though he wasn't looking at me to see it. "Listen, Will," I said, preparing myself to confess the hardest and deepest thing I'd ever confided in my life. *You can do this.* "About what you said-"

He turned to face me, drink in hand, immediately cutting off my ability to continue. Had he always looked this beautiful? "Yeah?" he prompted.

I couldn't handle this face-to-face. I spun around,

realising that, in actuality, I couldn't handle this at all. "Never mind."

"You're acting weird again," he accused.

"No, I'm not."

"Then why aren't you looking at me?"

I turned, putting on a calm mask that contradicted the erratic beating of my heart. "I was just thinking that if you're never going to wear the suit, why don't you show it to me now?"

"That's not what you were thinking."

I wished I weren't so easy to read. "Yes, it was. I was just too embarrassed to say it."

He narrowed his eyes. "You actually want to see me wearing it?"

"Will in a suit, why wouldn't I?" I held his stare, but it took everything within me to do it.

"Okay," he shrugged, placing his drink on the counter. "At least someone will get to see it." He proceeded to lift up his shirt.

Realising that he was about to strip right here, right in front of me, I quickly extended my hand. "What are you doing?" I protested.

He paused, looking at me with an innocence that didn't quite match the mischievous sparkle in his eyes. "What do you mean?"

"Go and get changed somewhere else!" I could *not* see shirtless Will right now.

He pulled his shirt down and swooped up the bag, smirking as he passed me. I gulped, fearing he somehow knew my thoughts. That I both wanted to see Will half-naked, but if I did, I'd probably explode on the spot.

When Will swept back into the kitchen, I hadn't moved.

One look at him had me crumbling at my knees.

Nothing could have prepared me for Will in a suit. My already thrashing heart beat faster as my eyes roamed over every glorious inch of him. He didn't just look hot; he looked… *gorgeous*. Mindbogglingly, out of this world, *gorgeous*. It made my body react in ways I didn't expect.

The suit was a deep green, woven with flecks of gold that reminded me of the sun casting soft shimmers across the surface of a rainforest. It was thick, like tweed, but moulded around muscles I hadn't known existed before now. Will stood with his legs slightly apart, lean and strong, with his hair ruffled like he'd run a hand through it several times already.

"So," he said, moving from one foot to the other, "how does it look?"

I realised my mouth hung open and quickly closed it.

"It's-" my voice came out embarrassingly hitched. I tried again. "It's… nice." Nice was an understatement, but I wasn't about to tell him what I really thought.

That puzzled look returned to Will's face. Whatever he saw as he examined me made his lips fall a little. "You hate it."

"No!" I quickly shook my head. "You look…" *gorgeous, sexy, unfairly beautiful.* "Look…" *like someone I want to see without clothes on.* "I'm sorry."

His frown deepened. "What?"

I shook my head when I realised I'd apologised for

something I hadn't said aloud. "I need to go." I rushed past him, swerving away from his hand as he reached for me.

"Wait, Dani, what's the matter?"

He followed after me, but I shoved on my shoes and bolted from the house before he could begin to understand why I did it.

My many attempts at telling him how I felt went about as successfully as the first time.

I became nervous. A downright jittery wreck. And, as the week went by, things got out of control. My nerves meant that I couldn't be myself around Will. Which, in turn, meant that I avoided him at all costs.

Avoiding him came easy at work since that's what we did anyway. But I did catch him looking at me in puzzlement more than once. I'd just look down at my desk and pretend I hadn't noticed.

Once, toward the end of the week, he'd gently grabbed my hand and pleaded to speak with me. Luckily, no one was around, but the desperation in his eyes almost had me following him into an empty pod. Then I'd remember him in his suit, and my cheeks would burn at the thought of being so close to him. Of confessing my feelings to him. I'd flee back to my desk and stay glued there for the rest of the day like the coward I was.

Avoiding him at home came harder. Impossible, even– because I needed to leave my room at some point, whether for food, drink, or the bathroom. Vigilance aided me. I'd only use the bathroom if I knew Will was downstairs, and I'd make food as soon as I got home before he returned. If I did bump into him, I'd come up with some excuse to quickly get out of there.

But the hardest part wasn't avoiding him–it was how much I *missed* him while doing it. By the end of the week, I was practically pulling my hair out because we'd barely said more than two words together. It was all my fault, of course. But there was a nervousness inside me, an unexplained giddiness and my-heart-won't-stop-racing-ness that increased tenfold whenever Will was around. I thought I'd explode from being in the same room as him.

I threw myself into work. The illustrations Chrissie had asked from me were well on their way to getting done, and my game demo for the competition slowly edged toward completion.

I was sitting at the kitchen table, distracted by work, when hands came thundering down onto the counter.

I started, more surprised at seeing Will in front of me than at his outburst, as he turned to look at me with eyes that could only be described as tortured.

"I can't take this anymore," he said with a strained voice.

"Why aren't you at work?" Indeed, that was the only reason I was in here with my guards down. Finn had told me they were all working late.

"Oh, you'd like that, wouldn't you?" He sounded uncharacteristically sardonic. "You'd prefer me to be anywhere than around you, right?"

Something on my face must've told him he'd hit the nail on the head because his features suddenly twisted. I wondered if, until this moment, his fear had just been suspicion. And now I'd just confirmed it.

I chewed on my bottom lip. "That isn't the case."

"Oh yeah?" he pushed away from the counter, taking a step toward me. "Then do you mind if I sit here?" My eyes followed as he pointed to the chair opposite me. Before I could answer, he ran a hand through his hair and spun away again. His knuckles turned white as he gripped the edge of the counter. "I should not have told you how I felt," he said, his hair ruffling as he shook his head. "That's why you're avoiding me, isn't it?" he turned his gaze on me. Once again, I saw the pain in his eyes.

My throat clogged up. "Will, that's not…,"

"Idiot." He ducked his head. "I was an idiot for telling you how I felt and putting you in this situation. Now you can't even be in the same room as me."

At that moment, I realised what a horrible mistake I'd made by avoiding him. I'd been selfish, and that selfishness had caused him pain. Will had been brave by being honest with his feelings, by being honest with *me*, and I'd kept him in the dark about my own. In doing so, I'd made him feel like he was wrong to confess. When he should never, *ever* think for one second that it's better to stifle his feelings than express them.

Coward. Coward. Coward. I got to my feet, unable to take his pain any longer.

"Will," I said, extending my hand. I placed it on his shoulder. "I'm sorry." He twisted to look at me, his head still ducked. "You're right. I have been avoiding you. But that's on *me*, not you. I'm glad you told me how you felt, but it's made me… flustered. A downright nervous wreck. It's not often someone tells me they're in love with me, you know.

Even less often that I live with the person who does." I smiled gently, wanting badly to see one on his lips.

They did tug up a little. "Flustered, huh?"

"Oh, so flustered. I've been having heart palpitations all week."

He chuckled. "I made the great Dani Scott flustered. That's got to count for something, right?" he straightened. "I get it. It's a big bomb to have dropped on you, and you need time to adjust. Just please…" he closed his eyes for a second. "Stop avoiding me. I'd rather get rejected than that."

A flicker of pain returned to his face.

I gripped his hand. "I won't avoid you anymore. Okay? I won't." I waited until I saw the pain disappear before continuing. "So, now that you know it was just a healthy dose of nerves, should we get back to normal? Fancy a movie night?"

His lips pulled up some more. "Only if I get to choose the movie."

Twenty minutes later, we sat in the front room with snacks sprawled across the table and the lights dimmed. Will sat beside me, and I didn't object. I liked the closeness. I wanted the closeness.

As he flicked the movie on and settled back, his hand falling beside him, the memory of our trip to the cinema flooded my mind. I hadn't watched the film back then because I'd been too distracted by whatever energy pulsated between us. And he'd held my hand, his warm, gentle touch causing my skin to shiver in a way I never thought possible. The darkness had been like a blanket… safe, comforting, *daring*. The soft glow of the living room had a similar effect.

I gulped, feeling that strange energy stir again. My eyes darting to his hand, I wondered if I should hold it like he'd held mine. I wanted to. I yearned to. Moving my eyes back to the TV, I willed myself to do it. Wasn't this the perfect time to not just tell but to *show* him how I felt?

That time, he'd held my hand.

This time, I would hold his.

My heart thundered as I reached out slowly, my fingers making their way to what I knew would feel like home.

The first touch was electric–like a current had literally shot through my fingertips. My breathing hitched, and I swear Will froze with me.

But then he relaxed, allowing his fingers to curl around mine. We kept our eyes on the screen, breathing heavy, as our hands found their home. Using his other hand, Will began to trace lazy patterns up and down my arm.

I struggled to breathe again. I had to concentrate on keeping the rhythm steady–in, out, in, out–but the air got caught in my throat like I was bracing for something. I exhaled slowly, and then I caved, allowing my impulses to take control of my body. They guided my every movement. Wanting the space between us to disappear, I shifted so that our arms touched and our legs pressed flush against each other.

I still hadn't looked at him yet. But I wanted to. I wanted to watch his face far more than I wanted to watch the movie. To read his eyes, his expression... to see his lips.

Releasing a steadying breath, I turned to face him. My breath caught when I found him looking back at me with eyes so longing, I thought I'd lose it. But again, I exhaled slowly, allowing the process to steady me. Will seemed to be doing something similar. His eyes moved down to my lips, and then he raised his hand, reaching out to tuck my hair behind my ear. He kept it rested there, cupping my cheek, his touch like fire as he brushed his thumb across my cheekbone.

His eyes stayed glued to my lips as he leaned toward me. Mine fluttered closed. Impatience flared within me as I waited for the moment his lips would touch mine. They pressed softly against me, warm, tender, almost as if testing for something. More than anything, they felt *right*. I realised then that I'd never felt perfectly at ease before.

Far too soon, Will pulled away. I frowned, not ready for it to end, and his lips pulled up at one corner.

"Does this mean my feelings are mutual?" he whispered, leaning close to my ear.

A shiver ran through me. Nodding, I leaned back just enough to look into his eyes. "I'm in love with you, too."

His one-sided smirk turned into a full-blown smile, and then he kissed me with a crushing force that sent heat waves throughout my entire body. I leaned back, sinking into the sofa, and he lowered himself with me, our lips never breaking. Will's hand caught my head before it could hit the armrest, cushioning it against the hard edge. He reached for a pillow with his other hand, swapping it to free both hands. He leaned back just enough to pull off his hoodie.

"Is this alright?" he asked, pausing halfway up.

Silently, almost as if speaking would shatter something

precious, I nodded. Lifting my hand, I traced a finger down his torso, moving slowly down to the prominent V in awe. He shuddered, meeting my eye.

And then he was on me again. Kissing me, whispering my name, telling me he loved me. My body trembled as his hand moved beneath my sweater, sending fire blazing down my side.

How was it possible to love someone this much? To not only love who they are as a person, but to love every part of them. Their mind and their soul. Their flesh and their bone. *Everything.*

And to feel so at ease in their company, they become a part of you.

I leaned back enough to whisper, "I love you."

His eyes burned into mine, and then he planted the tenderest of kisses onto my lips. "I love you, too."

I could taste the words in my mouth. Taste him. It made me crave him more. My body yearned for him–my *soul* yearned for him–wanting him, wanting him, wanting him.

With a desperate desire to have him, I fisted my hands through his hair and ground against him. He released a low moan that sent ripples through me.

"Dani," he said, leaning back enough to look me in the eye. I could see the unspoken question burning within them–see the same desperate desire coursing through my veins.

"I want you," I choked in answer. "More than anything."

His eyes turned hungry. Running his hands beneath my sweater, he lifted it slowly. I leaned forward as he pulled it over my head, tossing it on the floor.

He moved to my lower half, removing my jeans with the same deliberate slowness, holding my eye the entire time.

"You're beautiful," he told me, moving up to kiss my lips again. I smiled against him. While I was well aware that I wasn't what many would describe as beautiful, coming from him, I believed it.

He removed his clothes next, and I felt my body come to life beneath the touch of his bare skin. Will, my best friend and so much more. I yearned for him. For all of him. He moved his kiss to my shoulder, my collarbone, my stomach. He kissed every inch of me as though he couldn't decide which part he wanted more. He stroked my hair, kissed my temple, the nape of my neck, all while moving his body against mine.

Fire burned through me. A fire that exploded and brought an ache between my thighs. I lifted my hips, wanting, needing, to be closer to him. His kiss deepened. He moved it downward, at first a gentle caress before becoming lightning, bringing my whole body to life.

"*Will*," my legs tightened around him, and he moaned, almost undoing me. Grabbing his arms, I pulled him upwards, wanting him closer somehow. Deeper.

He looked at me with hunger and love rolled into one. Sweat glistened in his brow, and I reached out to brush it with my thumb, stopping with my hand cupping his cheek.

"Should I get a condom?" he whispered, leaning into it.

My voice came out as breathless as his. "Yes." I leaned up to kiss him as he untangled himself from me. He deepened the kiss, continuing it for a moment before tearing himself away.

When he returned, that same look swirled in his eyes. He walked slowly towards me, aware, just as I was, of what we were about to do.

He repositioned himself between my legs.

"Let me know if you want me to stop, okay?"

As I felt him nudge against me, I reached up to cup his face in my hands. "I won't want that."

He pressed a soft kiss to my hand as he entered me.

"*Fuck*," he ducked his head, biting his bottom lip as he continued moving deeper. "It's never-" he moved deeper still, the bite on his lip hardening. "Felt like this before."

"I know what you mean," I lifted my hips to allow more of him, and my low moan came out with his.

He leaned down to press his forehead against mine. "I love you, Dani."

I leaned to the side to kiss his arm, and his grip on the sofa tightened, his bicep tensing. His slow rhythm became faster, and I rolled my hips with him, creating a rhythm that was ours and ours alone. I wondered why we hadn't found it sooner. Silly, afraid me. This was nothing to fear. Not with him. Not with us.

CHAPTER TWENTY-SEVEN

When I awoke in the morning, I was alone.

Still laying on the sofa, I had a blanket wrapped around me which hadn't been there when I'd fallen asleep. In Will's arms, I remembered with a shudder.

As my eyes adjusted to the light, the memories of last night came groggily back to me, and I smiled to myself.

Will had been gentle, sweet, and fierce all at once. Where was he now?

I lifted my head, panic building for a second as I searched for him. But he deserved more faith than for me to believe he'd bolted. As if to reward my trust, I heard a noise from the kitchen. Wrapping the blanket around me, I headed toward it, stopping to lean against the open door when I saw Will by the cooker.

"You're not going to ask me to kick myself out, are you?" I asked.

He turned, the smile on his face brighter than any I'd seen before. "Luckily for you, we have a contract which states I can't just kick you out. Otherwise, you'd already be out of here."

I snorted. "You couldn't get me past the front door."

"Is that a challenge?" he moved toward me, the smile on his lips predatory.

"Don't," I held up a finger in silent warning, but he was already sweeping me off my feet. I yelped as one arm swept beneath my knees while the other clasped my back. Will's cheeks were dimpled as he grinned down at me, his eyes dancing with playfulness. "Are you going to chuck me out?" I asked.

His chuckle came deep from his throat, and then he leaned down, planting a soft kiss on my lips. "I'd rather have you in here."

A blush crept up my neck, but before I could think of a reply, he winced in pain, placing me back down.

"What's the matter?" I asked, frowning as he rolled his neck.

"I didn't sleep in the best position last night."

I thought back, trying to remember exactly *where* he'd slept, but I couldn't remember anything past my own lids drooping closed. "Did you sleep on the sofa with me?" I asked in puzzlement. It was the last thing I remembered–falling asleep on his chest with his arms cocooning me.

"I did," he rolled his neck again. "And I didn't want to disturb you after you fell asleep, so I tried to stay still."

My heart turned to butter at the thought of him withstanding discomfort just so I wouldn't awaken. If it'd been the other way around, I probably would've kicked him off. "Move over," I said, nudging past him. I turned at the cooker, where he'd already started preparing something, and smiled. "Today, I make you breakfast."

While I worked, Will sat by the table and watched, smiling faintly.

"Do you not want to go up and shower?" I asked, thinking I'd be less likely to burn the sausages with him not here.

"I don't think I want to leave you."

My heart stuttered. "We'll probably both be late for work if one of us doesn't shower now."

"We could shower together," he suggested. I turned to raise a brow at him, and he laughed. "Right. Then we'd never leave." He wasn't wrong. "How about you shower first?" he suggested. "It doesn't matter if I'm late."

I tried not to think about Will in the shower as I finished cooking breakfast. His naked body dripping with water, his wet hair swept back...

"Here," I slid the food across to him, somehow managing not to burn it. "If we're both quick, neither of us will be late."

We left with barely any time to spare. Still, even with the pressure of time rushing us forward, we were smiling. I couldn't help mine. Not when Will had a huge grin on his face every time I looked at him. A grin that told me this might just be the happiest day of his existence.

"So," he said, using his thumb to stroke lazy patterns across the back of my hand. "I don't know if this is needed–after everything we've said, I mean–but I wanted to ask you anyway." His eyes met mine, and I knew I wanted to see these eyes for the rest of my life. "Will you be my girlfriend?"

What came out of my mouth was not at all representative

of the pleasure I felt.

"Did you just laugh?" he said, dropping my hand.

"I'm sorry!" I grabbed his hand again as he tried to stalk ahead. "It was a nervous laugh. Will, come one," I pulled him to a stop. He whirled on me, looking so disgruntled that I had to hold back another chuckle. "Would you ask me again?" I said. "*Please*?"

The blaze in his eyes made me doubt he would. But then he smirked, and that light danced across his face again. "Has that nervous laugh of yours ever gotten you in trouble?"

"More times than I can count."

His smirk deepened. "Will you be my girlfriend?"

Thankfully, I didn't laugh this time. Instead, I leaned up on my toes and planted a kiss on his lips. "Nothing would make me happier."

His eyes danced with delight. I stepped away, but his hand caught my back, pulling me toward him. My chest pressed against his midriff as he smiled down at me, the look on his face causing my breath to hitch. And then he kissed me with enough passion that, by the time I stumbled away from him, I was red-faced, wide-eyed and craving for more.

I looped my hand in his again as we started walking. His pace was quicker now, and I wondered if it was because he didn't want me to be late.

When we were close enough to the office that we were now in dangerous territory, we paused to look at each other.

Will's lips pulled down as he lifted our entwined fingers. "I wish we could go in together like this."

"Should we not just do it?" I asked, wanting the same

thing. "To hell with what people think?"

He shook his head. "That office is full of gossipers. It would make our lives harder if they knew about this." He met my eye. "But if you wanted to tell people, I would."

I shuddered at the thought of Finn knowing that I lived with Will. Or worst, at Chrissie. "No, you're right. It's nice having this privacy." I pulled my hand away and stepped back, even as my body screamed not to do it. "Do you think we'll be able to keep it a secret now that… you know… we're dating?"

He smiled at my use of the term. "We've managed to keep it together for this long, haven't we?"

And I knew he meant he'd had feelings for me since before now, and he'd still managed to keep them at bay at work. To draw the line.

"I'll head inside first," I said. "Don't be late!"

As seemed to be nearly always, Finn was outside the office when I got there. And as seemed to be nearly always, he spotted Will walking at a distance. It was frightening this ability of his.

We waited, and a large part of me felt happy to be walking in with Will in some form, even if we couldn't hold hands or be seen to have a deeper relationship. I caught his eye as we entered and clamped my teeth down to keep from smiling.

Inside the elevator, there was room enough to stand at opposite ends. We probably should've done that. I probably should've stridden straight to the far corner and turned my back on him. As it happened, I chose the space beside him, my desire to stay close too strong to fight. And while Finn flanked his other side, chatting about some work thing

I only half-heard, that strange energy stirred between us again. He shifted beside me, and I wondered whether he also felt it. His fingers brushed against mine, and I held my breath, fighting the urge to touch him outright. I could tell by the embers kindling within me that if I made one wrong move... all would be over.

I allowed Will and Finn to walk ahead when we stepped out of the elevator, needing a second to calm myself. The former glanced over his shoulder and offered me a knowing smile that in no way helped.

Sucking in a deep breath, I entered the office.

Chrissie immediately looked over at Will when he reached his desk, watching him with gleaming eyes as he hung up his jacket. I tried not to let it irk me so much. Being territorial was not something I admired.

"You're looking happier than usual today," she called out to him.

Will looked over his shoulder, careful not to glance at me, and grinned. "My roommate has become less bothersome."

I almost snorted. But when I noticed that the glint had left Chrissie's eyes, I quickly looked down at my desk.

About halfway through the day, Will sent me a text. *Why do I miss you when you aren't that far away?*

I looked up with a smirk, but I understood what he meant. We really weren't that far away, yet the distance felt magnified compared to how close we'd been the night before, bodies against each other on the sofa. Blushing at the thoughts now circling around my mind, I texted back, *And I thought you said this wouldn't be hard.*

Barely a heartbeat later, *Oh, it's hard. Very hard.*

I covered my mouth to hide the smile I was biting against before I texted back, *I have no words for you, Lovett. None.*

And here's me thinking I can never get you to shut up, Scott.

I glared up at him and saw that he was wearing his smile for all to see.

Perhaps this was going to be much, much harder than we thought.

It was ridiculously harder than we'd thought.

Keeping our relationship a secret at work now that we were actually *in* a relationship was a challenge, at best. An impossible mission, at worst. It was as if Will had somehow levelled up, and his pull was more alluring to me than ever. I used every ounce of my willpower to keep myself away from him. Even when my bones screamed in protest, even when that pull tugged hard against my chest.

But every time I saw him go to the kitchen, I wanted to follow. Whenever I caught him alone, I immediately wanted to be in his company. We were like two circling magnets, north and south, keeping just the right distance apart to stop us from snapping together.

It was actually a mystery how we *didn't* get caught. While we tried to be careful, sometimes the temptation became too intense to resist.

Will started it.

Perhaps our first elevator trip had caused quite the stir in him because the next time we were side-by-side, his fingers didn't just brush mine–they played with them. A mischievous cat toying with its prey. We kept casual about it, continuing our conversations like the other wasn't there… but I had to keep my breathing in check as my heart thumped in exhilaration. And if it wasn't the elevator… it was a sly whisper in my ear, a wink whenever we crossed paths, a kiss when nobody was around. I liked this game so much that I started to initiate it myself.

Until one day.

The office was already abuzz, particularly the first years, because we'd finally submitted our final game demos for the competition that morning. And to celebrate, our team leaders were taking us out for a meal after work, which we'd be finishing early.

I was happy because my demo was finally done, over, and I'd resisted any offer of help coming from Will. To keep me from doing anything mentally strenuous as a reward, Chrissie had assigned me the task of filing paperwork in the filing cabinet.

I stood on a stool, reaching for a higher-level folder when I lost my balance. Unable to get it back, I tumbled to the floor, the heavy folder clasped in my hand falling with me.

I heard a shout of panic coming from Will as the folder collided with my face.

He was by my side within seconds.

Swearing beneath his breath, he pulled me into a sitting position, brushing the hair from my face with shaking fingers. I saw the blood on his hands before he called over his shoulder, "I need a first aid kit! Now!" He turned back to me, eyes wide and full of fear. "Are you alright?" he asked with a jagged breath.

"I think so," I moved slightly, feeling several aches at once. "Although I've probably got a lot of bruises." He winced. "Where did that blood come from?" I asked, nodding at his hand.

"Your cheek," he brushed it gently with his thumb. "It's cut, but it doesn't look deep enough for stitches."

Somebody cleared their throat. Will whirled. From where I was positioned, still in his arms, I could see Jasmine standing nearby with a first aid kit. And in the office behind her... many eyes. Most panicked, some with a glint like they'd just been let in on the juiciest secret.

Will seemed to realise what he'd done then. He slowly removed his arms from around me, raising himself into a standing position. He cleared his throat. "I've never seen someone fall like that," he said as an excuse.

"Do you want to be the one to clear the cut?" Jasmine asked, holding the kit out to him.

"I think it would be more comfortable for Dani if you did it." He walked away, knowing full well it wouldn't be, yet needing to mend any damage he may have just caused.

Jasmine took me into an empty meeting room and away from prying eyes while she worked the first aid kit. I winced as she dabbed something wet on my cut.

She gave me a look of apology before observing, "I've never seen Will so worked up like that before."

It took me a second to form my response. "Has anyone ever fallen off a stool and had a folder smash into their face before?"

She smiled. "Fair point. But it's good to know that he cares for his colleagues."

Yes. That was how we could spin this. "I'd hate to think what he'd do if someone in his team fell," I joked. "He probably would've fainted."

Jasmine chuckled. "Are you hurt anywhere else?"

After assuring her I wasn't and getting a bandage stuck to my face, we returned to our desks. People voiced their concerns as I walked past, but it was Chrissie who I most worried about. While her face did nothing to indicate whether she thought anything about Will's earlier panic, she did seem quieter than usual.

I texted him, *Anyone seem suspicious about us?*

I almost snorted at his response. *The entire office now seems to think I'm some kind of hero who protects his co-workers. I hate it.*

You always were the office favourite. Why not add to it?

I tucked my phone away and prepared to leave for the restaurant.

As we made our way there, everyone but Will, it seemed, had forgotten about my fall. He still seemed slightly shaken, and his smile faded every time he looked at my cheek. I tried to laugh as much as possible to assure him I didn't feel pain.

At the restaurant, I managed to get a seat opposite him. Next to him might've been too suspicious, and Chrissie and Finn had already snagged those seats anyway. Again, I tried not to let Chrissie's obvious affections irk me.

Jasmine stood and raised her wine glass. "Congratulations on getting your demos submitted," she said, eyeing all of us first years. "I can't wait to test and vote on them. Cheers."

"Cheers," we all echoed, clinking glasses.

The food tasted delicious except for one thing: mushrooms. The chef had gone heavy on them. Which was fine–I could push them to the side without effort. But when I accidentally chewed on one, I had to swallow it down in disgust instead of spitting it out like I had that time with Will.

Who watched me now, I realised.

Something seemed to flicker in Will's memory because a second later, he reached across the table with his fork. Before I could stop him or find a discreet way to remind him that we were in public, he speared the pile of mushrooms on my plate and moved them across to his.

And then he seemed to remember where we were. Peeking up from his lashes with the mushrooms not far from his open mouth, he searched the table for any witnesses.

"Did you ask Dani if you could take her mushrooms, Will?" Jasmine said. She eyed him with a frown.

More eyes turned to us, taking in the mushrooms still hovering by Will's open mouth.

He rubbed the back of his neck and cleared his throat, cheeks turning pink. "Sorry about that," he made a weird laughing sound as he dropped the mushrooms back on my plate. "I just love them." He cleared his throat again, ducking his head as he took a bite out of his food.

I tried my hardest not to laugh. But one look over at Will, whose face burned red, had one bursting out of me.

"Here," Finn said, shuffling every mushroom he could find onto Will's plate. "You can have mine."

"Thanks, Finn," Will smiled, but I could see the pain behind it.

I almost laughed again.

CHAPTER TWENTY-EIGHT

I waited for Will around the corner of the restaurant. Or, to be more precise, I waited until enough time passed for him to slip out after me.

Out of sheer boredom, I touched the dressing on my cheek and winced at the sudden strike of pain.

"Are you alright?" Will asked. I turned to find him approaching me. He wore a frown on his face, a frown which told me he was remembering my fall and that folder hitting me.

I held back another wince. "I'm fine. Honestly. Jasmine did a great job at patching me up."

He leaned against the wall beside me and slid his hands into his pockets, reflective. After a moment, he said, "I'm sorry about my reaction. If anyone has any suspicions about us now, it's my fault."

His words tore a hole through me. Not because I was bothered about anyone suspecting, but... he sounded so guilty. "No one suspects anything," I assured him. "And you shouldn't apologise for caring. It felt... nice to have you by my side, worried for me."

His lips tugged up at that. "What would you have done if it'd been the other way around?"

"Oh, I would've left you for sure." He scowled, so I added, "There are plenty of people in that office who would've made sure that their precious Will didn't bleed to death."

His face was calm and poised as he said, "I'm only your Will."

Heat crept up my neck. I swallowed against a sudden urge to throw my arms around him as I said, "Now I know why you did so well with women. You're flirting is shameless."

He laughed. "I've actually never said that before. Or felt the need to say it."

"Really? Not even with-" I almost said *with your previous girlfriend*, but thankfully I had more sense than that. I didn't need to remind him of the girl who'd once broken his heart.

But he seemed to read the unfinished question on my face. "No, not even then," he answered, holding my stare. And I could see the honesty in his eyes. "I've never felt anything remotely like what I feel for you."

A weight that I hadn't known I'd been holding lifted. I took his hand in mine. "Should we go home?"

He stepped away from the wall with a devilish smile. "Please. I need to find a way to get you to like mushrooms before I die of embarrassment again."

When we got home, we both took turns using the bathroom to get ready for bed. I found Will waiting for me outside his bedroom door when I finished brushing my teeth.

"Goodnight," was all he said. But as I made the steps over

to my bedroom, I thought I could see unspoken words in his eyes.

I paused with my hand on the door handle. "Goodnight," I said, looking over at him.

He swallowed. "Do you want to stay with me tonight?"

The question was tentative, almost as if he feared my answer.

But I didn't want to leave him any more than he seemed to want to leave me.

I nodded. "Just let me get changed."

"Do you not want to wear something of mine?" His eyes danced as he waited for my answer.

I rolled my eyes, but a thrill ran through me at the thought of wearing something of his. Of *smelling* like him. "What is it with boys wanting women to wear their clothing?" I said, trying to feign calmness.

He shrugged. "It's... appealing."

I gulped. "Fine," I strode past him into his bedroom. "But it'd better be a top *and* bottom."

Once clad in a baggy t-shirt and joggers so long that they covered my heel, I crawled beneath the sheets. I didn't want to think about how different I looked from those girls in movies who somehow managed to pull off their partners' shirts. Or how *un*appealing I looked. Will didn't seem to think that, anyway.

He climbed into the space beside me. We glanced at each other with a sudden awkwardness that surprised me. I didn't think I could still feel that way around him.

But I supposed we'd never shared a room like this before. Or a bed.

Will's eyes shot away just as mine did. When our eyes met again, the awkwardness remained, but something else rumbled through me, escaping in a laugh. Will chuckled, bursting the tension like a knife slicing a balloon.

"This is awkward, isn't it?" I asked.

"Oh, yeah." He grinned, leaning back against his hand. "But it's something we'll get over. I like sharing this newness with you."

I slid down the bed, propping myself up on my elbow. "I never thought I'd be sharing a bed with you."

He glanced down. "I never thought so, either. I only wished it." After looking at me for a moment longer, his eyes shatteringly tender, he slid down until we were side by side, faces next to each other.

I held my breath as my heart rate picked up. Will leaned closer, his eyes on mine, and kissed me. I smiled as he pulled back, his eyes blazing. And then my treacherous mouth opened up into a yawn.

"You're tired," he said. Not a question.

"I'm not."

Will smirked, seeing the lie for what it was. Wrapping his arm around me, he twisted me to my other side, planting a kiss on the top of my hair. "You should sleep. You've been working late every night this week."

Just as my exhaustion hit me–finishing my game demo meant I'd barely slept–Will reached over to switch off the lamp. The room went dark.

I let my eyes flutter closed, savouring the warmth of his body moulded around mine. His hand, which had laid flat on my stomach, started stroking my skin. I felt his breath whisper against my neck as he kissed just below my ear, my jawline, my shoulder...

I arched into him. "You know I'm not going to want to sleep if you're doing that."

He chuckled but stopped kissing me. Instead, he stroked my arm, moving his finger in circular motions. He traced all the way to my side, my stomach, lower...I shivered. "Or that."

He smiled into my neck. "Do I really have that effect on you?"

I nudged him with my elbow and then spun to face him. Ignoring his surprise, I moved my fingers to his chest, gently caressing his neckline, his sculpted torso, lower, lower, lower...

His eyes turned hungry.

I smiled, raising a brow. "I seem to have the same effect on you." And then I turned back, smug.

Will heaved out a sigh and wrapped his arm around me again. "Point matched." He lifted my head gently to tuck his arm beneath me, wrapping me in a hug. "I could do this every night," he whispered.

I smiled. "Me too."

The smile stayed on my face as I finally drifted to sleep.

I let Will sleep in as I slipped out of bed and crept downstairs. It was already late morning, but he'd seemed so peaceful in his slumber that I didn't want to wake him.

Before I'd arisen, I'd allowed myself a minute of just savouring the sight of him. My eyes moved from his bed-strewn hair to his slightly parted lips and long, dark lashes.

I smiled as I flicked the kettle on. While I let my teabag stew, I was too caught up enjoying my thoughts to hear him enter the kitchen. He wrapped his arms around my stomach, kissing my cheek. "Good morning."

I smiled over my shoulder. "It's almost the afternoon, you know."

"Well, then, maybe we should go back to bed until it is. Or the evening. Or midnight."

"You want a bed day?" I raised a brow. "Don't try and be a bad influence on me, Will Lovett."

He opened his mouth to argue, but someone knocked on the door. We both looked toward the sound.

"I'll get it," I said, pushing past him. "You can finish the brews." He was much better at making them than me, anyway.

I swung the door open, fully expecting to see the mailman, and stumbled back at what I saw.

My mouth gaped open as Chrissie gawked back at me. She had a folder in her hand, her excuse to drop by to see Will on a weekend. I wanted to run away and hide, but I knew it was useless. She'd already seen me.

I had no words to say. No explanation as to why I was here. But her eyes raked over me, undoubtedly coming up with her own explanation. And I knew what she saw.

Will's clothes.

I was still wearing Will's clothes.

This was bad.

"Who's here?" Will appeared behind me, far too close for us to spin this as anything but what it was. The look on his face as he beheld Chrissie was enough to tell me how bad this was. "Chrissie…"

She spun on her heel, running out of the garden so fast that neither of us had the chance to try and stop her.

"Chrissie, wait!" Will shoved on some trainers and chased after her. When he reached the gate, he spun back to me. "I'll fix this."

What exactly needed fixing was something I didn't want to think about. But the cold dread swirling in my stomach told me this wasn't good.

No. Will *would* fix this. He'd explain to Chrissie our situation, and she'd understand. It wasn't a crime what we were doing. Far from it. So what if we lived together? We hadn't told anyone about it because it was our business, not theirs. We were perfectly within our rights to keep whatever privacy we wanted.

But Chrissie had feelings for Will. And that look on her face…

I swallowed.

I could almost hear the thoughts that must surely be whirling around her brain. Running over every work interaction we'd had together and every conversation she'd had with Will about his 'roommate'.

I swallowed again, wondering how my throat wasn't dry. Suddenly, I no longer felt worried about myself or Will. My anxiety reached out to Chrissie. I knew deep in my bones that if it'd been the other way around, I would feel betrayed, whether rightly so or not. I'd feel hurt.

Will found me in the living room when he returned, quietly watching a black screen.

He paced before me, running a distressed hand through

his hair. "She wouldn't listen to me. When I tried to speak, she just ran away."

"Can we really blame her? Give her a few days. I'm sure she'll come around."

"Dani!" he stopped his pacing and looked at me. "She doesn't know that we live together. To her, it probably looks like I'm just sleeping with you."

"Does it matter?"

"I'd rather she knew your truth than think you're just a hook-up."

I swallowed. "You don't think she'd tell anyone at work, do you? Not- not before speaking to you about it."

He shook his head. "No, Chrissie wouldn't do that." I relaxed, but then he said, "She wouldn't." And he didn't sound as convinced this time.

"I guess we'll find out on Monday," I said.

Will tried to speak to Chrissie before the new work week arrived, but with no success. She ignored all his calls, and when he messaged her instead, she blocked his number.

I tried not to let it fill me with dread as I got ready for work, but it did. Dark, looming dread that screamed at me to stay home.

"I can call off the meeting," Will said, eyeing me with concern as I entered the kitchen.

"Absolutely not." His meeting this morning was with an important distributor, and he could not miss it. "I'm a big girl," I assured him. "I can take care of myself."

His concern eased. "You are tougher than most."

"Besides," I plonked myself onto a chair, "won't you be

back early afternoon?" He nodded. "And I very much doubt Chrissie's told anyone about what she saw. If she's willing, maybe I can speak to her." I really, really wanted to. Just to make sure that she was alright.

"Okay." Will nodded as though to convince himself that I'd be alright. "In that case, I'll get going. Hopefully, I'll be at the office before the morning ends." He gave me a long kiss before leaving.

I released my pent-up sigh, telling myself again that everything would be fine at work. That *I'd* be fine.

But as soon as I got into the office, I knew things were different. People were looking at me, and not in a particularly nice way. Some wore sneers on their faces as I walked past, while others looked surprised or disgusted. I thought I imagined it at first–maybe I'd worked myself up into paranoia. But when I said good morning to Lily, she turned her back on me.

I tried Finn next. "Do you know what's going on?" I asked although something told me I already knew the answer.

"Oh, Dani…" he looked at me like he wished he was anywhere else. Like I was the school outcast, and he'd join me just by speaking to me. "I don't want to upset you, but…," He dropped his voice to a whisper. "There's a rumour going around the office that you're sleeping with Will to get a promotion."

"*What?!*"

I spun on my heel, steely eyes going straight to where Chrissie sat. And whose desk currently sat empty. *So she spread rumours about me and then decided she was too cowardly to show her face?*

And then another voice, *would she really do that?*

I slammed into my seat, trying to pretend that the eyes on me were on something else. Rumours, it seemed, spread fast. Will had been right about that.

And the news that I was sleeping with him wasn't the only rumour going around. Throughout the rest of the morning, I heard others. That I was sleeping with him to win the competition I'd worked so hard for. That he was the reason that I got through to the next round. That he *did* the work for me. That he got me the job here in the first place, taking the opportunity away from someone who actually deserved it.

My stomach churned by the time noon arrived. I knew I wouldn't be able to eat. Knew that, even if I'd had an appetite, I'd probably hurl it back up.

"Dani, can I speak to you for a minute?"

I looked up to find Jasmine beside me. Her eyes held no scorn, just a gentle request.

I nodded.

She led me into an empty meeting room and closed the door. I sat opposite her, bracing myself for what I knew would come.

She heaved out a sigh. "So… can you tell me what the hell these rumours are about? I haven't heard this kind of stir in the office for a very long time."

I opened my mouth and then closed it. The rumours still upset me. Even more so now that I knew my team leader had heard them. So I told her. I told her how I'd met Will, how I'd moved in with him, and how we decided to keep our roommate status a secret from co-workers. Her eyes grew more concerned the more I progressed.

"Is there... a relationship involved?" she asked once I'd finished.

I knew she didn't just mean friendship. "Yes."

It wasn't the answer she wanted to hear. She closed her eyes, rubbing at her temples. "We have a policy here that relationships of that kind are disclosed."

"I... didn't know."

"And I bet Will forgot." She opened her eyes and smiled. "It's not something that's regularly refreshed at training, so I don't blame you for it."

"But..."

"But given the current stir around the office, we're in a bit of trouble."

I nodded. And then it all rolled out. "I swear that none of the rumours are true. Me and Will... we're new in that sense. And even so, I'd never ask him to help me in a way that's unfair to others. And I doubt he would if I asked. What I've achieved, I've achieved by myself." My chin lifted slightly at that. I went on, "I honestly didn't think we were doing anything wrong. We just... wanted privacy." At least she looked like she understood that. "And Will... he didn't want anyone thinking that he helped me in any way. He thought if people knew I lived with him, they'd automatically assume my achievements were due to him. A lot like what they're assuming now, actually."

Her eyes softened as I frowned. When she spoke, it was with sympathy. "I don't think Will helped you with anything here. He wouldn't do that. And more importantly," she reached out to touch my hand. "You wouldn't do that."

I fought back a sob. "I didn't even know he worked here when I moved in with him."

She nodded. "The issue is that people don't know this or are choosing not to believe it. We need to somehow diffuse the situation."

"How?"

"I'm supposed to suspend the two of you for something like this. But I won't," she added, seeing my devastation. "Still, I think it will be smart if you take a week or two off while we satisfy everyone with an investigation. Prove you've done nothing wrong."

"That sounds a lot like suspension," I croaked.

"It won't go on your record."

"To hell, it won't."

We both spun as the door slammed open. Will stormed inside.

"What the hell is going on?" he asked, his voice more furious than I'd ever heard. His eyes turned to Jasmine. "Why am I hearing rumours that Dani's been sleeping with me to get her game crowned as the winner?"

I winced.

"We're diffusing the situation," Jasmine soothed.

"Diffusing it how?" Yes. He was furious. "Why is Dani getting suspended when it should be those," he thrust his thumb over his shoulder, "who's getting it instead? How can they get away with saying those vile things without waiting to hear the truth?"

"Dani isn't getting suspended." Jasmine's voice remained calm, but there was a strain to it. I guessed she'd never heard

Will angry like this, either. "I just think it would be best for everyone if she took a few weeks off." *So now it was a few weeks?* "Why don't you take a seat?"

Will shook his head, refusing to yield. "That isn't fair, and you know it." When Jasmine didn't answer, he continued, "If Dani stays off, so do I."

Panic flickered behind Jasmine's eyes. "You know the company needs you."

"And they don't need Dani?"

Never mind the situation out there, I needed to somehow find a way to diffuse the one in *here*.

"Will," Jasmine's voice came out shaky, as though she couldn't believe what she heard. "You know that you're working on an important project. That you're the *lead designer*. Without you here, the whole place falls apart."

"So Dani gets punished because you deem me more important?" His words were like venom. I was surprised that he had it in him. "We are two people, not one. If there's a punishment–*when there shouldn't be*–then it's going to be equal. If anything, I should be in a worse position for forgetting about that damned disclosure."

"Will," I spoke in a way that drew his eyes to me. The storm in them calmed, but only slightly. "Please don't do anything rash. What Jasmine said is right. You *are* important here. And I, as a first-year, am not. I can take a *few*,"–I stumbled over that last word–"weeks off while they do an investigation and everyone realises that they're wrong. That *we* did nothing wrong."

"I'm not going to let you take the fall for this on your own," he said.

And I could see it in his eyes that he would take those weeks off with me. And I knew that I couldn't let it happen. "Alright," I said softly. "I appreciate you having my back on this. I really, *really* appreciate it. Could you give me some minutes alone with Jasmine, please? She is my lead, after all."

He nodded. But as he reached the door, he turned back to me to say, "You are not on your own."

I forced a smile onto my face. It hurt more than it should.

When the door closed, I turned back to Jasmine, who looked truly frightened by the thought of losing Will for a few weeks. "What would happen if he did stay off with me?" I asked.

She tore her eyes from the door to meet mine, that fear remaining. "Will is a critical part of this company. If he stayed off work without approval, two things would happen. First, the company would fall heavily back on its deadlines and lose money. Second, the board might be angry enough about it that they try to replace him."

I shivered. "*Can* they replace him?"

"It'd be hard, but the point is that they'd try."

"But he's worked so hard to get here," I whispered.

"You must mean a lot to him." I met her eye, which held a flicker of curiosity. "I'd be tempted to keep it a secret if he decided to go through with it, but it'd be impossible to hide the destruction."

Thoughts whirled in my brain, trying to sift through possible ways to avoid such destruction. To prevent Will from making a mistake that would cost him big. Too big. A mistake that I couldn't let happen...

I looked up at Jasmine. "Is there any way you can keep Will working late tonight?"

She frowned. "I'm sure I can find some reason. Why?"

"Because I'll take that time off for this to blow over." Although I couldn't see how this *would* blow over, not when the people here were so ready to believe lies... I pushed the dread down as I said, "And I can't let Will do it with me."

When I got back to my desk, I made my face impassive. The only emotion I showed was the reassuring smile I gave to Will. I ignored everyone else entirely.

And when the day was over, I quietly packed up my desk, only taking what I'd brought to avoid suspicion. And then I left through the doors, knowing Will would be staying back for a while.

He sent me a text when I got to the house.

Are you alright?

I let the tears fall as I replied, *I'm fine. Don't worry about me.*

I worked quickly, lest he returned home before I finished. With my bags packed–I had more now than when I first came here–I locked the front door and posted the key through the letterbox. I followed it with a letter for Will.

I almost shattered as I unlatched the garden gate, but I forced myself to hold it together.

For him.

And for me.

Because I wasn't going to let *anyone*–not Chrissie, not people who so readily believed the rumours–ruin the career we'd both worked so hard for.

CHAPTER TWENTY-NINE

Well, this was familiar.

I looked up at the ceiling, then across at the computer desk that no longer housed a computer. I wondered what they did with it. Recycled? eBay? It'd been so long since I'd last been in this room that it could be anywhere.

When I first came here, Nick had been less than satisfied. I assured him that it wouldn't be for long. I couldn't have stressed that enough. But even a mere few days would've been too much for him. Never mind weeks.

I wished I could tell him this was my last option as much as my first. My only. Some things never changed.

My phone buzzed, but I'd long stopped hoping it would be from the person I missed the most. The person who my heart and soul longed for. No, Will had stopped messaging me two weeks ago.

And I couldn't blame him. I'd left him without so much as a goodbye. Worst, I hadn't told him where I'd gone or if I was coming back. I'd blind-sighted him to a horrible degree. And if it'd been the other way around, I knew in my bones that

whatever panic I'd feel about being left would quickly turn
to anger. He was probably seething at me right this second.
If he was thinking about me at all.

But what I'd done had worked. In fact, it was the only
thing keeping me sane.

I'd received word from Jasmine that Will still turned up
to work. He'd thrown himself into it with an unstoppable
force that wouldn't go unrecognised. There was no more
talk about leaving with me... because I was no longer there
to follow.

My throat bobbed as I swung my legs from the bed. I
missed Will more than I thought humanly possible. It was
as if someone tore a hole in my chest, seared it, and plunged
a knife into my heart.

And I missed Bluebird. I missed going to the office and
doing the work that I loved, that I'd dreamed about doing
for years. As if damaging my heart wasn't enough, someone
else clawed at my stomach.

I didn't know if I'd ever be allowed back.

"Good morning!" Holly said as I made my way into the
kitchen. She sounded unusually bright, but she'd sounded
that way ever since I'd moved back in.

"Morning," I said, trying my utmost to sound cheerful
with her.

The last thing she needed was a grump living under her
roof.

Not when she already had one.

I moved my eyes over to Nick, who leaned against the
counter with a coffee in his hand. He didn't hide his
contempt from me. He'd worn that look from the moment

I'd got here. But today, there seemed to be something else gleaming in his expression. An amused kind of sneering.

I ignored him as I walked over to the table.

"We saw someone yesterday," he said, his eyes laser-focused on me.

Holly shot him a warning look that I pretended not to see. I also refused to be provoked by him.

"Who?" I asked, dragging out a chair.

"Will."

I paused. Everything else stopped with me–my heart, my breathing, my ability to think. I didn't dare look at Nick. I didn't want to give him the satisfaction of seeing me crumble. Instead, I took a seat and pretended like my heart wasn't shattering because of the name he'd just said.

"He was with a girl," he continued, clearly trying to provoke me and loving it. I wouldn't tell him that it worked. That his words did far worse damage than the dagger in my heart.

"That's enough," Holly hissed at him. She laid a hand on mine. "I'm sure it was nothing. Has he- has he messaged you recently?"

I shook my head, feeling my eyes warm.

"See?" Nick drawled. "I just thought Dani should know that her boyfriend is cheating on her."

I turned eyes full of hatred on him. "Will would never do that."

"Oh, really?" he raised an innocent brow, inviting me to argue. "Then why was he nose to nose with a very pretty girl in a cocktail bar?"

Nausea whirled in my stomach. But I could not–*would*

not–give Nick the satisfaction. "Will would never do that," I repeated through gritted teeth. I wanted to believe that. I *did* believe that. But it didn't stop the image from cutting deep.

Nick saw the pain on my face and smirked. "Maybe you leaving was the blessing he'd been waiting for. I mean, who wants to live with their girlfriend straight after getting together? He was probably planning on kicking you out soon, anyway."

"*Nick*," Holly hissed again.

I pushed my chair back, not caring that it scraped across the floor. "I'll be in my room," I told Holly.

"*Our* room," he corrected. "You're just borrowing it." And from his tone, I knew he wouldn't allow me to borrow it for much longer.

I tore my glare from him to face Holly, who looked like she wanted to melt into the wall and stay there forever. That softened me a little. *Sorry*, I mouthed before running up to hide in the room I'd borrowed.

Will was with another girl. Will was with another girl. Will was with another girl.

I threw myself onto the bed, face down, and screamed into the pillow. It helped release the pent-up anger Nick had managed to build in me. It did not, however, release the pain I felt.

Will was with another girl.

I sat on the side of the bed and dropped my face into my hands. Tears pooled in my palm.

I didn't believe Nick when he'd said Will was cheating on me. But maybe, just maybe, I was no longer his girlfriend to cheat on. It wasn't like I'd given him a chance to break up with me.

I just never, for a moment, thought something like this would happen when I left. I had too much faith in my love for him, in his love for me. Not only as partners... but as *friends*.

But maybe he was angry. Maybe he was hurting.

And I'd left him.

The weekend came and went, and I spent it in the dark, feeling cold and sorry for myself. I stayed wrapped beneath the quilt, only leaving the room when necessity called for it.

I brooded. Maybe it was a pathetic thing to do, but I didn't care. Sometimes self-care involves allowing yourself to crumble and not feeling bad about it.

I repeated Nick's words, over and over, each one like a pierce from a venomous fang.

He was with a girl.

Maybe you leaving was the blessing he'd been waiting for.

And then I cried. Cried from someplace deep in my soul, the part tethered to Will. And when it got too much, I rang him, desperate to hear his voice and the comfort it brought. But it went straight to voicemail, so I cried some more.

By the time Monday morning came around, I was all cried out and ready to face some light again.

I heard Holly outside my door and opened it. She looked at me tentatively, eyes full of concern. I smiled, allowing her inside.

"I'm so sorry about what Nick said," she apologised again. "How are you feeling?"

"You have nothing to apologise for," I said. "And I'm alright. Sort of."

She laid a hand on mine. "Why don't you speak to Will? I think you've done what you needed to do now. I don't think he'll be in danger of losing his job anymore."

I swallowed. "I know. I want to, I just-," my voice dropped to a whisper. "I'm scared he won't want me back." That's the fear that I hadn't dared voice.

Holly's grip tightened. "Don't you dare think like that. Of course, he will. He lo-" she cut off as the doorbell chimed through the house.

We both turned as the door opened, and then we heard the sound of muffled voices. Nick came upstairs a moment later.

The look on his face as he met my eye could only be described as irritated. And maybe a little ashamed. When he spoke, every word seemed forced, as though they caused him discomfort. "There's someone at the door for you," he told me.

Someone...

I leapt to my feet. Without thinking of who it might be or who it might not, I hurdled down the stairs, almost colliding with the wall at the bottom.

My heart soared when I saw him standing there.

"Will," his name came out as a sob of pure relief. I flew into his arms. Doubt jolted through me as I wondered if he wanted me there. But then his grip tightened, and he pressed a kiss to my hair.

"I've missed you," he murmured.

My laugh came out broken. "You have no idea."

I saw Jasmine then. She stood a few feet back, her eyes thoughtful and sympathetic. Blushing, I stepped away from the embrace, but my eyes gravitated toward Will again.

He had a twinkle in his eye, and my favourite smile touched his lips. But there was also something pained in the way he looked at me.

"Have you been watching a tragic movie," he asked, keeping his tone light. "Or have you missed me that much?"

I turned a glare that I didn't feel on him. That humour… that tone… I'd missed him. "I think we both know that you're the one who cries at movies."

He grinned, and a lump rose in my throat.

But then I realised that I hadn't asked the most important question. "What are you both doing here?"

"To give you this," Jasmine stepped forward, pulling something bulky from her bag. A trophy, I realised. Made of clear glass and shaped as a gaming pad.

I took it from her, reading the inscription.

Dani Scott,
Winner of the eleventh annual Gaming Contest

"What?" I stroked my name before looking up at them. "I won?"

Will's smile stretched even wider.

"Your game was amazing, Dani," Jasmine said. "The whole voting committee was impressed."

"And the best part about it," Will interjected, his eyes sparkling. "Is that I wasn't involved at all. I didn't see the demos, wasn't allowed to talk to anyone about them and was banned from voting at all."

"Which was your idea," Jasmine slipped in.

"I'm known to have some brilliant ones," Will gave me a wink that made my heart soar.

"Basically, Dani," Jasmine said, ignoring Will's self-appraisal. "The entire office realises what awful jerks they were to you and that you're an employee we're lucky to have." *Present tense.*

"Who would've thought you refilled the printer ink, stocked up on paper, and made sure empty milk cartons were always replaced?" Will asked.

I smiled at him. "I'm not one to brag. Just someone who likes to help." I thought of another question. "How did you know I was here?" I aimed the question at Will, but Jasmine answered.

"It was the address you gave on your application. Will made a calculated guess that you'd be here. Although I think he would've knocked on every door in the city if you weren't," she gave him a knowing look.

Will just smirked, eyes on me. Eyes that said, *I absolutely would have.*

"We want you back," Jasmine continued. "Immediately."

I wanted to grab my coat and go there now. But then I remembered how terrible I must look. All puffy-eyed and red-faced. "How immediately?"

She understood what I meant. "Tomorrow, if that's alright with you. In fact, Will, why don't you also take the day off? You've earned it."

Will's eyes danced as he watched me. "I know how we can spend it."

CHAPTER THIRTY

"So this is where you've been hiding?" Will walked around my temporary room, eyeing it up, as I quickly packed my bags.

Holly and Nick had left for work already. I'd told the former that I'd leave the key beneath the plant pot and almost stuck my middle finger up at the latter. Before Holly had left, she'd pulled me to the side and whispered that Jasmine was the girl they'd seen with Will. My relief had been immeasurable, but then I felt guilty for having felt relief in the first place.

"I have to say," Will continued, running his fingers across the empty computer desk, "I prefer your room at my house."

My house.

Cruel and unwanted, Nick's words rang through my mind. *Who wants to live with their girlfriend straight after getting together? He was probably planning on kicking you out soon, anyway.* Self-doubt hit me like a punch to the gut. I glanced at Will, still standing by the computer desk, and wondered what he thought about us living together. We were boyfriend-girlfriend now, not just roommates. Was he okay with that?

But he'd said *my* house. Not *ours*.

And the tenancy agreement was ending soon.

Will must've seen a shift in my expression because he suddenly frowned. "They didn't give you a hard time while you were here, did they?" By *they*, I knew he meant Nick.

I rolled my eyes. "Nick was as delightful as ever. And Holly helped in every way she could." At least the last part wasn't sarcastic. Zipping up the final bag, I heaved it onto my shoulder. "All packed."

After gathering up my other bags, he reached his free hand out to me. "Ready to go home?"

My throat clogged up at the word, but I managed to choke, "I'm ready to go home."

Smiling, Will led me from the room, his hand feeling like home already.

We walked in silence. Neither of us had mentioned our weeks apart yet–why I'd left, how he'd felt upon returning home and finding me gone, and how we both felt now. His fingers curled around mine tightly, almost as if he were afraid to let go. Mine clung to him with the same dependency.

Once back, we dumped my bags in the hallway before walking silently to the kitchen. A well of emotion almost overwhelmed me as I devoured the sight of the home I so dearly loved.

Will flicked on the kettle as I took a seat. I watched in mute as he poured us a drink and set them on the table with a smile.

"You don't look... angry," I noted with relief.

"Why would I be angry?"

I had to force the words through my throat. "Because I left."

He winced, but he managed to quickly smooth it out. "I can't say I wasn't angry when I saw your note," he said. He raised a brow. "Thanks for that, by the way."

I smiled apologetically. The note I'd left read: *I love you*. It was the only thing I could think of to convey that what I did was *for* him and not to hurt him.

"But," he continued, cupping his hands around his mug, "I understood." His eyes shone as he looked at me. "It may have taken me a week or so to understand it, but I did in the end." A week. That was about the time when he'd stopped trying to ring me. He leaned across the table, bringing his face closer to mine. "Thank you."

I blinked. "What?"

"Thank you," he said again, leaning back. "I know you did what you did for me, so I couldn't possibly be angry at you for that. You left here without telling me because you knew I'd leave with you if you didn't. It was brilliant blind-sighting," he gave me a small smile of approval before continuing. "Because I would've left Bluebird in a heartbeat for what they were saying about you, and that wouldn't have helped either of us. So, thank you."

"I think I'm going to cry," I admitted.

He laughed. I cherished the sound of it. "It turns out that staying at Bluebird did a lot of good. People felt your absence. An absence they would've convinced themselves was mine if I hadn't been there. So, knowing what you did for me, I was able to keep a cool head and wait for the competition results to come out before finding you, knowing that I had zero involvement in it. For you." He held my gaze for a second before saying, "I mean, it can't have been easy for you to move back in with *Nick*."

I laughed as he rolled his eyes. "He's certainly no Will."

"Your game is brilliant, by the way," he said. "I've tried it myself now that I'm allowed. Chrissie's impressed by it, too."

From how he said her name, I knew there was more to this story.

"Has she…" I let the words trail off.

"I told her everything. About you, about me, about us." His eyes burned into mine. "I told her that she deserves a love that's all-consuming. Someone who will cherish and adore her and look at her like he's the luckiest man in the world because he's found the one thing everyone wants. A best friend and life partner rolled into one." Silence stretched over us as we continued to stare at each other. The love in his eyes made my throat clog up.

"She's sorry, you know," he continued. "About drawing conclusions too soon. She's one of the reasons why those in the office feel so bad about what they said."

I knew the floodgates would open if I responded to any of that now. Instead, I breathed, "You said you waited for the competition results to come out before finding me. How did you know that I'd win?"

He didn't break eye contact as he said, "I believed in you."

My vision blurred. Wetness soaked my cheeks. "Thank you for believing in me."

He got to his feet and walked over to me, pulling me into a

hug. A hug that I'd missed so, so much. "I will always believe in you."

"I've missed you," I whispered.

He stepped back, brushing my tears away with a smirk on his lips. "You have *no* idea."

"I don't think I can do this," I said to Will as we walked hand-in-hand to the office.

He gave my fingers a squeeze. "You have nothing to feel nervous about. It's *those* in there who should be feeling worried."

I looked at him sideways. The blaze in his eyes told me that he hadn't quite gotten over what they'd said about me.

I mustered up my courage for him. "You're right. I'll be fine."

Lifting our entwined hands to his lips, he brushed a kiss against my knuckles.

There was no hiding our relationship now. While we'd keep PDA to a minimum inside the office for obvious reasons, until we actually got *inside* it, we refused to break apart. No hiding. No pretending we didn't know each other. Just us.

There was no one from our office in the elevator when we got there, which surprised me. But at least it meant I could keep holding Will's hand for a while longer.

As the doors opened to our level, he pressed a kiss to my forehead and stepped away from me. I followed him inside, my nerves picking up with every step. I frowned when I saw rows of empty desks, but my confused look at Will gave me no answers.

Then I saw it.

A swarm of people around a desk, around *my* desk. As I got nearer, I saw the balloons and banners that read *congratulations*.

They broke apart when we reached them, allowing me to get through.

"What's going on?" I asked, hoping my face wasn't as red as it felt. I spotted Will's floating, smiling head at the back of the row and realised that he'd known about this... and had kept it a secret.

"We all wanted to band together and congratulate you on your game demo," Jasmine said from her chair. "We've already got a team of volunteers who want to develop it. And," she moved her eyes over those who surrounded us. A warm smile spread on her lips. "We wanted to welcome you back."

That opened up a floodgate of apologies, the sorriest coming from Lily and Finn. Once those were over with, people offered their congratulations. When it looked like I might faint from the attention, Will finally beckoned everyone to get back to their desks and start working.

My face still burned when I felt a tap on my shoulder. Turning, I saw Chrissie before me. She wrung her hands together, looking like something tortured her from the inside out.

"Can I speak to you privately for a minute?" she asked quietly.

I nodded, following her through the room. Will caught my eye and gave me a supportive nod. I returned it with a smile.

Chrissie closed the door and kept her back to me for a second. After sucking in a deep breath, she turned to face me.

"Dani, I am so sorry."

I held up a hand. "I already forgive you."

She blinked in surprise. "You do?"

"Honestly, I understand it. I know how upset you must've been after what you saw and that you've liked Will for a while. I also know that you probably regretted what you said about me the moment you said it. And from how sorry you look now... yes, I forgive you."

For a second, I thought she might cry. "I was upset after seeing you that day," she sniffed. "I didn't...," she shook her head as if something heavy weighed on her heart. "After seeing how Will's been these past few weeks without you... I don't want to be someone who drives two people apart. Two people who clearly love each other. I thought I loved him, but I guess it wasn't that. But after speaking to Will, I realise I *do* want that for myself."

Her eyes were full of sadness when she stopped speaking. I did know what to say, so I pulled her into a hug.

"You deserve that love, Chrissie."

She wiped her nose. "Do you really forgive me?"

What she'd said had caused me weeks of torment, but I knew it was better to live in peace than anger. So I said, "Of course, I forgive you."

She stepped back with a smile. "Will gave me the illustrations I had you working on. They're brilliant. You've real talent, you know."

I smiled back. "Then I'm looking forward to learning

from you."

It didn't take me long to feel comfortable at work again. And now that everything was semi-normal once more, I was back to mulling over what Nick had said to me. The self-doubts I'd let him plant into my mind.

With the expiration of our tenancy agreement looming near, I wondered if Will really did want to live with his girlfriend or if he might prefer separate living spaces. Maybe Nick was right. Not many couples lived together from day one, after all.

I booked a viewing for a flat, just to be on the safe side. I'd tried to ask him outright, but I didn't think it was fair to put him in a position of saying yes or no. He might've said no just to keep from hurting me.

I decided to tell him about the viewing when he found me alone in the kitchen at work.

"Oh?" I thought I saw devastation in those lovely eyes, but he nodded. "Your viewing is tonight?"

I bit back my disappointment at his lack of resistance. "Yep."

"Hmm. Can I come with you?"

Do you really want me to move out?

"S-sure."

As we made our way to the flat, I told myself this was for the best. We needed space. We needed somewhere we could go that was private and alone.

I told myself that–but I didn't believe it.

My entire being ached to stay with Will. I wanted to go home to him and hear the rattle of the keys as he came home to me. I longed to wake up beside him, eat breakfast with him, and stay up late watching movies. And, if we needed space, we could have it. There were two rooms.

But I guessed that wasn't what he wanted.

I felt a gnawing in my stomach as we stopped outside the flat and looked up at it.

"So this is it," I said, forcing a smile.

He frowned. "I'm not sure I like it."

Well, you won't be moving into it, I wanted to grumble. We followed the agent inside and allowed him to show us around. Once the initial viewing was over, he left us to inspect and discuss in private.

Will looked like he was inspecting every inch of the place. Disheartened, I stood in the dingy open living space and watched as he sized up my potential future accommodation. He opened cupboards and looked inside, poked his head inside tiny rooms, and checked the efficiency of appliances. With his scrutiny over, he came over to where I stood, slipping his hands inside his pockets.

"I think it's a bit small for us," he said seriously. "I want enough space to keep work and fun separate, and I'm sure we'll need a bigger bathroom than *that*. There's also a certain smell that I don't think I'll ever get used to," he wrinkled his nose.

I blinked, too focused on his use of the terms *us* and *we* to be distracted by the smell that indeed existed. "What do you mean?"

He smirked, pulling me in closer. "You didn't think I came all this way because I want you to leave me, did you?"

I looked at his face, searching for a sign that told me he

was kidding. Relief flooded through me when I found none. "You don't... want me to move out?"

"I think I'd miss you every day if you did. Unless," uncertainty flickered behind his eyes as he leaned back. "Unless you want to move out. In which case, I would never stop you."

"I think I'd miss you every day if I did."

His smile mirrored mine, but then he frowned. "Why did you think I'd want you to move out?"

"Nick..." I shook my head, feeling ashamed to be saying it out loud. "I thought you might not want to live with your girlfriend so soon. And the other day... you'd said *my* house instead of *ours*. I thought that might've been a subtle way of reminding me." I ducked my head, but he gently lifted it again with his finger.

Guilt blazed in his eyes. "I'm sorry that I said that. It was a stupid slip that I didn't mean. And," his lips tugged up as if a sudden memory amused him. "It stopped being my house the day you had the nerve to turn up on my doorstep without an agent."

I laughed. "And now?"

"Now it's our home."

Home. I'd never had one of those before. Always a roof above my head, but never somewhere I truly belonged.

Swallowing down a sudden wave of emotion, I said, "So, will I need to sign another tenancy agreement? What will the rules be this time?"

He shook his head. "You aren't moving in as my tenant, Dani, and there will be no rules. In fact, I'd rather we wipe out the previous rules altogether."

I ticked them off my finger, "Rule one, we don't go into each other's rooms. Rule two, no strangers without warning. Rule three, no walking around the house naked,"– His eyes glinted at that–"Rule four, no invading each other's space. And rule five," I held my hand up for him to see, "No falling for each other."

He tilted his head to the side, but the glint in his eyes practically burned. "You memorised all of that?"

I shrugged, "I'm a stickler for breaking the rules."

"And I let you break them all," he tutted. "What a pushover."

"Are you sure there aren't any more rules you want me to break?"

A laugh rumbled against my lips as he kissed me. "Rule six," he said, kissing my jawline, "no sleeping in the same bed. Rule seven," he moved the kiss to below my ear, "no waking up together. Rule eight," the kiss moved to my neck, "no sharing each other's secrets. Rule nine…" On and on he went, making each rule more tantalising than the last. Until he reached one that made my body and soul shake with pleasure. "No honeymoon."

I leaned back. "You know I'm going to break all those rules, right?"

His lips pulled up into my favourite smile. "I'm counting on it."

AFTERWORD

If you enjoyed reading this book, please consider leaving it a review. It's a huge help for self-published authors! With love and appreciation, C.L. Sharples x

Printed in Great Britain
by Amazon

83440256R00207